"Without Fu-Manchu we wouldn't have Dr. No, Doctor Doom or Dr. Evil. Sax Rohmer created the first truly great evil mastermind. Devious, inventive, complex, and fascinating. These novels inspired a century of great thrillers!"
—Jonathan Maberry, *New York Times* bestselling author of *Assassin's Code* and *Patient Zero*

"The true king of the pulp mystery is Sax Rohmer—and the shining ruby in his crown is without a doubt his Fu-Manchu stories."
—James Rollins, *New York Times* bestselling author of *The Devil Colony*

"Fu-Manchu remains the definitive diabolical mastermind of the 20th Century. Though the arch-villain is 'the Yellow Peril incarnate,' Rohmer shows an interest in other cultures and allows his protagonist a complex set of motivations and a code of honor which often make him seem a better man than his Western antagonists. At their best, these books are very superior pulp fiction... at their worst, they're still gruesomely readable."
—Kim Newman, award-winning author of *Anno Dracula*

"Sax Rohmer is one of the great thriller writers of all time! Rohmer created in Fu-Manchu the model for the super-villains of James Bond, and his hero Nayland Smith and Dr. Petrie are worthy stand-ins for Holmes and Watson... though Fu-Manchu makes Professor Moriarty seem an under-achiever."
—Max Allan Collins, *New York Times* bestselling author of *The Road to Perdition*

"I grew up reading Sax Rohmer's Fu-Manchu novels, in cheap paperback editions with appropriately lurid covers. They completely entranced me with their vision of a world constantly simmering with intrigue and wildly overheated ambitions. Even without all the exotic detail supplied by Rohmer's imagination, I knew full well that world wasn't the same as the one I lived in... For that alone, I'm grateful for all the hours I spent chasing around with Nayland Smith and his stalwart associates, though really my heart was always on their intimidating opponent's side."
—K. W. Jeter, acclaimed author of *Infernal Devices*

D1707648

THE WRATH OF FU-MANCHU

THE COMPLETE FU-MANCHU SERIES BY SAX ROHMER

THE WRATH OF FU-MANCHU AND OTHER STORIES

SAX ROHMER

TITAN BOOKS

THE WRATH OF FU-MANCHU
Print edition ISBN: 9780857686169
E-book edition ISBN: 9780857686824

Published by Titan Books
A division of Titan Publishing Group Ltd
144 Southwark Street, London SE1 0UP

First published as a novel in the UK by Tom Stacey, 1973
First published as a novel in the US by DAW, 1976

First Titan Books edition: March 2016
10 9 8 7 6 5 4 3 2 1

The Authors League of America and the Society of Authors assert the moral right to be identified as the author of this work.

Visit our website: www.titanbooks.com

Did you enjoy this book? We love to hear from our readers. Please email us at readerfeedback@titanemail.com or write to us at Reader Feedback at the above address.

To receive advance information, news, competitions, and exclusive offers online, please sign up for the Titan newsletter on our website: www.titanbooks.com

Frontispiece illustration from Liberty magazine, Nov. 16, 1940, art by Arnold Freberg. Special Thanks to Dr. Lawrence Knapp for the illustration as it appeared on "The Page of Fu Manchu," http://njedge.net/~knapp/FuFrames.htm.

A CIP catalogue record for this title is available from the British Library.

Printed and bound in the United States.

From the cover of *Liberty* magazine, November 16, 1940, art by Arnold Freberg.

THE WRATH OF FU-MANCHU

"By your leave, sir!"

Thurston stepped quickly to the side of the carpeted alleyway, as a steward pushing a trolley stocked with baggage went past. His traveller's eye noted Dutch Airlines labels on some of the pieces. But he was more interested in a man who followed the trolley.

He was of thickset, shortish figure and wore a chauffeur's uniform. His yellow, pock-pitted face and sunken eyes were vaguely menacing and his walk more nearly resembled a lope, catlike and agile.

"What a dangerous looking brute," was the thought which crossed Thurston's mind. He asked himself by which of the passengers now joining the *Lauretania* at Cherbourg this forbidding servant could be employed.

He hadn't long to wait for an answer.

A Chinese cook (or Thurston thought he was Chinese) hurried along just ahead of him in the direction of the square before the purser's office. He carried something on a tray, wrapped in a white napkin. There was no one else in the alleyway until a woman turned into it and began to saunter in Thurston's direction.

The cook, seeing her, behaved in so incredible a manner that Thurston felt tempted to close his eyes, count ten and then look again. He set the tray down, dropped to his knees and touched the carpet with his forehead!

The woman showed no surprise, never even glanced at the crouching white figure, but continued calmly on her way. As she passed by, the man gathered up his tray, and without once looking back, hurried on. The mysterious passenger had now drawn near enough for Thurston to get a clear impression. She carried a small handbag to which was tied another of the KLM tags.

It was alligator leather, similar to several piled on the trolley.

Thurston tried not to stare, tried to pretend that he hadn't noticed the singular behaviour of the Chinese cook. But this chivalrous effort was wasted.

Apparently, the woman remained unaware of his presence as she had been unaware of the prostrate Chinese. Her gait was leisurely, almost languid. She wore a cream shantung suit which displayed her graceful figure to perfection. A green scarf wound turban fashion (perhaps because of the high wind in the harbour) lent her features some of the quality of a delicate ivory mask. Except for superciliously curved lips, her face could not be said to bear any expression whatever.

She was beautiful, but unapproachable.

Like a vision she appeared, and was gone. He was left with a picture of half-closed, jade-green eyes, of slender white hands, hands nurtured in indolence.

Thurston was too experienced a voyager to bother his friend, Burns, the purser, until the *Lauretania* had cleared Cherbourg. But he meant to find out all that Burns knew about this imperious beauty attended by an Oriental manservant and whom a Chinese member of the crew treated as a goddess.

Having time on his hands, for he travelled light and had already unpacked, he roamed the ship, drawing room, smoking room, lounges, decks, but never had a glimpse of the jade-eyed woman of mystery.

When he took his seat at the purser's table for dinner, Thurston read a signal from Burns and lingered until the others had gone;

"Come along to my room," the purser invited. "Haven't had a moment to spare until now."

When they were in Burns' room, the door closed and drinks set out, Burns unburdened himself.

"Glad to have someone like you to talk to. I mean someone not officially concerned. We often have difficult passengers, but this time we've got a woman who is a number one headache. Good looker, too. Jenkins, the chief steward, is raising hell. She won't have a steward or stewardess in her room. She's got a yellow faced manservant on board, and he's to take care of everything. Bit irregular?"

Thurston put his glass down.

"Woman with green eyes? Ivory skin? Wonderful figure?"

Burns' eyes, which were not green, but blue, twinkled.

"Powers of observation good! That's the dame. Her papers show that she's from the Dutch East Indies."

"Ah! That may explain it. A yellow streak?"

"Could be. She's Mrs van Roorden, widow of a Javanese planter. But her pock-marked attendant, who's in the servant's quarters, of course, is Burmese! Add that up."

"I can't," Thurston confessed. "Is she travelling alone—I mean, except for the manservant?"

Burns nodded and began to light his pipe.

"More or less, yes. She came on board with a Mr Fordwich, whom I don't know anything about, except that I'm told he's a member of a big Chicago concern with overseas interests. He came from Java to England and then flew over to France. That is, according to his passport."

Thurston, accepting a nod from Burns, passed his glass for a refill and smiled.

"I can add to your information about the mysterious Mrs van Roorden. Listen to this."

He told the purser what he had seen in the alleyway. Burns' eyes opened even more widely than usual.

"Damn funny! I'll get Jenkins to check on the cook's staff. We have some Chinese boys down there, I know. Sure he was Chinese?"

Thurston considered. He was not well up on Far Eastern types.

"Almost sure," he said at last. "You see, I had only a glimpse of the man. But I'm certain he was an Asiatic."

Burns nodded thoughtfully.

"Now, on our last run, we had a mutual friend on board who could have settled the point out of hand! Sir Denis Nayland Smith."

"What! He may be in New York when I get there. I'll look him up. Amazing man, isn't he? I knew him very well when he was head of the CID at Scotland Yard. Member of my club. Smith's a fellow who has crowded more adventure into his life than any ten ordinary men. He must be out on a job. Wonder what it is?"

"Communists, I expect," Burns murmured.

But Burns happened to be wrong, as Thurston was to find out.

In fact, at about the time that he sat talking to the purser of the *Lauretania,* the centre of a stormcloud the existence of which had brought Nayland Smith to New York was actually located in Cairo.

In an old Arab house not far from the Mosque of El Ashraf, a house still undisturbed by Western "improvements," a tall, gaunt man paced slowly up and down a room which once had been the *Na'ah* or saloon of the *harêm*.

Lofty, and lighted by a lantern in the painted roof, it was tastefully paved in the Arabian manner, had elaborate panelled walls and two *mushrabiyeh* windows. Before one of these recessed windows a screen had been placed.

The man pacing the tiled floor wore a loose yellow robe, a black cap on his massive skull. Although unmistakably Chinese, his finely lined features were those of a scholar who had never spared himself in his quest of knowledge. It was a wonderful face. It might have belonged to a saint—or to the Fallen Angel in person.

His walk was feline, silent. He seemed to be listening for some expected sound. Suddenly he paused, turned.

A door opened at the end of the saloon and a man entered quietly, an old white-bearded man who wore Arab dress. He was met and challenged by a glance from emerald green eyes. Momentarily, an expression of eagerness crept across the impassive Chinese face.

"You have it, *hakîm*?"

The words were spoken in Arabic, sibilantly. They were answered by a deep bow.

"I have it, Excellency."

From under his black robe, the old physician took out a small phial, half filled with a nearly colourless liquid.

"You guarantee its absolute purity?"

"I swear to it. Am I a fool to dream of deceiving Dr Fu-Manchu?"

Dr Fu-Manchu's nearly unendurable gaze remained focussed on the bearded face a while longer, and then:

"Follow," he directed.

He walked under a decorated arch into a neighbouring room

equipped as a laboratory. Much of the apparatus in this singular apartment would have puzzled any living man of science to define its purpose or application. On a long, glass-topped table a number of test tubes was ranged in a rack.

Dr Fu-Manchu seated himself at the table and held out his hand for the phial. Watched by the Arab physician, he removed the stopper and inserted a glass dipper. The unerring delicacy of touch displayed by those long-nailed fingers was miraculous. He replaced the stopper and smeared a spot from the dipper on to a slide, putting the slide into place in a large microscope. Stooping, he stared through the lens, which he slightly adjusted. Without looking up:

"You are sure of hormone B?" he challenged harshly.

"Positive, Excellency. I extracted it myself."

Then Fu-Manchu raised his head and pressed one of several studs on a switchboard. A door opened and a young Japanese came in. He wore a chemist's white tunic. Fu-Manchu indicated the phial.

"The missing elements, at last, Matsukata. Use sparingly." He spoke in Japanese. "Above all, watch the temperature. Inoculate a rat, a guinea pig and two rabbits. Report to me at ten minute intervals. Proceed."

Matsukata took the phial, three of the test tubes, bowed, and went out. Dr Fu-Manchu turned to the Arab physician.

"How long have you known me, *hakîm?*"

He spoke softly.

The old Arab stroked his beard as if in meditation.

"Since I was twenty years of age, Excellency."

"And what age was I then?"

"I could not say."

"What age did I appear to be?"

"As you appear now, Excellency."

Fu-Manchu stood up.

"Follow."

They returned to the long saloon. Fu-Manchu crossed to the screen set before a *mushrabiyeh* window and moved it aside. In the recess, motionless in a silk-padded basket, lay a tiny grey marmoset!

"My little friend, Peko." Dr Fu-Manchu spoke in a sibilant whisper. "The companion of my wanderings."

The old physician conquered his astonishment. Unmistakably, Dr Fu-Manchu was deeply moved.

"He is asleep?"

"No. He is dying."

"Of tuberculosis? These creatures are subject to it."

"No. Of senility."

"What, then, is his age, Excellency?"

"The same as my own."

"What do you say?… Pardon me, Excellency. I was startled. Such a thing seems impossible."

Dr Fu-Manchu replaced the screen. They stepped down again into the saloon; and the Arab physician found himself called upon to sustain the fixed regard of those hypnotic eyes.

"Peko had already reached his normal, allotted span of years at the time that I completed my long experiments so vainly attempted by the old alchemists. Yes—I had discovered what they termed the *Elixir Vitae*: The Elixir of Life! Upon Peko I made the first injection; upon myself, the second."

"And now?" It was a hushed murmur.

"Failure threatens my science. Peko was not due for treatment until next spring. Yet—you see? I found myself unprovided with the materials. I searched Cairo. I laboured in the laboratory day and night. Can you understand?"

His voice rose harshly on a note of frenzy. His eyes blazed.

"Yes, Excellency… I do understand."

"If death claims him, I am defeated. A plan upon which may rest the peace of the world, even the survival of man, demands my presence in America. But, if I fail to fan that tiny spark which still smoulders within Peko into a flame, of life, this means that I too—I, Fu-Manchu—may die at any hour!"

Weather remained fresh, but clear and fine throughout the *Lauretania*'s run. Thurston, that unimaginative man of business, had no suspicion as yet of the rôle for which Fate had cast him. But he found a magnetic attraction in the personality of Mrs van Roorden.

This beautiful enigma, always correctly but exquisitely dressed, engrossed his attention to the exclusion of everybody else on board. Nor was he alone in this. Mrs van Roorden would have become a focus of interest in any community.

She was much in the company of Mr Fordwich. He was a man of middle height and spare build, his skin yellowed as if by long residence in the tropics. A heavy stick with a rubber ferule was never far from his hand, for he was afflicted by a slight limp. His keen, dark eyes lighted up at times, as if a laughing dare-devil lay hidden under the cool facade which he showed to the world. Without being handsome in the Hollywood sense, Thurston could well believe that Fordwich might be attractive to women. They were an intriguing pair.

Mrs van Roorden rarely permitted her graceful languor to become disturbed. She possessed an aura of sublime self-confidence, as if some invulnerable power protected her from any intrusion upon her queenly serenity. Sometimes, when in Fordwich's company, she smiled. It was a strange smile, secretly voluptuous. But it promised little and revealed nothing.

There was acid comment amongst the passengers and ship's officers concerning the strange arrangement whereby no one was permitted to enter Mrs van Roorden's cabin except her dangerous looking Burmese manservant. Whenever she took one of her leisurely constitutional strolls, a barrage of glances fell upon her from the massed batteries of deck-chairs.

The Sphinx could not have shown more perfect indifference.

Thurston, in his quest of information, seized every opportunity to talk to Mr Fordwich, with whom he sometimes had a drink in the smoking room. But Mr Fordwich proved himself a master of reticence.

And so it was not until their last night at sea that Thurston met Mrs van Roorden. She was one of the guests at a cocktail party in the purser's quarters. Somewhat to his surprise, Mr Fordwich was not present. Mrs van Roorden wore a green backless frock entirely justified by her faultless ivory arms and shoulders. A band of emeralds was clasped around her throat.

Burns presented his friend, at the same time treating him to a sly wink.

"I'm very glad to meet you at last, Mrs van Roorden," Thurston declared. "It would be annoying to have to leave the ship without making the acquaintance of the most beautiful woman on board."

That vague smile curved disdainful lips as she glanced at him when he sat down beside her. Her eyes slanted very slightly.

"A compliment from an Englishman is as unexpected as an Ave Maria from a tabby."

What a lovely voice she had, Thurston thought! A wall-lamp just behind her touched bronze highlights in her hair, which he had believed to be quite black.

"A compliment may sometimes be a fact. Are you staying in New York, Mrs van Roorden?"

She shrugged slightly.

"Perhaps for a little while. This journey is not of my choosing. But there are some duties which must override personal inclination."

"Then what does personal inclination suggest?"

She turned and looked at him directly. He started, rebuked himself. He was an experienced man of the world... But he had the utmost difficulty in meeting that penetrating gaze. Then Mrs van Roorden seemed to be satisfied. She turned her head aside again, languidly.

"I belong to the old world. The new world has little to offer me."

Thurston recovered himself.

"You are too young to be cynical."

"I am too old to embrace shadows. Truth is dying today. We are all so smug, although we dance on the edge of a precipice. Where are the men, who can see—the great adventurers who put self last?"

"Not all dead, I assure you! I should like you to meet my friend, Nayland Smith, for instance."

Mrs van Roorden seemed to become quite still, statuesque. At last, she stirred, turned her head, and again he found himself claimed by those jade-green eyes.

"Sir Denis Nayland Smith?"

"Yes. Do you know him?"

Her lips curved in that provocative, voluptuous yet impersonal smile. She glanced aside as a steward offered a selection of cocktails. Taking one:

"I used to know him," she replied, a deep, caressing note in her musical voice. "Were you ever in Java, Mr Thurston?"

Her wish to change the subject was so unmistakable that Thurston had no choice but that of following her lead. So that when the party broke up, although he knew that the Communists in the Dutch Indies were worse than the Japanese, he knew no more about Mrs van Roorden than he had ever known.

But he wondered very much why she had steered him off the subject of Nayland Smith…

During belated dinner, an urgent message came for the purser. He excused himself and hurried out.

Thurston, later, passing his door and finding it open, rapped and went in.

Burns was sitting in an armchair, smoking his pipe.

"Sit down, old man. There's something very queer going on aboard this ship."

"Why—what's happened?"

Thurston sat down.

"Well, the steward who generally looks after the room occupied by Mrs van Roorden nearly ran into her as she rushed out into the alleyway. She said that a thief had been in there!"

"What!"

"Fact. The man reported to Jenkins, and Jenkins sent for me. I went along. Mrs van Roorden opened the door when I knocked. She was as cool as an icicle, but those eyes of hers were just blazing. She stuck to the story, but said that she didn't intend to make an official complaint. Insisted, in fact."

"This is all very strange."

"There's more to come. This man of hers, who I believe acts as her bodyguard as much as anything else, was found in his cabin—insensible!"

"You mean—he'd been assaulted?"

"Rubber truncheon, the doctor thinks! This is all off the record. Not a word. The cops would hold us up for hours if they got on to it."

"But, what—"

"Yes." Burns stood up. "That's what *I'm* wondering. Let's have a drink."

Landing was delayed the next day by unexpected mist which blanketed East River. Thurston, taking a final look into closets and drawers, heard a rap on the door, and supposed his steward had come for the baggage.

"All ready!"

Mr Fordwich entered, leaning on his stick.

"Thought I might catch you," he said, smiling. "The fact is, I owe you a drink, and I don't know a better time to balance the account than when the bars are sealed on a foggy morning!"

From his pockets he produced a large flask and a bottle of soda water.

"That's a pleasant sight," Thurston confessed. "I admit my own reserve is exhausted. Thought we'd be ashore by now."

Fordwich mixed two tepid drinks and glanced around. His eyes rested on a well-filled golf bag.

"I see you're a golfer? Expect to get much play?"

"Well, I'm spending a week with a friend in Connecticut who lives near a good course. I'm no plus man. Never got below eighteen!"

They talked about golf, and other things. Thurston gave Fordwich the name of his New York hotel and Fordwich promised to call him later. He wondered if Fordwich knew what had happened to Mrs van Roorden and her Burmese servant, but, although burning with curiosity, he was bound to silence.

Another rap on the door interrupted them. A page came in.

"Mr Thurston?"

"I am Mr Thurston."

"Note for you, sir."

Thurston glanced at the scribbled chit. It said, "Please call at Purser's office immediately."

"Excuse me." He turned to Fordwich. "Make yourself comfortable. Shan't be a minute."

He went out and along the alleyway to the office. Pandemonium reigned in that area, but Thurston managed to catch the eye of an assistant whom he knew.

"Want to see me?" he asked.

He handed in the note.

The assistant purser stared at it, with a puzzled frown, then went away. He wasn't gone long.

"There must be some mistake, Mr Thurston, I can find no one who sent you this thing."

Deeply mystified, Thurston returned to his room, when he had a second surprise.

The silver flask and the soda water remained on the table, but Mr Fordwich had disappeared. Thurston concluded that he had been called away and would return, but as the steward came at that moment to collect his things, he put the flask in his pocket and left the room.

Up to the time that the *Lauretania* docked, he never had a glimpse of Mr Fordwich, nor, which disappointed him more, of Mrs van Roorden. As he waited under the letter T for his steward with the baggage, he watched all the passengers in sight, but failed to find either of those he was looking for.

He was quietly clear of the Customs, for he carried only a suitcase, a valise and his golf bag. These he gave to a porter and headed for the exit. This route took him past the letter F, and here he pulled up.

SAX ROHMER

Fordwich, leaning on his heavy stick, was explaining something to two Customs officers bending over an open handbag.

Thurston's insatiable curiosity prompted him to draw nearer. Across the shoulder of an interested bystander he saw what lay in the bag.

It was a grotesque green mask of Eastern workmanship. He had a hazy idea that it should be described as a devil mask. He could hear Fordwich's voice:

"I picked it up in Java. It's of small intrinsic value. Merely a curiosity..."

Thurston moved on. He didn't want to appear to be eavesdropping. But his glimpse of the green mask had given him an uncomfortable, and indescribable sensation. Who was this man, Fordwich? He had felt all along there was something mysterious about him. And what lay behind the raid on Mrs van Roorden's cabin and the assault on her servant?

Above all, why had she declined an official inquiry?

If, at about the time the *Lauretania* had reached mid-ocean, Thurston could have been transported to that old Arab mansion near the Mosque of El Ashraf, he might now have held a clue to some of these riddles.

It was midnight, and the lofty saloon was dimly lighted by a number of hanging lamps of perforated brass. The screen had been moved from the *mushrabiyeh* window. Dr Fu-Manchu, seated in a chair of native inlay workmanship, bent over the padded basket in which the tiny monkey lay.

He had been seated there for four hours.

It was literally true that vast issues hung upon the life or death of a marmoset.

Native Cairo slumbered. No sound came from the narrow street upon which the gate of a tree-shaded courtyard opened. Inside the house there was unbroken silence. And Dr Fu-Manchu never stirred.

His elbows resting on the chair arms, his long fingers pressed together, he watched, tirelessly. An emerald signet ring which he wore glittered in the light of a shaded lamp. He was so still that a marked resemblance which his gaunt features bore to those of the mummy of Seti I in the Cairo Museum became uncannily increased. It was as if the dead Pharaoh had awakened from his age-long sleep.

Sometimes the strange green eyes filmed over queerly, as if from great weariness. Then at the appearance of some symptom so slight as to be visible only to the inspired physician, they glowed again like living gems.

But when the great change came, it was unmistakable.

Peko moved his tiny arms, almost exactly like a human baby waking up, yawned, stretched and opened beady eyes.

Fu-Manchu's lips moved, but no sound issued from them. A spot of perspiration trickled from under the black cap and crept down his high forehead. Peko looked up at him, chattered furiously, and then sprung in one bound onto the bowed shoulders.

There the little creature perched, slapping the yellow face of his master in an ecstasy either of rage or of happiness. Only Dr Fu-Manchu could know.

Rising and stepping down into the saloon, Fu-Manchu struck a silver gong. Peko responded with a sound like a shrill whistle and leapt onto a brass lamp hanging directly overhead. Here he swung, looking down and chattering volubly.

Matsukata came in from the laboratory.

"Triumph!"

Dr Fu-Manchu pointed to the swinging marmoset.

Matsukata bowed deeply.

"I salute the genius of the master scientist."

"Advise General Huan Tsung that we leave in an hour. It is still possible to be there in time. Proceed."

Matsukata bowed again, and went out. Dr Fu-Manchu dried his high forehead with a silk handkerchief which he drew from the sleeve of his robe, and crossing the saloon, his gait slow and catlike, he mounted a *leewan* at the further end and opened a cupboard.

From the cupboard he took a flat cedarwood box and raised the lid.

Inside lay a green mask—identical with that which, later, George Thurston was to see in a Manhattan Customs shed…

The phone buzzed in Thurston's hotel apartment.

He was unpacking his suitcase. He crossed and called:

"Hullo!"

"That you, Thurston?" came a vaguely familiar voice. "Fordwich here. Got my flask, haven't you?"

"Yes. I lost sight of you. What happened?"

"Called away. Hang on to the flask. Be seeing you around cocktail time. That all right?"

"Quite."

"Did you get your golf clubs through safely?"

"Golf clubs? Of course. Why not?"

A chuckle of laughter.

"Just asking! See you about six."

Fordwich hung up.

Thurston scratched his head reflectively, then returned to his unpacking. He took out a lounge suit, a Tuxedo and black trousers.

He put them on hangers in the wardrobe, turned, and stared at his golf-bag.

Slowly, he went over and inspected it.

Amongst the club-heads he saw a rubber ferule sticking out!

He grabbed it, trying to pull the thing free. But he had to remove a niblick, a mid-iron and a mashie before he succeeded.

Then—he held Fordwich's walking stick in his hand!

"Phew!"

Thurston sat down on the side of the bed. The stick was unmistakable. It was of some dark, heavy wood, smooth, nearly black. The handle curved above a plain gold band. There was no inscription.

He couldn't doubt that the stick he held in his hands was the one upon which Fordwich had been leaning in the Customs shed!

"It isn't possible!"

Thurston spoke the words aloud. He was startled out of his normal self. This inexplicable incident crowned all the others. What on earth did it mean? Why should the mysterious Mr Fordwich assume that he was a suitable subject for conjuring tricks? And when had the trick been performed?

He thought of the green devil mask. He recalled a conversation with an Anglo-Indian at his club. This man had assured him that, for all science might say to the contrary, the powers of magic were very real in the East.

Hurriedly completing his unpacking, he went down to the bar.

The delay in getting ashore had upset his plans. He didn't know what to do with himself, or how to spend the evening.

Six o'clock came; half past.

Still there was no word from Fordwich. Thurston sat down and stared at the black walking stick. He didn't touch it. He was aroused from amorous musings, in which the ivory arms of Mrs van Roorden figured prominently, by a disturbance in the corridor outside.

Someone seemed to be persistently banging on a door, and he could hear the dim ringing of a bell.

As the row continued, Thurston stood up, crossed the apartment and looked out.

The disturbance came from a door almost immediately opposite his own... and the main who rang and banged was *Nayland Smith!*

"Smith!"

Nayland Smith had turned, was staring at Thurston across the width of the corridor. His skin had been permanently darkened by years of tropical suns, so that it was impossible to detect pallor. But Thurston thought that some of the old, eager vitality was lacking tonight. The silver at his temples had become more marked.

"Hullo, Thurston!" he rapped (the quick-fire speech remained unimpaired). "Didn't expect to see *you* here. Come into your apartment and phone if I may."

"You're very welcome."

But, when the door was closed, Nayland Smith dropped wearily into an armchair, and Thurston saw that he looked almost haggard. Something had taxed this man of iron to the limit of his endurance.

"I'm up against one of my toughest problems, Thurston," he began in his abrupt, staccato way. "Can talk to *you*. Glad to. There's a gigantic plot about to mature—a plot to destroy Fort Knox, and the gold reserve upon which the financial power of the United States largely depends!"

"Destroy Fort Knox! It's just impossible! Communists?"

Nayland Smith shook his head, smiled grimly, and taking out a charred briar pipe, began to charge it from a dilapidated pouch.

"No. What d'you think *I'm* doing here? If it had been the Communists I might have agreed with you. But it's something far more serious. Did you ever hear of the Si-Fan?"

Thurston stared blankly.

"Never."

"It's the most powerful secret society in the world today. It is directed by a man who is probably the supreme genius of all time. He has more scientific knowledge in that one phenomenal brain than any ten men alive. He is called Dr Fu-Manchu. You have heard the name?"

"As a name, yes." Thurston was awed. "No more!"

Nayland Smith replaced his pouch and lighted his pipe.

"I sincerely hope you may never have occasion to learn more! We are uncertain of the details of the scheme. But we think some kind of guided missile is involved—probably with an atomic warhead, or something even more destructive!"

"But where could such a thing be assembled?"

"Several thousand men are engaged, at this very moment, trying to find out! One man, a brilliant FBI operative, has actually succeeded in becoming a *member* of the Si-Fan!"

"Is he an Oriental?" Thurston gasped.

Nayland Smith smoked feverishly.

"Not a bit of it. Don't run away with the idea that the Si-Fan is a Far Eastern group. It's international. That's the danger. It's true that Selwyn Orson—the FBI man—joined it somewhere in the East. He's a wonderful linguist. He's just back, with vital information."

"Where is he?"

"That's his room over there. And, although he called me only half an hour ago, I can get no reply. Hasn't gone out. Checked that."

He grabbed up the 'phone. Thurston stared.

"Put me through to Mr Wylie. This is Sir Denis Nayland Smith."

He glanced aside at Thurston.

"When do you think this horror is timed to happen?" Thurston asked in a hushed voice.

Nayland Smith shook his head, and then:

"Hullo—Mr Wylie?" he asked. "Nayland Smith here. I'm in Number 114, Mr Thurston's apartment. Be good enough to send a boy up with a key to Number 113. Yes, at once, please."

He hung up.

"I don't know the exact time, Thurston. But all my information suggests that it may happen at almost any hour now!"

The speed with which the key was delivered by the management indicated the authority vested in Nayland Smith, and when the boy had gone away, they crossed the corridor, and Nayland Smith unlocked the door of Number 113.

On the threshold he stood still, barring Thurston's entrance.

"What is it, Smith?"

"You don't have to come in, Thurston." He spoke without turning. "If you do, prepare for a dreadful sight!"

Nayland Smith went in, and Thurston followed him. The warning had been timely; for even now Thurston pulled up, uttered a smothered cry.

Face downward in the lobby, and so near the door that it was only just possible to open it, lay a blue-clad stocky figure. The man's outstretched hands were still plunged into an open suitcase, from which a variety of articles had been thrown out on to the floor.

"Good God!" Thurston muttered. He felt deathly sick. "What does this mean?"

"Murder!" snapped Nayland Smith. "He's been shot through the head—from behind."

"There's blood—a trail of it—leading into the room."

Nayland Smith nodded and went in. Thurston, trying to avoid wet patches on the carpet, followed. Inside, he clutched Smith's arm.

"Smith! This is horrible! The place is a *morgue*!"

Another dead man was seated beside the table on which the 'phone stood!

His arms were stretched out on either side of a Manhattan Directory, and he had slumped forward so that his head rested slantwise on the book. The effect was grotesque. He seemed to be leering up at the intruders.

"Merciful God! It's *Fordwich*!"

The whisper came from Thurston's pale lips.

Nayland Smith hardly glanced at him. He sprang to the dead man's side, touched cold fingers, and stooping, peered into sightless eyes. He stood upright.

"Too late! And you're mistaken. This was Selwyn Orson—the finest investigator who ever worked with the FBI!"

Thurston said nothing. Words were failing him. He had been swept into a world of mystery, of horror, for which his orderly life had not equipped him.

The apartment bore every evidence of a frantic search. An automatic fitted with a silencer tube lay beside the table. Only one shell had been used. And then, half under the bed, came a discovery which completed Thurston's sick bewilderment. This was Fordwich's black walking stick—snapped in half…

"Poor Orson was stabbed," Nayland Smith rapped out the words at top speed. "Almost certainly by that brute lying in the lobby. It was a surprise attack. How the man got in we are never likely to know, now. Orson collapsed. The killer went to work. Orson revived, dragged himself out, silently, to where the man was busy on another suitcase in the lobby, and shot him. Then, he dragged himself back to the phone—but died before he got his message through."

The languor had gone. Nayland Smith was revivified. His grey eyes shone like steel. His reconstruction of the crime had been a matter of minutes. He stood for a moment looking about him, pulling reflectively at the lobe of his ear, then went out to the lobby. Thurston followed, dizzily, trying to conquer his nausea.

Nayland Smith bent over the prone figure.

"We shall find the knife with which Orson was murdered, unless I'm greatly mistaken."

"But I thought," Thurston began—and said no more.

Vaguely, he was beginning to grasp the fact that those strict police regulations which prohibit the disturbing of the body of a homicide corpse did not apply to Sir Denis.

"In the other pocket, then." Smith turned the body over. "Ah! Here it is!"

And, as he drew a bloodstained knife from the blue coat, Thurston had a glimpse of a distorted, pock-marked face.

"Smith!" His voice shook emotionally. "Smith! This is Mrs van Roorden's Burmese servant!"

"There's no doubt," said Nayland Smith, "that you have been chosen by Higher Powers to save the United States from disaster!"

Thurston helped himself to a third brandy. Some trace of colour was returning to his face.

They sat now in his apartment, already foggy with tobacco smoke from Smith's pipe. The handbag (its lock smashed) which contained the green mask, and the mask itself, intact, lay on the bed; Fordwich's black stick lay beside it—the one that had been in the golf bag.

"I have told you all I have to tell, Smith. But I haven't the very slightest idea what it adds up to!"

"This," Smith rapped. "In the first place, after the medical examiner has made his report, Number 113 must be sealed. No whisper of what lies there has to leak out. So much I have arranged with Raymond Harkness of the FBI, who is co-operating with me. In the second place, poor Selwyn Orson must have known he was spotted. He chose *you* to bring his stick ashore!"

"But…"

"He had a duplicate, which he had kept hidden during the crossing. The note you received, asking you to call at the purser's office, was sent, of course, by Orson—whom you knew as Fordwich. He wanted you out of the cabin long enough to slip the stick into your golf-bag. He must have noted that you carried one."

"But why? Why *two* sticks?"

Nayland Smith began to knock ashes from his fuming pipe.

"That I hope to find out. The smashed duplicate across in his room suggests that his killer—who, by the way was a professional thug, a Burmese dacoit—had special instructions on this point."

"And the green mask?"

Nayland Smith shook his head.

"One mystery at a time, Thurston! Suppose we start with the stick."

He took it up and examined it closely. He tapped it, and endeavoured to unscrew the crooked handle. It appeared to be solid. Smith clicked his teeth together irritably.

"Of course, it's a smuggler's stick. But how does it open?… *Ah!*"

He begun to detach the rubber ferule. It was not easy, but at last he had it off. Under the rubber was a brass ferule. Attempts to remove it defied all his efforts, until, with the ferule wedged in the hinge of the bathroom door and while he turned the shank firmly, it began to unscrew.

There was a cavity in the base of the big stick, from which protruded a roll of paper!

Nayland Smith pulled it out. It proved to consist of a number of closely typed and very thin pages, wound around a sort of slender jade baton most curiously carved.

At this he stared with deep curiosity. He examined the delicate carving.

"What the devil have we here?"

Then, with care, he turned the baton in his fingers. It opened without difficulty. It unscrewed in the middle. And Smith tapped out into the palm of his left hand a single sheet of parchment on which appeared some lines of writing in heavy, black letters.

At the foot of the parchment was a small seal.

He glanced at the seal, rapidly scanned the typescript, and then shot a steely glance at Thurston.

"I believe you told me that you found Mrs van Roorden dangerously alluring?"

"I did."

"She is! She's Dr Fu-Manchu's daughter!"

Thurston stared almost stupidly.

"But, Smith—she is quite young."

"She has always appeared so," Nayland Smith snapped, "from the first time I met her up to her last attempt to seduce me!"

At about which time, Dr Fu-Manchu, wrapped in a fur-lined coat and having an astrakhan cap pulled well down over his massive skull, glanced back at old Huan Tsung, his chief-of-staff, who sat behind him in the plane. Matsukata was the pilot.

"I seem to hear your teeth chattering, Huan Tsung?"

"Your hearing does not mislead you, Excellency."

"Yet Peko, here in my arms, sleeps peacefully."

"Even if men derive from apes, some small differences distinguish us from our remote ancestors. Monkeys may be immune. But at our present height, without aid of oxygen, I confess that my old heart falters."

"We could touch the outer atmosphere, encased as we are in the new amalgam. Imagination, Huan Tsung, is a two-edged sword." Fu-Manchu glanced at the instrument board. "We are far above the commercial air lanes, but we continue to receive absurd signals from military bases. I anticipate that we shall be reported once more as a 'flying saucer'."

"Excellency, surely life is a flying saucer, a saucer in which we are whirled out of eternity into eternity…"

"It's now quite evident," Nayland Smith was saying, "that Orson must have been responsible for searching the stateroom of the woman you knew as Mrs van Roorden while she was at the purser's cocktail party. No doubt it was Orson, too, who put her Burmese bodyguard to sleep. These typed notes wrapped around the jade baton make it clear that he had risen high in the Si-Fan organisation."

"What an amazing man!" Thurston exclaimed.

"Amazing indeed. It's to Selwyn Orson that we owed the first news of the Fort Knox conspiracy. At that time he was in Egypt, where he had been called to a personal interview with the president of the Si-Fan. Steps were taken here. And an attempt was made to find the Cairo headquarters of the society." Nayland Smith snapped his fingers irritably. "Next to impossible to get action under the present Egyptian government."

He was pacing up and down the room like a caged tiger, smoking almost ceaselessly.

"Do you mean," Thurston asked, "that these people have agents in Egypt?"

"All over the world! The Si-Fan has expanded enormously since I first came in touch with it. Orson seems to have posed as a Frenchman, which he could do very easily, as he had lived for many years in Paris. He was one of the deputies selected by the Si-Fan to attend a secret conference here in New York!"

"But how do you suppose he discovered the real identity of Mrs van Roorden?"

"I don't think he *had* discovered it, until the night he burgled her cabin. He makes it quite plain in these notes, and in his earlier despatch from Cairo (which I have seen), that no officer of the Si-Fan knows another by sight. But he knows all the lesser members under his immediate control. He was evidently sent from Egypt to Java. The Si-Fan has been very busy there, rubbing out some of the leading Communists!"

"What! The Si-Fan is anti-Communist?"

"Somewhat!" snapped Nayland Smith grimly. "Orson, I believe, met Mrs van Roorden in Java, and then, later, on the *Lauretania*. He doesn't state, here, what aroused his suspicion, but he *does* say that he was waiting for a chance to search her cabin." He pointed to the jade baton. "This is what he found."

Thurston picked up and stared again at the sheet of thin parchment which the baton had contained. It was half covered with heavy, square writing.

The message, in English, was in cramped script resembling old Black Letter. It authorised the bearer, referred to as "my daughter," to preside at the conference in the unavoidable absence of "the President."

"I don't understand," Thurston said, "how such a conference could take place, if it's true that no officer of this society knows another by sight."

Nayland Smith paused in his restless promenade, picked up the green mask and dropped it back in the bag.

"Clearly, they all wear these things—not to frighten one another, but simply to conceal their identity. It's not a new trick. It was used, in the form of hoods, by Inquisitors of the Holy Office in Spain and is still popular with the Ku Klux Klan."

Thurston was studying a sort of crest which served as letterhead:

"What does this thing mean?" he asked.

Nayland Smith glanced aside and then continued his pacing.

"I have come across it only once before. Out of context, it really means nothing. But it could be construed to mean 'The higher' or 'The one above'. it is evidently the sign of the Si-Fan."

The message bore no name; only the imprint of a seal on green wax:

"And this seal?"

"Is the seal of *Dr Fu-Manchu*…"

The door-bell buzzed.

"That will be Harkness."

Smith crossed the lobby and threw the door open. Raymond Harkness, of the FBI, came in, a slight man with gentle, hazel eyes and the manner of a family doctor.

"Have you made all arrangements?" Smith rapped.

"Yes." Harkness spoke softly. "Poor old Orson. Our star man, Sir Denis."

"He didn't sacrifice himself for nothing," said Nayland Smith grimly. "Thanks to him, we hold most of the threads in our hands. We owe this to Mr Thurston here. He became unavoidably mixed up in the thing."

Harkness turned his quiet regard on Thurston.

"Take my advice," he said. "Step out of this affair just as soon as you can—and stay out. Also keep your mouth shut as tightly as if the air was poisoned."

Thurston was not one of those "great adventurers who put self last" referred to by Mrs van Roorden. He was a plain man of business. Fate had made him an unconscious messenger, had plunged him into deep, dark mysteries. He sighed, for sometimes he had longed for such adventure. But he decided that Raymond Harkness' advice was good…

Mrs van Roorden stepped out of the shower and critically considered her gleaming ivory body in a long pier glass. She could detect no sign of age's encroachments. Her cool flesh was firm; the contours remained perfect.

She wrapped herself in a woolly robe and returned to the bedroom.

A contrast to other rooms in the apartment, this was equipped in the Parisian manner; a fragrant nest for loveliness. She lingered over creams and perfumes in crystal bottles ranged on a cedarwood dressing-table inlaid with mother-of-pearl, took up a hand mirror, the back delicately enamelled on gold, and studied her profile.

She was satisfied; she was still beautiful.

But she was ill at ease.

The frock which she had decided to wear lay draped over a chair, with appropriate shoes and stockings beside it. Mai Cha was perfect in her attentions, as should be expected from the daughter of a Chinese aristocrat. But Mrs van Roorden had never met this youngest child of the aged but prolific Mandarin Huan Tsung before. She had been received as a princess, but all the members of the household were strangers.

If only Huan Tsung had been there! Old Huan Tsung who used to smuggle sweetmeats to her in baby days, who had given her that pet name of Fah Lo Suee, because, he said, she was like a budding lily blossom.

She stood up restlessly and went out into an adjoining room equipped in purely Chinese fashion. There were panels of ivory and jade, rare and beautiful rugs, rose porcelain. The furniture might have, and possibly had, come from an Emperor's palace. There was a faint perfume, blended of musk and sandalwood, and the lamps were hidden in frames of painted silk.

Mrs van Roorden crossed to windows screened by ebony fretwork, and opened a screen. A warm breeze met her as she stepped out on to the balcony and stood there looking down at Fifth Avenue far below and then across the Park to where tall buildings on Central Park West loomed up, monstrous, against the evening sky.

What, she asked herself for the hundredth time, had become of Sha Mu?

Had he failed altogether—been arrested? She was not prepared to believe this. His stealthy cunning had never failed before. It was barely possible that he might still be waiting for an opportunity. Even the uncanny skill with which he could make himself almost invisible would not have enabled him to hide in the hotel so long without being challenged.

Who was the man who called himself Fordwich?

Only by a fleeting glance in a mirror had Sha Mu been able to identify his attacker. And it had proved hopeless to attempt anything on the ship. Something was seriously wrong. But she dare not call the hotel.

Mrs van Roorden returned to the softly lighted room. A Chinese girl stood there. She wore native dress, and her eyes were modestly downcast. She had a shy grace of movement which remained one of a gazelle.

"My lady lacks something?"

Mrs van Roorden smiled.

"Nothing that *you* can find for me, Mai Cha! Tell me, dear, when did you see your father last?"

"It was nearly a year ago."

"And where is he now?"

Mai Cha shook her glossy head.

"I cannot say. I never know."

"But this apartment is always kept open?"

"Always, my lady. He might return at any time."

"How I wish he would return tonight," Mrs van Roorden murmured; and then: "May I ask you something, Mai Cha?"

"Anything you wish."

"Has Sir Denis Nayland Smith ever been here?"

The dark eyes were raised to her in mild astonishment.

"But no. Of course not. He is my father's enemy. He has never known that we live here. The apartment was bought by someone else—on my father's behalf."

"But you know Nayland Smith?"

"I have seen him, my lady. But not for many, many months."

Mrs van Roorden moved towards the bedroom.

"Don't bother about me, Mai Cha," she smiled. "I shall not be going out for a long time yet…"

Centre Street that night resembled a wasp's nest.

An inoffensive businessman, purely because of deep interest in the fascinating Mrs van Roorden, which had impelled him to force his acquaintance upon Mr Fordwich, had become an instrument of justice. Unwittingly he had carried on the work of a star secret agent.

Motorcycle patrolmen, radio cars, shot into the dusk like earth-bound rockets. Phones buzzed. The private line to Washington stayed red hot for hours. And Nayland Smith, in the office of his old friend, Deputy Commissioner Burke, a heavy powerful man with black, tufted eyebrows and greying hair, smoked his foul pipe incessantly as if in competition with Burke's strong cigars.

Raymond Harkness inhaled cigarettes in swift succession, each neatly fitted into a tortoiseshell holder. He displayed no other signs of excitement.

"This card," said Nayland Smith, "which Harkness found wedged between the leather cover and the silver of poor Orson's flask, is clearly intended to admit him to a meeting at the house of Kwang T'see, wherever that may be, at two a.m. tomorrow morning, September 10th—that is, tonight. It has the Si-Fan crest at the top."

"Not a doubt of it," Burke growled in his deep bass. "He meant to pick up the stick and the flask just as soon as he thought it was safe.

If I could have a hand in cleaning up this Fu-Manchu gang before I retire next year, I'd go to growing watermelons with a light heart."

"The Fu-Manchu gang," Smith rapped back, "is too big to be cleaned up overnight. But we have a chance to get some of the high executives and to break the Fort Knox scheme." He glanced at a clock over Burke's desk. "I'm waiting for news about the house of Kwang T'see!"

"So am I," Burke agreed, and was about to ring when a rap sounded on the door and Police Captain Rafferty came in.

He saluted Burke with the deference due to a dreaded but respected chief.

"I have a report on Kwang Tsee, sir."

"Spill it."

"The only man of that name known in the Chinatown area is the proprietor of a store formerly owned by old Huan Tsung."

"That settles it!" said Nayland Smith drily. "Go ahead."

"Huan Tsung disappeared about a year ago. We wanted him, you may remember, but we could pin nothing on him. This man, Kwang T'see, bought the business. He's enlarged it. He owns a big warehouse in the next street, same block, stocked with antiques from the East. He lives somewhere on the premises. Nothing against him…"

When Rafferty was gone, with a number of instructions:

"I guess this Kwang T'see is a dummy, Smith," said Burke. "What's your idea?"

"The same as yours. A Chinatown base is characteristic of Dr Fu-Manchu."

"You knew Huan Tsung fairly well, didn't you?"

Raymond Harkness smiled but said nothing.

"You exaggerate!" Nayland Smith assured him. "I never really knew him at all. He was once governor of a Chinese province. He is now Dr Fu-Manchu's chief aide. He's a first-class soldier, although of incalculable age. If Chiang Kai-shek had had him on his staff, the Communists would lie nowhere in China today. I have had several skirmishes with General Huan Tsung Chao, to give him his full name, but never won one yet!"

"The whole thing drops dead," Burke declared, "if any news has leaked about the slaughter in Room 113."

"No leakage has occurred," came Harkness' gentle assurance. "No one saw the baskets taken out. The room remains sealed. I arranged for Mr Thurston to dine and spend the night with friends of mine in Bronxville, where there is gay company. He has driven there in one of our cars."

Nayland Smith's grim face relaxed in a smile. It was a smile which betrayed the schoolboy who had never grown up.

"Clean, smart, efficient work," he commented. "Satisfied, Burke?"

"I guess so. It's up to us, now. We know that Fu-Manchu is playing for recognition. He figures that if performers with records like that old cross-talk act, Hitler and Mussolini, not to mention artists still with us, have been allowed a place in public life—why not Dr Fu-Manchu?"

"And why not?" Nayland Smith challenged. "He has the brains of all of them rolled into one."

"Must have," Burke agreed. "You've been down to Fort Knox and you know that a consignment of gold in one of the vaults, still in the boxes it was shipped in, has been turned into something that looks like lead!"

"Quite so! In accordance with Fu-Manchu's threat to Washington. Contents of the other twenty-seven vaults are still intact."

"But the Treasury's nearly crazy," Harkness said quietly. "Already, the loss is enormous. If the further threat of the Si-Fan to destroy the entire reserve is made good, the financial stability of the United States will lie in the hands of those people!"

"And we can't find out how it was done," Burke groaned. "It sounds like a miracle. Fu-Manchu knows that such losses have to be officially denied. Otherwise we'd have a financial panic. He aims to *blackmail* Washington into recognising him."

"He wants to see the Si-Fan where the Nazis and the Fascists stood—where the Soviets stand today!"

"When this conference assembles," Burke pointed out, "even if we manage to grab the lot we shan't know what we want to know."

"There's another point." Harkness fitted a fresh cigarette into his holder. "News of it might speed up the action we want to stop. Our information clearly indicates that Fu-Manchu won't be present, and we may have no evidence whatever against the others."

Nayland Smith began to walk about restlessly.

"The meeting must not be disturbed. It's the best chance we're ever likely to have of finding out what happened to that gold in Fort Knox, and of taking steps to see that it doesn't happen again."

"But *how*?" Burke shouted.

"Surely it's obvious. They will all be masked. I regard it as highly unlikely—a hundred to one against—that Mrs van Roorden ever suspected Orson of being a Si-Fan deputy. What could be more simple… I'll take his place."

Mrs van Roorden leaned over the balcony, watching two streams of light, one north bound, the other south, which represented Fifth Avenue, below. No individual light could be picked out; just two long, luminous ribbons broken only when a red traffic signal checked their flow.

She wore the green gown which she had worn at the purser's party on the *Lauretania*. This, for two reasons: the first that she despised ideas of good and bad luck, the second, that it amused her to dress to the green mask she must wear at the Si-Fan conference.

The unaccountable disappearance of Sha Mu, her Burmese bodyguard, was disturbing and ominous.

But, whatever the explanation, she could do nothing at all about it—yet.

No amount of interrogation would extract anything from Sha Mu. What little he knew was negligible and he spoke no language other than the Shan dialect.

So that, whatever had happened, no clue could be picked up from it leading either to the time of to the place of the Si-Fan meeting. As to the man, Fordwich, there was no longer any room for doubt... He had been covering her since their first meeting in Java. He was a secret service agent, either of Great Britain or of the United States.

But, although she taxed her memory unmercifully she could recall not one slip she had made. All the same, it must have occurred; for he had searched her room, and had taken nothing but the letter from her father which betrayed her identity.

Where was that letter now?

Highly probable that every precinct in New York City had a description of the appearance of Dr Fu-Manchu's daughter!

She smiled, turned, and went into the softly lighted room, redolent of old memories. Mai Cha, Who had been seated, reading, stood up as the graceful figure appeared.

"Sit down, dear. There's no need for ceremony when we are alone."

She addressed the girl in English, which she spoke without trace of accent.

"Thank you," Mai Cha said simply, and obeyed.

"I have had the same training as you." Mrs van Roorden sank onto a low settee. "The beautiful old courtesies. But we both live in a new world. Perhaps we shall never know that old world of ours again. You are to be my guide tonight?"

"Yes, my lady. Those are my orders. But I was told…"

Mai Cha hesitated.

"Yes, dear, what were you told?"

"That Sha Mu would follow, to protect us if necessary."

"You know Sha Mu?"

"He was here a year ago."

"He landed with me. But I am sorry to say he has disappeared!"

"That is bad," Mai Cha murmured.

Mrs van Roorden studied her. She was very young to be a child of Huan Tsung. Her mother must have been pretty, for beauty was not a characteristic of the old mandarin.

"We must go alone. I am a stranger to New York, Mai Cha. Is it far?"

"Quite a long way. We can take the car nearly to where we are going and then we must walk."

"I wonder if you can find me a cloak to put over my frock?"

"Certainly, my lady. I was told to do so."

The careful staff work of Huan Tsung could be detected in this. What he had not foreseen was the loss of her credentials—so that she must convince six men, each one risking his liberty, six men who had never met her before, that she was authorised to preside over their conference…

The car in which Nayland Smith was being driven to Kwang T'see's house of mystery slowed up at a selected point, and Harkness got in. Although the black sedan belonged to Headquarters, there was nothing visible to indicate this fact, and the police driver wore plain clothes.

"Turn right at the lights," Harkness directed, "and cruise along the river front slowly."

"What news?" Nayland Smith asked.

"The meeting is at Kwang's beyond doubt." Harkness fitted a cigarette into his holder. "Something afoot there all right. And we have settled one point that was bothering you. Visitors aren't going in at the store; they're ringing a private bell beside the door on the other street. Small office belonging to the warehouse."

"There have been visitors, then?" Smith rapped. "How many?"

Harkness nodded as he lighted his cigarette.

"Two, so far. Strangers to the area. And both carried cases."

"Similar to Orson's which I have here?"

"That's it. The first man arrived on the dot of one-thirty-five. Exactly at one-forty, the second came along… Ah! Here's a report."

He lifted the 'phone, listened, said "Go on reporting," then hung up.

"Another?"

"Number three was there on the stroke of one-forty-five. I expect you follow my line of reasoning, Sir Denis?"

"Clearly. The cards are timed so that no two deputies arrive together. My card says: 'Two a.m.'—So I'm evidently expected to be the sixth arrival. Do they all come alone?"

"Yes. On foot."

"H'm."

Nayland Smith stared out across the River, through a gap in dock buildings, to where the Jersey City skyline stretched like far-flung ramparts of some giant castle. A launch of the Harbour Patrol went by, its crew ignorant of the fact that a conspiracy to upset the stability of the United States was brewing close on shore.

"I don't like this business," Harkness remarked in his gentle way.

"It's believed, but has never been proved, that the cellars under both those places intercommunicate, in fact form a perfect warren in the time-honoured Chinese style."

"What of it? You may remember that I know something about Huian Tsung's cellars, anyway. Been down there before. Point is, if anything goes wrong, you know I'm there and you know where to look for me."

"Yes. But I feel this should be my job, not yours."

"The hell you do!" rapped Nayland Smith, his eyes suddenly steely. "Don't misunderstand me, Harkness. I quite follow and I appreciate. But now that poor Orson is gone, there's probably no man outside the Si-Fan who knows more about the organisation than I do. No. Definitely it's my job."

Harkness sighed.

"You have memorised the notes pencilled on Orson's report?"

"I have. But I don't know what some of them mean. I wonder if he had a premonition of what was to happen? Or were they intended to refresh his own memory?"

The notes referred to had been scribbled on the back of one of the typed pages hidden in Orson's hollow stick. They were:

Ring seven times
Si-Fan. The Seven
Give up card
Mask. Gown
Seven rings. Sixth bell

"The first one's clear enough," Harkness said. "You ring the doorbell seven times. The others are incomprehensible. I can only hope that their meaning will come to you when you get inside. But if anything goes wrong, you know what to do?"

"Certainly. But I should hate to disturb the party before it had properly begun."

The arrival of a fourth man at Kwang's door had been reported:

"Time we were moving," Smith said, rapidly, and glanced at the illuminated dial of his wrist-watch. "Better put the glasses on!"

At a word from Harkness, the sedan shot forward at sudden speed, swerved swiftly left and swept almost noiselessly into a dark street. At this hour of the night on the outskirts of the Asiatic quarter, windows were blackened, there were few people on the sidewalk. These mean houses might have been uninhabited.

Even the show places on Mott and Pell Street would be closing. Only one prepared to explore deep in secret burrows could hope to penetrate to the shady side of Eastern life in Manhattan's Chinatown.

The big car came to a sudden halt.

"You can't miss the door," Harkness said. "Remember—I'm standing by!"

Nayland Smith, wearing no disguise other than heavy-rimmed glasses (with plain lenses), got out. He carried Selwyn Orson's small leather case. They had driven past the establishment of Kwang T'see an hour before, and it was impossible for him to make any mistake.

As he walked slowly along, he paid an unspoken compliment to the police arrangements, whereby several men had been placed, earlier, so that they commanded a view of Kwang T'see's office door. The store on the next street was also under close observation.

He had the whole of the New York Police Department behind him... and the unknown before...

"We must walk from here, my lady."

Mrs van Roorden alighted from the car. Her green gown was

hidden by a dark rainproof coat, the hood pulled over her head. A satchel hung from a strap across her shoulder. Mai Cha, hatless, and wearing a cheap frock in place of her native dress, had stepped out first and held the car door open. The chauffeur sat, silent, at the wheel.

There was garbage piled on the dirty sidewalk. The dingy houses looked as though they had been deserted in a plague. Two or three dilapidated automobiles were parked along the street.

"This is a dreadful neighbourhood, Mai Cha."

"Yes. It is bad. I worked near here for a long time. But further up it is better."

"Which way do we go?"

"To the corner. Then around, half way along the block."

"The car will wait?"

"Of course, my lady."

The warmth of the night had grown sultry. Clouds gathered, to add to the gloom of the depressing street. They had nearly reached the corner when Mrs van Roorden heard the sound of a started engine. She stopped, turned.

"You told me the chauffeur would wait!"

"He will wait, my lady." Mai Cha's placid voice remained soft, soothing. "I shall know where to find him."

They came to the corner, and Mrs van Roorden stood back against a wall decorated with a Chinese poster. A heavily built man, a half-caste of some sort, picturesquely drunk, had almost bumped into her. He pulled up, stared at her, stared at Mai Cha, and staggered on.

"Let's hurry!"

Mrs van Roorden was coolly composed, but delicately disgusted. Her composure might have faltered if she had known that the drunken half-caste was one of Raymond Harkness' men. That he had returned to the corner to watch them and that, two minutes later, he would report: "The woman has gone in."

They hurried along to a door set beside double, barred gates.

"Here is the bell, my lady. I shall be waiting for you to come out."

Nayland Smith five minutes before, had pressed the same bell—seven times.

An interval followed, during which nothing happened. Then, there was a faint clicking sound. Realising that it operated mechanically, Smith pushed the door—and found himself in a complete blackout, stuffy, airless. The door closed behind him.

He stood still for a moment, trying to get his bearings in the dark. But he could see nothing, hear nothing. He wondered what he should do next, thought of Orson's notes—and had an idea.

"Si-Fan. The Seven!" he called.

A mechanical rumbling followed, heavy, dull, thunderous. A second door was being opened. In that utter darkness he saw a panel of faint green light. It enlarged as he watched, became a wide rectangular gap.

He found himself looking out into a dimly illuminated place which resembled Aladdin's cave. It was the warehouse referred to by Police Captain Rafferty.

This green light came from a solitary lamp far away in cavernous darkness, but coming out of even more complete darkness, Nayland Smith's eyes quickly became accustomed to it. He glanced around—and was amazed.

Here was a fabulous treasure-house.

The distant light was from a silver mosque lamp fitted with green glass; one of the objects of art with which this incredible place was crowded. Piled upon the floor were rugs and carpets of Kermanshah, of Khorassan, of the looms of China. Here was furniture of lemonwood, ivory, exquisitely inlaid, some of it with semi-precious stones; lacquer and enamel caskets, robes heavy with gold brocades and gems, pagan gods, swords, jars and bowls of delicate porcelain.

He looked back at the door by which he had entered, for he had heard it closing.

It was a metal door, set in a steel frame.

Clearly, Kwang T'see did not rely on burglary insurance. But, setting aside certain qualms aroused by this unbreakable door, Nayland Smith concentrated upon the next move.

It was highly probable that the real delegates were familiar with the routine, and his only chance of safety lay in divining what this routine was. He hesitated for no more than twenty seconds.

Picking a route along a sort of alleyway amid priceless pieces, some of them fragile, he paused under the green lamp. It was suspended before a drapery of magnificent Chinese tapestry which only partly concealed another metal door. The ingenuity of the scheme, carried out without care for cost, earned his admiration.

These steel doors could be explained readily by the proprietor of such a collection as this. But other than a bank strongroom, no safer place could well be imagined for a meeting of conspirators.

A ticking sound, ominously like that of a time-bomb, drew his glance swiftly upward.

From somewhere in the shadowy roof an object that looked like a lacquered tray, suspended on thin metal chains, was descending slowly! Lower it came, and lower, until it swung within reach of his hand.

Feverishly, Nayland Smith reviewed the pencilled notes.

Give up card…

He might be right, he might be wrong. But to hesitate would certainly be fatal.

Taking from his pocket the card found in Orson's flask, Smith dropped it in the tray and gently twitched the chain.

The tray was wound up again.

A moment after it had been swallowed in the shadows of the roof beams, that now familiar rumbling was repeated. He saw that the half-draped door had begun to open. When the opening became wide enough, he stepped through.

The rumbling ceased for three seconds, was renewed—and the metal door closed upon his entrance.

He was in a small, square room, unfurnished except for a long couch and a row of pegs on the wall, and lighted by one ceiling lamp. A number of cases and handbags lay on the settee. Two robes, or gowns, rather like those of university bachelors but of a dull green colour, hung on the pegs.

His next step was crystal clear... *Mask. Gown.*

Taking out the hideous green mask, he removed his glasses and fitted it onto his head. It was contrived so as to cover the hair, and made of some flexible, lightweight material. The mouth aperture was hidden by a sort of grating, but the eyeholes were not obstructed in any way.

Orson's case he laid on the settee, where five others lay already. None of the cases was initialled, he noted. Then he draped one of the two voluminous gowns over his shoulders.

And now came the crucial test:

Seven rings. Sixth bell.

What in the name of reason, did that mean?

He inspected the room closely. Apart from the heavy, mechanical door now shutting him off from the world of normal men, he could see no other way in or out. But he saw something else: a narrow board, with seven green buttons. Reaching out, Nayland Smith pressed the button numbered six. He pressed it seven times.

Throughout, no human sound had reached him; but he could not dismiss an impression of being covertly watched. So far, he believed, he had done nothing to betray himself. So that, unless the unseen watcher had recognised him, his course still remained clear.

As for anything which might happen now, he was totally without guidance and must rely on his wits.

His pressure on the bell-push had produced no audible result. Complete silence claimed the small room. He was just beginning to wonder, uneasily, if he had misread Orson's last note, when a second door, camouflaged so cleverly in a wall that he had overlooked it, slid almost noiselessly open.

Nayland Smith stood at the head of a flight of concrete stairs.

He was about to enter the secret cellars!

Smiling grimly (from now onward he stood alone against the Si-Fan) he began to go down.

The stairs led to a long, paved passage. It seemed to end before semi-transparent green draperies. Evidently green was the Si-Fan colour. Light showed through the drapes.

And then, at last, a silence which had been disturbed only by the sound of his footsteps on the stair, was broken.

It was broken so sharply that he started, clenched his fists.

Six strokes on a deep-toned gong echoed, eerily, from wall to wall of the passage…

Raymond Harkness had just received the report, "The woman has gone in," when he noted a disturbance outside the yard in which the black sedan was parked. He stubbed out a cigarette he had been inhaling and sat quite still to listen.

A bulky figure appeared——and came right up to the open window.

"Who is it?" Harkness asked, sharply.

The glowing end of a big cigar was poked right in.

"Who does it look like?" Burke's growling bass inquired. "Your Aunt Fanny? Suppose I could wear out the seat of my pants with a show like this on? I have all the dope up to Smith going in. What's new since then?"

"The woman has gone in."

"Was she alone?"

"She went in alone. But a girl came out with her."

"Where's this girl?"

"She walked around to Kwang T'see's store."

"Fine! We know where to find her. Did they come in a car?"

"Yes. But they left it too far away for anybody to pick it up. The car was driven off."

"Lousy!" Burke growled. "Oh, lousy! Nobody tailing it?"

"Rafferty reports there wasn't time. It was off the moment the owner got out."

"I'll talk to Rafferty, later. Is it certain, stone-sure certain, that every possible bolt-hole is plugged up?"

"There's a cordon right around the two blocks. You see, this car stopped outside the netted area—'

"Forget it! How long are we to give Smith to try to find out what we want to know before we go look for him?"

Harkness fitted a cigarette into his holder. "As I'm not in charge tonight, sir, that must rest with you."

Nayland Smith pulled the green draperies aside and stepped into a room which challenged his sanity.

It was a square room having no visible opening except the one through which he had come in. The green draperies were carried around all four walls and up to the centre of the ceiling, so that the interior resembled a tent. Its sole furniture consisted of a shaded lamp suspended on a chain over a circular ebony table around which were placed seven ebony chairs. Before each of the chairs a disk with a number stood on the gleaming surface.

Five green-masked, green-robed figures arose as he entered. Nayland Smith clenched his teeth, trying to assure himself that he had not been drugged in some subtle way, that this was not delirium.

Five pairs of eyes stared from five masks as the deputies saluted him by swinging their right hand across so that it rested, palm outward, over the heart. No word was spoken. Reverberations of six gong strokes still haunted the air.

He returned the salute, and sat down in an ebony chair placed before a disk numbered six.

The five masked men resumed their seats in silence.

Was he accepted—or did this ominous and unnatural silence mean that they were waiting for him to carry out some part of the ritual not mentioned in poor Orson's hastily scribbled notes?

Furtively, he glanced from mask to mask, trying to detect any signal one to another. No such communion was visible. These men were waiting—but for what?

It was a nightmare. Temptation to exchange some word with his neighbours became nearly irresistible. His heart was beating over-fast. Perhaps he wasn't the man he had been. His mental reserves might be failing him. He fixed his gaze on the only vacant place at the circular table. It faced him almost directly.

And it was numbered *One.*

Nayland Smith reviewed the mumbo-jumbo practised by other

secret societies of which he had knowledge, the Fascist and the
Nazi ceremonies, hunting for some parallel. In fact, this silence was
getting his nerves on edge.

Almost with relief, although it startled him, he heard a deep
gong note.

One!

The five masked men stood up, and Nayland Smith did the same.
Light footsteps became audible beyond the green draperies. The
curtain was swept aside and a masked woman entered the room.

Her entrance was a signal for the first human sound to disturb that
ghostly company. A wordless murmur swept around the ebony table.

Ignoring it, the woman gave the Si-Fan salute, walking slowly
to the vacant chair. The salute was returned. But a new silence had
fallen. It was an uneasy silence.

She carried the green cloak on her arm, and now draped it over
the back of her chair. Light from the hanging lamp gleamed on white
shoulders as she took her seat. The men, imitated by Nayland Smith,
slowly sat down. But many glances were exchanged across the table.
Her face concealed by the grotesque mask, Fu-Manchu's daughter
looked like an incarnation of the goddess Ishtar.

Coolly, without hesitation, she began to speak in that bell-like
voice which Nayland Smith remembered—had good reason never
to forget.

She greeted the deputies briefly, in French, English, German and
Arabic. Unmistakably the French greeting was addressed to him.
His deduction, from certain evidence, that Selwyn Orson had posed
as a Frenchman had apparently been correct. Greetings over, she
continued in English.

"You were expecting the President, my father. This I know, for
he has appointed me to act for him in his unavoidable absence. As I

am a stranger to all present tonight, he gave me his sealed authority to represent him." She shrugged nonchalantly. "It was stolen from my cabin on the ship by a dangerously clever agent who evidently knows far too much about the Si-Fan for our safety."

Number Five, who sat next to Nayland Smith, speaking English with a German accent, said that it was well known they had a clever agent somewhere amongst them; for top secrets had already leaked out.

There was a loud murmur of agreement. Unfriendly eyes became focussed on the woman; but:

"A great decision has to be made tonight," she went on coolly. "You are aware that we have brought pressure to bear upon Washington in an effort to induce the United States Government to give support to our president's plan to drive Communism out of the East."

No one spoke. Six pairs of eyes watched her.

"It was decided to implement words by action. Washington was notified that unless our friendly intentions were recognised and our proposals considered, a small demonstration of the powers at our disposal would be made: the gold in one of the vaults at Fort Knox would be destroyed."

"This," (it was the guttural voice again) "is knowledge common to ourselves and also to the United States authorities. I have a question to put…"

There were assenting murmurs.

"Later, if you please." Through the openings in her mask Smith could see those blazing jade-green eyes. "*I* have more to say."

The musical, imperious voice reduced the meeting to silence.

"What is not common knowledge—a fact known only to a few of us and to a few United States officials—is that the threat was carried out. No one knows, but I am authorised to tell you, how it was done."

Nayland Smith almost literally held his breath. A mystery which had defied scientists and expert investigators, himself among them, was about to be unveiled. Furthermore, he was fascinated, wholly enthralled, by the magnetic personality of this woman, her power to dominate desperate men who doubted her identity, who knew that life or liberty might be the forfeit of accepting an imposter.

"My father," she continued quietly, "has always known that the old alchemists were wrong only in one vital particular. Whilst it is impracticable to transmute base metal to gold, it is practicable to transmute gold to base metal. For many years he carried out experiments with a Rünsen beam. The Rünsen beam, as you may be aware, is a kind of super X-ray."

And now—it seemed, against their better judgement—the five men were listening intently as Nayland Smith listened.

"It has the property of penetrating nearly everything even steel or concrete. It is invisible. But gold resists the beam, which cannot penetrate it. Dr Fu-Manchu succeeded in amplifying the Rünsen process, producing a Rünsen Beam II. Gold still resisted it, but, to speak unscientifically, died in the attempt."

"Explain further, if you please."

The request came from Number Two. Nayland Smith had already noted his slim, Arab hands.

"But certainly. The effect is to disturb what my father described as the 'atomic poise' of gold, and to break it down (I quote him again) 'to its primeval elements'."

"But how," (the guttural once more) "was this beam operated Upon Fort Knox?"

White shoulders dimpled in a shrug.

"It was not operated upon Fort Knox. A consignment of gold, worth twenty-four million dollars and meant to be stored there, was dealt with on the high seas. A plane circled low over the ship and a Rünsen Beam II was directed upon the bullion-room in which the gold was packed. The sealed cases were never opened until Washington was advised by the president of our council to examine their contents."

Excitement became vibrant, but no word was uttered until a third voice, speaking cultured English (Nayland Smith identified Number Three), asked:

"Assuming, Madame, without prejudice, that what you tell us is true, how are we to proceed if Washington remains obstinate, to any further demonstration of what you termed 'the powers at our disposal'?"

Without hesitation, the bell voice replied:

"Quite simply."

Nayland Smith clenched his teeth, glancing swiftly right and left. A pad and pencil were placed before each delegate, and one of them (number Seven) had already made several notes. Smith's Germanic neighbour seemed to have brought notes with him. A large wallet lay at his elbow and he was fingering a card on which appeared a mass of neat writing.

But, as the silvery voice paused, and jade-green eyes searched each mask in turn, no one spoke.

"Quite simply. We have a plane with a maximum ceiling of 45,000 feet."

A sound of sharply drawn breaths alone interrupted.

"At a height of 40,000 feet it is already beyond interception by any type of fighter possessed by the United States Air Force, and ground defences are useless. Dr Fu-Manchu has completed a radio-controlled torpedo equipped with a proximity fuse. Its explosion releases energy almost identical with that of Rünsen Beam II."

Nayland Smith scribbled rapidly, in shorthand, which he hoped neither of his immediate neighbours understood: "Bomber attack planned on Fort Knox from 40,000 feet. Fighter patrol at highest ceiling might intercept or at least give warning…"

"Some of the energy would be dispersed, but a considerable quantity of gold could be transmuted to that metal new to metallurgists which my father has named *voluminum.*"

"Madame." The light voice was that of Number Seven. "Is there any substance which is non-conductive of this energy?"

"Only one," came a prompt reply. "*Voluminum.* A thin coat of *voluminum* would suffice."

Nayland Smith wrote rapidly: "All gold at Fort Knox must, immediately, be protected by a thin coating of the unknown metal found in those cases which were recently opened. Urgent. Nayland Smith."

There came slight, nervous movement around the table; glances were exchanged. But that compelling voice continued:

"From such a height, accurate observation is impossible. As it is vital that the first attack shall succeed (for when it takes place, the remaining gold will certainly be removed elsewhere), the purpose of this meeting is to select from among ourselves reliable ground observers. They must be near enough to Fort Knox to be able to report correctly, by radio, to the attacking plane which will carry four torpedoes. You have all been chosen for your special knowledge and experience. Several amongst you are intimately acquainted with the district. Great ingenuity will be called for. Great danger must be incurred. But ground observers are indispensable. A second pilot must also be appointed. I await your suggestions."

Number Four, who had not spoken yet, anticipated everybody. He had fat, white hands and curiously oily tones. "My first suggestion is this: that before we commit ourselves any further, we take steps to make sure that the extraordinary absence of our honoured president and the appearance here of a charming lady none of us knows does not mean that we have all walked into a trap!"

The German beside Nayland Smith banged the table and sprang to his feet.

"This is just what I have been wanting to say! All she has told us may be fabrication! Where, I demand, is Dr Fu-Manchu? Who, I demand, is this lady?"

Nayland Smith quietly tore off his shorthand note, folded it neatly on his knees—and by an apparent accident knocked the speaker's wallet off the table.

"Pardon, M'sieu."

He' stooped, slipped his note in amongst a number of papers, and restored the wallet to its place. He was adopting the tactics of the late Selwyn Orson. His own life hung in the balance here, but when the men left Kwang T'see's premises it was near-certain they would be picked up by the cordon of FBI agents and police surrounding the block.

"I agree," came the English voice, "that we are entitled to ask for a few more particulars."

Mrs van Roorden stood up, slowly, languidly, and faced the German.

"So! You have the audacity to challenge your president's daughter! You are so great a fool that you think *I* am the spy in our ranks!" Her glance moved from mask to mask. "Is there no sane man amongst you? Are you so ready to invite the anger of Dr Fu-Manchu?"

Nayland Smith's brain was working at top speed. This situation did not suit him. The meeting must adjourn amicably. Any change of plan might ruin everything.

He inhaled a deep breath, wondered if he had chosen the right tack, and spoke stiffly in French.

"Madame—fellow deputies. It chances that this lady is wrong in supposing that none of us knows her by sight. *I* know Dr Fu-Manchu's daughter. You will agree that she cannot unmask before us all. And so I suggest that she and I retire for a few moments so that I may verify my belief that this is indeed the daughter of our honoured president. If it is so, I have means to enable her to convince you."

There was a momentary silence, broken by the German.

"To this I can see no objection. I ask for a show of hands."

All hands were raised.

Nayland Smith bowed to Mrs van Roorden, crossed and held the green drapes aside. They went into the paved passage. A babel of words burst behind them.

They had walked right to the foot of the stairs before the woman halted. There, she turned, impatiently removed the green mask and faced Nayland Smith, a contemptuous smile upon her lips.

"Well, monsieur? You claim to know me. Are you satisfied?"

He was accepted. She spoke in French. He was amazed, as always, vaguely disturbed, by her beauty. Aspasia, Leontium, Faustine must have been such women. He had no idea of her age, had never known what mother bore her, but she was dangerously alluring. Her jade-green eyes had some of the hypnotic quality of her father's, allied to an appeal seductively feminine.

"I have known all along," he replied, continuing in French, which he spoke accurately but awkwardly. "In fact, to provide against misadventure, Madame, I carry a second sealed authority from the president."

He handed her the parchment found in the jade baton.

She glanced at it, then fixed the penetrating gaze of those wonderful eyes upon him.

"You are therefore a high initiate, monsieur. I had not been informed of this. What are the wishes of my honoured father?"

"That you adjourn the meeting, Madame."

He was answered by a smile, at once voluptuous and mocking. She replaced her mask.

"Let us go back."

Excited voices died away as Nayland Smith held the green curtain aside and Fu-Manchu's daughter walked slowly to her chair. The five masked men stood up until Nayland Smith had resumed his place, and then:

"Be seated, if you please," the bell voice ordered.

All resumed their seats—except the last speaker. She stood for a moment, a graceful, indolent figure, and then tossed the sealed document across the table to the German.

"My father, who foresees most things, took the precaution of sending a second authority, bearing his seal, by the hand of Deputy Six. When you have satisfied yourself, be good enough to pass it around."

Number Five no more than glanced at the parchment. He stood up, bowed, and gave the Si-Fan salute. Mrs van Roorden resumed her seat, resting one ivory arm across the carved ebony back of her chair as if deliberately to display the beauty of its curves.

The letter passed from hand to hand. One deputy after another rose and gave the Si-Fan salute. When the parchment was returned to the slender hand which had thrown it on the table, Mrs van Roorden stood up again.

"I am adjourning the meeting." Another murmur, in which fear might be detected, swept around the board. "You will await instructions as to time and place of the next. I am instructed to tell you that you leave by another route, to which you will be guided, one by one, and in the order of your arrival. Masks to be worn until you reach the door."

The six men stood up and saluted. Number Three bowed and went out.

Nayland Smith silently repeated those words, "the order of your arrival."

He would be left alone with Fu-Manchu's daughter.

Deputy Commissioner Burke was getting restive; so much so that he had allowed his cigar to go out. He had just begun to growl something when the 'phone in the control car buzzed. Harkness took it up. Listening, he whistled softly, asked several questions and hung up.

"What's moving?"

"The first man to go in has just come out. But he came out of Kwang's store!"

"Who is he?"

"You'll be surprised; Sir Mostyn Bierce, English baronet, ex-Member of Parliament."

"Jumping Jupiter!"

"He was suspected of Fascist sympathies at one time. He's a celebrated racing motorist. And he's married to an American wife with a home not fifty miles from Fort Knox. Anyway, he's in the bag."

"You're dead sure he was picked up far enough off to escape observation by the gang?"

"He was covered until he had reached his Cadillac, which he

had parked half a mile away. When he stepped in, two of the boys stepped in behind him."

The next catch was Colonel Otto von Seidler, German gunnery expert, and a former military attaché in Washington.

Then came Dr Griswal, atomic scientist; quickly followed by Captain Cooper, ex-pilot United States Air Force. Cooper for a time had been in charge of the air defences of Fort Knox. Lastly, they picked up the Emir Abdulla al-Abbas, prominent left-wing politician from Trans-Jordania; well-known in diplomatic society and an international polo player.

"There's nothing against any of them," Harkness remarked, "except that they all carry green masks."

"There'll be plenty against 'em by the time I'm through!" Burke predicted darkly. "Where's Smith? Where's this woman? If they aren't out in five minutes, we're going in."

Another buzz sounded.

"This may be news of them!" Harkness took up the phone, listened, and then: "Hold the line for the Deputy Commissioner," he said, and turned to Burke.

"They've just finished working over Colonel Seidler. Among a lot of papers in his wallet they found a shorthand message which he swears he didn't know was there. It says a bomber attack is planned on Fort Knox, and that all the gold has to be protected in some way I'm not clear about... the message is signed *Nayland Smith*."

"By God! They've got him!" Burke snatched the phone. "Commissioner Burke here. I'm coming right over." He hung up. "This is where we divide forces. Break Kwang's place wide open. Explore every rathole. Use dynamite if necessary."

* * *

When Deputy Number Two—last to leave—had performed the Si-Fan salute with that delicate but muscular brown hand, had bowed and retired, there followed a few moments of almost unendurable silence. Nayland Smith, staring fixedly at a draped wall half-right of where he sat, tried to avoid those jade-green eyes. But always, he knew that they were watching him.

What was this incalculable woman going to do? What was a "high-initiate"? How could he hope, alone with her, to keep up such a part?

The effort was not called for.

As the footsteps of the outgoing man died into silence she raised her arms and removed the mask.

"Surely," she said, her voice very soft, "it is time we tried to understand one another, Sir Denis."

Nayland Smith clenched his hands, stood up, took off his mask and threw it on the ebony table. Perhaps he should have foreseen that this woman he had known by her childish name of Fah Lo Suee, later as Madame Ingomar, now as Mrs van Roorden, could not be deceived.

He met the gaze of green eyes with the challenge of grey. A panorama of past encounters swept before him. He saw her as she had looked under the skies of Egypt; in an ancient palace on the Grand Canal of Venice; in the more prosaic setting of a London house; he saw her triumphant, he saw her humiliated. When he spoke, his voice sounded harsh in his own ears.

"What do you propose to do?"

She walked, in her indolent fashion, around the table until she was beside him. Then, resting against it, her fingers on its edge, she faced him again, and smiled.

"I suppose," she said, "as *you* are here, that all the members whom I dismissed will now be in the hands of the police? I am not infallible, you know. Your French, which is not good, and which you speak slowly, disguised your voice. I grasped the opportunity you offered. Shall I tell you how you betrayed yourself?"

"If it would amuse you."

"By your hands——when you found yourself alone with me. I could never forget that nervous movement of your hands."

She bent towards him, her lips taunting.

Nayland Smith, conscious of a heightened pulse, for Fah Lo Suee was beautifully dangerous, continued to watch her grimly. The perfume of her near presence must have conquered a lesser man.

"As you forget so little, no doubt you remember that you are the daughter of Dr Fu-Manchu, his second self, and that, between you and me, Fah Lo Suee, there can never be compromise."

She bent closer. Raising one hand, she rested it on his shoulder. Her wonderful eyes were claiming, absorbing him.

"I have suggested no compromise. You say I am my father's second self." She laughed softly; the laughter of bells. "I am his second self only in this: I know what I want... And I want to be free, forever, of the Si-Fan!"

Her hand glided across his shoulder, her arm brushing his cheek. Her lips were very near.

"You are a fascinating woman, Fah Lo Suee, but I locked the door on women and the ways of women one day before you were born— at least, as I have no idea when or where you were born, probably before your birth."

But the white arm coiled around his neck, half parted lips drew even closer.

"You think so, Denis, you think so. To yourself, you are an old man, because there is silver in your hair. To me you are the dream-man of my life—because I could never make you love me. You are strong, inflexible. So am I. In the service of the Si-Fan, failure is not permitted. Excuses are not listened to. I have failed—and I dare not go back."

Her lips now were trembling on his own. He seemed to be losing his soul in the deep green pools of her eyes…

"There is a third exit from this place, of which I have of course been told. None of your police will be watching it. Had I recognized you in time, I could have saved all those men." Her voice had dropped to a whisper, her lithe body was pressed to him. "For *you* there is no exit—unless I choose to guide you to it."

Calling upon the last atom of a weakening resolution, Nayland Smith unloosed those seductive arms, and, his hands grasping her shoulders, held Fah Lo Suee away from him, looking into her face.

His glance was met by a mocking smile. She knew, had sensed, her power, knew that this iron-willed man was not entirely immune—that she might conquer yet.

"I don't know your object—but you are planning some trap."

"No." She shook her head; she triumphed in the nervous tension of his hands on her bare shoulders. "I am planning to save you from one. It would take a rescue party hours, perhaps days to reach this room. And it can be flooded to the roof in four minutes."

"But suppose I held you here, my prisoner?"

"You must know there is assistance within reach, if I care to call upon it."

"Then—quickly," he rasped: "Say what you mean, and I will give you my answer."

"I mean that I want to come with you! Oh, God! Take me away with you, away from all this—anywhere, anywhere! All I know of the Si-Fan I will tell you. I will bring a flame of passion into your cold, lonely life that will alter the face of the world. Take me with you!"

"The offer," came a quivering sibilant voice, "is an attractive one. I should advise you to accept it, Sir Denis."

Nayland Smith turned in a flash. Fah Lo Suee's face blanched to the whiteness of her shoulders.

The tent-like room appeared to be empty behind him, undisturbed—until one of the green draperies was swept aside, revealing a doorway.

Dr Fu-Manchu stood in it watching them.

He wore a long black, fur-lined coat, as if newly arrived from a cold journey. His massive head was uncovered, save for its scanty, neutral-coloured hair. And his features were contorted with a fury almost maniacal.

Hampered by the gown, Nayland Smith's attempt to draw his automatic was fumbled.

"Glance beyond me!"'

It was a sibilant command. Smith obeyed it. From shadows of a stairway at the foot of which Fu-Manchu was standing, two blue-grey barrels glittered.

Dr Fu-Manchu came in, and began, step by feline step, slowly, to approach the cringing woman. His taloned fingers opened and closed as though itching to clutch her throat. A pair of those stocky Burmese whom he used as bodyguards stepped in behind him. They carried heavy automatics.

"Little serpent!" he hissed in Chinese. "Bred of an evil mother. Why have I cherished you so long? Again and again you have struck at me, treacherously. Again and again I have relented in my purpose to destroy you."

Fah Lo Suee shrank back and back. Relentlessly, he continued to draw nearer. Without removing that deathly glance from her face, he spoke aside:

"One movement, Nayland Smith, and it will be your last." He advanced another step towards his daughter. "I know, now, but too late, why you begged to be transferred from Java and sent here upon this mission. To betray me! To ruin my labours! To seek out this man—my deadliest enemy—for whom your sensual infatuation has already cost me so dearly!"

"It isn't true!"

The words came as a whisper, from blanched lips.

"Be silent. Prepare to die with dignity."

As if this sentence of death, for it was no less, had struck some new chord in that complex soul, Fah Lo Suee raised her dark head, and pale, motionless, faced the terrible Doctor.

"You have seen death by the Wire Jacket, in the Six Gates of Wisdom. Such a death as this you merit." Fah Lo Suee did not flinch—but Nayland Smith did. "Since you must die tonight, this cannot be. When your body is found, it will be known that in death as in life you belonged to the Si-Fan."

From an inner pocket, Dr Fu-Manchu took out a small metal box, opened it and snapped up a blue flame. It emitted a slight hissing sound. Nayland Smith clenched his fists, but the bodyguard had drawn nearer. Two barrels were jammed into his ribs.

Fu-Manchu delicately extracted a metal seal from the box; grasped Fah Lo Suee with his left arm and pressed the seal to her shoulder. She uttered never a sound. But Smith had a glimpse of clenched white teeth between parted lips.

A muffled explosion shook the cellar. The lamp went out. Harkness' raiding party had blasted one of the steel doors.

Out of utter darkness, Fu-Manchu spoke:

"Your last triumph, Sir Denis! My careful plans to force the United States government to act with me, and not against me, are shattered. And so, we must part."

The presence of the pistol barrels prohibited any action. Nayland Smith stood still. A theory which he had always held that Dr Fu-Manchu could see in the dark, was now strengthened. Horror, a frenzied imagination, might have been responsible. But he thought those emerald green eyes were *visibly* watching him!

Then, they were gone.

A sharp order in what he recognised as a Shan dialect was spoken. There were faint movements.

The beam of a lamp was directed fully upon him from the hidden opening. The two men retired, covering him all the time. The light was switched off.

"Good-by, Sir Denis," he heard, in that unforgettable voice.

Silence.

Drenched in perspiration, he threw off the green gown, dragged out his pocket torch, snapped it on and ran to the draped wall.

He wrenched the hangings bodily from their moorings; and began feverishly, to examine the surface behind.

He could find no trace of the concealed door.

But he was still searching for it, when clinging arms crept around him. He turned. And, before he could resist her, Fah Lo Suee's lips were locked to his own.

"Our long battles are over, Denis!" It was a breathless whisper. "We shall die together."

A second explosion rocked the cellar.

Nayland Smith freed himself—but gently. There was madness in that possessive kiss, and he had seen, indelibly seared on one white shoulder, the sign of the Si-Fan:

"What of the stairs?"

He spoke hoarsely.

"The door at the top is locked. Those in charge will have escaped. Forgive me for all that has been in the past—for this, too. Promise, when the end comes, that you will hold me in your arms. My courage—might fail."

"I am far from beaten, yet!"

"But listen!"

Nayland Smith listened… to a sound which chilled his heart.

"The cellars are being flooded!"

"Yes. We have four minutes."

A beam of light suddenly split the gloom, glittered evilly on rivulets of water pouring across the floor.

"Oh, God! *He* has returned!"

This time, Nayland Smith's automatic was ready as the hidden door slid noiselessly open. A cloaked figure stood there, stooping, peering in. Behind him, someone held a bright lamp.

"Who…?"

He was checked by a wild cry from Fah Lo Suee.

"Huan! Oh, my dearest old friend! God bless you! Dear Father Huan!"

She ran across and threw herself into the extended arms of Huan Tsung—for indeed it was that ancient mandarin who stood there. He clasped her, tenderly, stooping a wrinkled face to kiss her hair.

"Little white lily blossom! How your heart beats." He spoke Chinese, in which Fah Lo Suee had spoken. "Almost you adventured too greatly. But time heals all things—even the wrath of Dr Fu-Manchu. And a day must come when Excellency will rejoice to learn that his beloved daughter did not die the death of a drowned rat."

"Where is he?"

Fah Lo Suee's face was hidden against Huan Tsung's shoulder.

"I have induced Excellency, in this great urgency, to rejoin the plane in which we came—a mode of travel unsuited to my advanced years." He raised twinkling old eyes and spoke in English. "Sir Denis—you have never failed to exhibit towards me the most correct and formal courtesy. In return, I wish to give you some advice, and to make my own position clear."

"He must go free!" Fah Lo Suee raised her eyes to the parchment face. "I insist, *he* must go, too!"

Huang Tsung stroked her hair. But he was watching Nayland Smith.

"Beyond doubt, Sir Denis, those distinguished men now held at headquarters will be detained until these cellars have been pumped out. I fear, if your body should be found here, our five friends would proceed from prison to the execution shed."

"I agree," Smith rapped.

"But, failing such a discovery, it is not clear to me what charge can be preferred against them. You can do us no more harm than you have done already. Even if these men could be identified as members of our Order, they have committed no breach of the penal code with which I am familiar."

Nayland Smith remained silent. He knew exactly what the master diplomat was going to say.

"And I believe, Sir Denis, you yourself, an officer of the law, would hesitate to identify any one of them?"

It was an evasion, but in the circumstances, an acceptable evasion.

"Since I have not seen their faces, legally it would be improper for me to do so."

"A prudent decision. I fear they will be marked men. Yet, as no crime has been committed here tonight, I trust they will be released. But we are wasting time. The water already approaches my knees, which, as I am subject to rheumatism, is regrettable." He turned Fah Lo Suee about so that she faced the stair. "My daughter tells me that she promised to be waiting for you. Members of my family always fulfil their promises. Here she is."

It was Mai Cha who stood holding the light.

Fah Lo Suee twisted around, looked back.

"You promised…"

"Precede me, Lily Blossom, with Mai Cha. Sir Denis is safe."

"But…"

"Precede me, child!"

The suave diplomat had become submerged. It was the word of command, spoken by one used to obedience.

Fah Lo Suee looked back once more, but Nayland Smith and old General Huan Tsung Chao were lost in shadows far behind.

It was an incredible maze of passages through which Nayland Smith was led by his aged guide. Once they came out under the stars, in a narrow court, crossed it and entered a house beyond. Here, again, they descended to cellars, finally to climb up to an odorous Chinese grocery store.

Huan Tsung leaned heavily on the counter, breathing hard.

"When I unlock the door," he said slowly, "you will be free. I must exact one promise. It should not be hard to give. In whatever you may see fit to report concerning your escape, omit any reference to myself and to these premises. This—for Fah Lo Suee's sake."

"I promise, General."

"Good morning, Sir Denis."

Two minutes later, Nayland Smith stood in a silent, deserted street.

Reflectively, he began to fill his pipe.

THE EYES OF FU-MANCHU

"Dr Gregory Allen?" Gregory looked up from the newspaper he was reading in the lobby of his hotel. He recognised that clipped English voice but hadn't expected to hear it now in Paris.

He saw a tall, lean-faced man, his crisp hair silvered at the temples, a man who looked like a retired Indian Army officer but whose smile was thirty years too young.

"Nayland Smith!" Gregory jumped up, hand stretched out. "What a happy surprise! How did you trail me here?"

"Got your address from the Sorbonne." Sir Denis Nayland Smith dropped into a chair facing Gregory and began to fill his pipe. "I was one of your admiring audience in the lecture theatre. You speak French better than I do—in spite of your American accent.

"I didn't join the mob in the lecturer's room; but I enjoyed the account of your remarkable researches. For a youngster in his early thirties you have gone far."

"What were you doing there?"

"I have reached an age, Allen—" Nayland Smith gave the boyish grin—"when your theories of extending life far beyond its present span begin to interest me."

"You don't look as though you need any of my new chemical discoveries to keep you young."

"The fact is," Nayland Smith said seriously, "that I hoped to find a certain person in your audience, a person who illustrates in his own survival the truth of your theories; a man of fabulous age—beyond doubt scientifically prolonged.

"I refer, of course, to Dr Fu-Manchu. He will have followed your career with interest. We know he's in Paris. But we couldn't spot him, although the place bristled with detectives."

Gregory stared at the older man. An ex-Commissioner of Scotland Yard and now an agent of the British Secret Service, Nayland Smith couldn't be romancing.

"Does Fu-Manchu really exist?" Gregory asked incredulously.

"Indeed he does. He is both the greatest scientist and the most dangerous man alive. You must have heard his name."

"His name, yes! But I thought—"

"You thought Fu-Manchu was a myth. Others have made the same mistake."

"But a person of such unusual appearance in this country?"

"He has a variety of unusual appearances, Allen. He doesn't conform to the popular idea of a Chinese and can pose successfully as a European. He speaks several languages fluently. His green, oblique eyes and his hands betray the Asiatic; but in public he wears gloves and tinted glasses."

"To have escaped prison or the gallows for so long, he surely has a lot of helpers?"

Nayland Smith smiled—but it was a grim smile.

"He has an international organisation, men and women; scientists, politicians, watching eyes everywhere."

"But what kind of person would work for him?"

"Every kind. He has his own methods of recruiting assistants and seeing that they work. Tell me, where do you go next?"

"To London. I'm invited to repeat my lecture at King's College. My grant from Columbia University doesn't allow luxury, so I have reserved accommodation in a small hotel near the Strand."

"Give me the address. I'll look you up."

"Bring our mutual friend, Dr Petrie, if he's in town. I should love to see him again. I need hardly say how much I'd like to meet Dr Fu-Manchu as well."

"I hope you never do!" Nayland Smith replied…

It was crowded next day on the cross-Channel steamer. As the ship cleared Calais, Gregory found a quiet spot at the port-side rail, well forward. There were many things he wanted to think about, but the shadowy Dr Fu-Manchu kept returning to his thoughts. He found himself inspecting the passengers in search of a man wearing tinted glasses and gloves.

He hadn't seen one. But he had seen a very pretty girl coming on board alone, carrying a large artist's portfolio, and had imagined that she stared at him.

As she was passing him the ship suddenly rolled to port. She stumbled against him, and dropped the portfolio in the scuppers.

Gregory steadied himself against the rail, grabbed up the portfolio and turned. She was even prettier than he had thought in the first glimpse as she came on board.

The ship rolled to starboard and he grasped a slim shoulder to support her.

"I'm so sorry," he spoke awkwardly. "Are you feeling unwell?"

Her delicate colouring seemed to make the question absurd. "Oh, no," she assured him. "It was the so sudden lurch that nearly upset me." She had a delightful accent. "It made me feel a little—swimmy." She laughed. "Thank you very much."

"There's nothing to thank me for. Are you travelling alone?"

"Yes. I go to meet friends in London."

Rather reluctantly, Gregory relaxed his grip bf her shoulder. She had remarkable blue eyes which possessed the strange quality, even when her lips smiled, of retaining a look of sadness that he found haunting.

"I have a splendid prescription for that swimmy feeling," he told her in French, tucking her portfolio under his arm. "As a fellow artist, of sorts, please take my advice."

She hesitated for a moment. The blue eyes considered him. Then she nodded and they went off along the deck together. The swell was increasing. Presently they faced each other across a table in the nearly deserted dining room. Gregory ordered dry champagne.

Her name, he learned, was just "Mignon". She made her living by drawing caricatures for French weekly journals, and had already exhibited two paintings at the Salon.

"Your card says you are a doctor. I never heard of a doctor of painting."

Gregory laughed, and told her how during his two years at the Sorbonne, where he had completed his studies, he had found time also to study art, which had been his first choice as a profession.

"I, too, am a bred-in-the-bone Bohemian, Mignon."

"Oh, I know you are." Across her face a shadow of compassion passed. "What a pity you changed your mind. Don't you think science is going too far? Isn't it upsetting the balance of nature? Science creates horrible things, and art creates beauty."

"You have something there."

She watched him wistfully. "You must often think of those Paris days, of the carefree life of the students at the *atelier*. You lived in two different worlds. Do you ever regret the one you gave up?"

He refilled Mignon's glass. Those compassionate blue eyes were oddly disturbing. "I sometimes wonder…"

Gregory couldn't make out how he managed to miss Mignon at the customs shed, but, somehow, in the crowd at Dover he lost sight of her. He walked from one end of the boat train to the other, but couldn't see her anywhere, until, looking farther afield, he caught a glimpse of a Jaguar gliding away from the dock. Mignon was in the passenger's seat.

He concluded that black and white art paid better than science research and said goodbye to a dream…

It was raining by the time the train reached London. From his hotel suite, Gregory called King's College, but could find nobody there from whom to get particulars about arrangements for his lecture. He ordered whisky to be sent up and wondered how he was going to kill time until the rain stopped.

He wondered, too, if he would ever see Mignon again. Evidently the friends she had come to meet moved in a financial circle in which he would be a misfit. Mignon? She had given him no other name. But Mignon was exactly the right one for her.

She seemed completely a part of the Bohemian Paris that he loved. Gregory took out a sketching block and a soft pencil. He began to draw a figure. His knowledge of anatomy had helped him in the life class, and he drew sweeping, confident lines, blocked in the features with bold touches of light and shade. At last, he held the drawing away for a critical look—and saw a rough but recognisable sketch of Mignon.

One thing was wrong. He had captured her pose, the slim lines of her figure, the oval face and smiling lips. But her eyes had defeated his pencil.

He had been subconsciously aware for some time of a sound which resembled muffled footsteps, but had ignored it. And at this moment he became aware of the footsteps again.

They were soft but continuous. There was something furtive in this caseless padding, something eerie. At one moment he thought it came from a room above; at another from the passage outside his own room—a sort of phantom patrol. Once, when the footfalls seemed to be passing his door, he ran and opened it, and saw no one.

Gregory took a look out of the window. He felt nervous and decided that a brisk walk would be good for him. The rain had stopped.

His mood was an odd one, an unhappy one. He had succeeded in his chosen profession, had earned the respect of older scientists, whose accomplishments he revered. His researches had won him wide recognition. Yet tonight he wished he had chosen to be a painter; he longed to escape from his accepted self, to be his natural self. He was still young, and there was a world outside the world of science, a world in which there remained room for romance, for beauty.

In the lobby he paused to light a cigarette. A wave of self-contempt swept over him. Had he, a trained scientist, fallen for that romantic myth, love at first sight? He left a message at the desk that he would be back in half an hour, swung the door open and stepped out into the street.

He was greeted by a flash of lightning which changed the gloomy night into a sort of blue-white day. Then came a volley of thunder so awesome that it might have heralded the end of the world. It prefaced a fresh deluge.

Gregory retired inside the porch. Left and right the street was deserted, until a figure came running through the downpour, a girl caught in the storm.

She dashed into the shelter of the porch, and Gregory found himself looking down at the piquant face, wet with rain, into the blue eyes of Mignon.

They stood for a moment watching the rain and then went to Gregory's small suite.

She sat in the only comfortable chair which the living room offered. The expression in her eyes was almost tragic, but she forced a smile.

"It is the thunderstorm. They affect me very much."

Gregory sat on a hassock, looking at her. There came another electric flicker through the shaded window, a shattering crash of thunder. Mignon flinched; tried to control herself. Gregory took her hand reassuringly. "I don't know what you were doing out on such a night, Mignon."

"I came to look for you. At Dover you disappear. I don't know what has happened."

"Mignon!"

And in the sudden silence which fell as the thunder died, Gregory heard the footsteps again.

But their pattern had altered. At regular intervals the patrol was halted, and three deliberate beats came. Now, as he felt Mignon's grip tighten, he glanced back at her, and before she could lower her lashes, he caught an expression of such frantic compassion that it frightened him.

"Mignon, there's no danger," he said. "The storm is passing. It was very good of you to come."

But he knew that whatever she feared, it wasn't the storm. She opened her eyes, still clasping his hand.

"I am silly, Gregory. Try to forgive me. Why, oh why, didn't you stay an artist?"

Her manner, her disjointed phrases, told a story of nervous tension for which he could find no explanation.

"Listen, Mignon. Take it easy. Let me give you a cigarette and a little drink, so we can talk quietly."

"No, no!" She held onto his hand, detaining him. "I don't want a drink—yet. I want to talk to you—yes. But it is so hard."

"What do you want to tell me? That we're not going to see one another again?"

He knew that the words betrayed his secret dreams, but he didn't care; for he knew, now, that Mignon wasn't indifferent and he meant to hear the truth.

"No," she whispered.

Three soft taps sounded distinctly.

Gregory was on the point of asking Mignon if she had heard the queer sound when a third flicker of lightning came and another crack of thunder. She closed her eyes.

"Let's go downstairs," Gregory proposed, "and have a drink in the lounge. This room is suffocating."

He pulled her up from the chair and they moved toward the door. The three muffled taps were repeated.

It seemed to Gregory that Mignon stopped as suddenly as if unseen hands had grasped her.

"Oh, Gregory, I feel so—swimmy! I think I will have a drink now, after all."

Her manner certainly suggested that she needed one, as she turned and dropped back into the chair. Gregory poured out two drinks, glanced at Mignon's pale face, and hurried into the bathroom for water.

When he returned he found Mignon had recovered herself a little, and was looking at the sketch he had roughed out. She drank from her glass and looked at the sketch again.

"Is it very bad?" he asked.

She didn't look up. "No, it's very good. It was sweet of you."

Mignon raised her eyes as she spoke, and he had only time to see that they were cloudy with fears when the phone buzzed. Puzzled and bewildered, he took up the receiver.

"Gregory Allen?" a familiar voice demanded.

"Here, Sir Denis." The caller was Nayland Smith.

"Good. Listen. I have just arrived. Followed you by plane. This is urgent: Don't leave your apartment until I get there. On no account allow anyone in."

Gregory hung up, turned—and saw Mignon through a mist. He staggered to the couch, gulped the rest of the brandy. What was the word Mignon had used? *Swimmy.* Yes, that was what he felt, too.

He fell back. His mind began to wander. He tried to call Mignon, to explain to her—but his voice would not come. He tried to rise. He couldn't move. But he could hear Mignon's voice—as from a distance.

With one arm she supported his head. Her fingers caressed his hair. Something wetted his cheek. He looked up, and into her eyes. Mignon was crying. He wanted to console her, to warn her. But he couldn't speak, couldn't move a muscle.

"You must try to forgive me," she whispered. "Try to understand. One day, you will. How sorry I am…"

She had gone. He didn't see her go, for he couldn't turn his head. All he could see was the ceiling above him and part of the wall. His brain now was clear enough; but his heart was sick—for at last he guessed the truth. She had doped his drink, and those uncanny footsteps were drawing nearer.

A number of people came in. He recognised the voice of the hotel manager. "How lucky you were in the hotel, Dr Gottfeld."

Someone bent over Gregory: a tall man. He wore black silk gloves and tinted glasses, with a delicate thumb and forefinger he raised Gregory's lids. Then he removed the glasses and stared down at him with brilliant green eyes. And Gregory knew he was face to face with Dr Fu-Manchu.

"Very lucky." The words were spoken with a guttural German accent. "I see from his baggage labels that he is recently in lower Egypt. There was a mild outbreak there of plague two weeks ago. Do not be alarmed. There is no danger—yet. But we must act quickly."

Conscious—seeing, hearing, but incapable of speech or movement—Gregory heard the man they called Dr Gottfeld volunteer to drive him in his own car to the London Hospital for Tropical Diseases—"Where they know me well," he explained.

Mentally alert, but helpless as a dead man, Gregory heard that German voice giving explicit directions concerning locking the apartment, destruction of its contents, and fumigation of the rooms. Knowing the symptoms of every variety of plague, he was well aware that the man was a liar.

Why had he been doped by Mignon? Was she in the power of Fu-Manchu? He thought about the drug. Its composition was unknown to him, but he thought there might be some hyoscine. Then he heard a hurried exodus.

Fu-Manchu bent over him, again removing the tinted glasses, and Gregory knew that those hypnotic eyes were claiming him.

"I have studied your career with interest." The words now were spoken in perfect, curiously precise English. "I recently lost my chief assistant in your particular field of research, Dr Allen.

You have become indispensable to me in my search for a way to continue my life—indefinitely. Your service will not be unpleasant. There are rich rewards."

He was charging a hypodermic syringe when there came a faint buzzing.

A few words, harshly spoken, told him Dr Fu-Manchu carried some kind of two-way radio device which kept him in contact with his associates. When again the Chinese scientist bent over him, he knew that the message had been a warning. The green eyes blazed with frustration.

"Your death could avail me nothing. Your life may yet be of use. I bid you good night, Dr Allen. Convey my deep respects to Sir Denis Nayland Smith." Gregory was alone in the room.

He fought to retain the state of unreal consciousness in which he was held, but found that his over-taxed brain was defeating the effort. Sleep overcame him.

As something out of a dream, he heard Nayland Smith's voice: "What is it, Petrie? Are we too late?"

"Very simple. A knockout drop. It was in this glass—this one."

"I assure you gentlemen,"—the manager's frightened voice climbed to a falsetto—"it's *plague!*"

"Plague be damned!" Dr Petrie snapped. "He's been drugged. I don't know what's in it. But I suspect a proportion of hyoscine." Gregory silently applauded. "I'm going to take strong measures. Sheer luck, Smith, that I hurried straight from the hospital to meet you and had my bag with me."

Gregory caught a glimpse of Dr Petrie's earnest face bending over him, and knew that the doctor had administered an injection.

Recovery was slow, and nauseating, but at last he regained control of his muscles as well as of his brain, sat up and looked about him.

Dr Petrie was watching him with a professional regard.

"Thanks, Doctor!" Gregory grasped his hand. "I agree with you about hyoscine. But I wish I knew the other ingredients."

Nayland Smith was looking at the drawing of Mignon. He glanced up as Gregory spoke.

"Hullo, Allen. This must be the young lady who informed the management that you were taken seriously ill and then disappeared. They gave me her description."

Gregory nodded.

"I warned you Dr Fu-Manchu has eyes everywhere. You know now how fascinating those eyes can be. His scouts warned him in some way that I was close on his heels, and once again he has slipped away."

Nayland Smith put the drawing of Mignon where he found it and glanced at Gregory. There was sympathy in the grey eyes.

"Don't condemn her," he said. "She's in his power as, but for an act of Providence, *you* might have been." His voice hardened. "You must never under any circumstances try to see that girl again."

For the next few days Gregory Allen prowled the streets of London, driven by the ridiculous hope that somewhere in the crowds which thronged the Strand and Piccadilly he would see the auburn hair and piquant face of Mignon. His scientist's brain told him Nayland Smith had been right in warning him that he must never see her again. But against reason was set a desperate urge to find the girl, free her from the spell of Dr Fu-Manchu and take her back to New York with him.

Sometimes in his restless walks, he had the feeling he was followed, but whether by one of Fu-Manchu's assistants or a

Scotland Yard man assigned to protect him, he did not know. Nor did he know where to look for Mignon. He didn't even know her last name.

With faint hope he had written off to Paris to the weekly magazine which regularly published her sketches. An answer came back promptly. The magazine could not give out contributors' addresses. But they would see that his message reached Mignon.

The letter filled him with hope. When he returned to his hotel two days later, there was a plain white envelope with his mail: "Exhibition of French art at the Tate Gallery," it read. "Please come there at 5.30 this afternoon. Wait near the Gauguin paintings, but when I come in pretend not to recognise me. Destroy this note—Mignon."

Gregory approached the Tate Gallery at dusk. He told himself once again that he was playing with fire; but he could not blind himself to the fact that he had become hopelessly infatuated with the girl.

The building was all but deserted. It was near to closing time. He found the appointed spot and then decided to wait on the other side of the room, pretending to examine the sketches and charcoal studies.

Few visitors came. At every footstep Gregory turned. One man, dark, of a saturnine cast of features and wearing a white raincoat strolled through twice; but Gregory decided that he was probably a gallery detective. He glanced anxiously at his watch. And still Mignon didn't come.

He had begun to lose heart when he heard light footsteps, and a girl came into the gallery. She wore a scarlet cape, her auburn hair almost entirely hidden by a close-fitting beret.

It was Mignon. But she gave no sign of recognising him.

The dark man strolled in, glanced round, and went out by another door. Mignon, a moment later, went out, too. Gregory followed. She passed through several other rooms and stopped in an empty room devoted to French drawings.

"Mignon!" He grasped her shoulders. "How wonderful!"

She turned her head aside. "I am glad to see you, too, Gregory. But you must be mad. You should hate me—I have done you only harm."

"I *am* mad, Mignon—mad about *you*. Look at me. I understand it all. Nayland Smith has told me. Don't reproach yourself."

She glanced up at him, furtively, timidly. "You should not have come. Nor should I. You had one narrow escape from Fu-Manchu. Why do you take another risk? You must forget me—forget we ever met."

"I can't forget you," he said, "and I won't even try unless you tell me, here and now, that I have no right to think about you as I do."

"There is no one else, in the sense you mean," she whispered. "Think of me, Gregory, as someone inaccessible, a slave."

He held her. "There are no slaves," he said tensely. "Come with me—now. Back to America. Nayland Smith has the power of the government behind him. You will be safe from Dr Fu-Manchu."

Mignon rested her head against his shoulder.

"How I wish it could be, Gregory. It is my father, hopelessly under the power of Fu-Manchu, whom I must protect." She looked up swiftly. "Every moment you stay with me you are in danger. My father is in danger. So am I."

He bent to her lips. Mignon thrust her hand against his mouth. Her eyes were wild. "If you value my life, Gregory, dear, please let me go. I mean it. Don't even look back. Don't try to follow me."

She slipped from his arms. He dared not ignore the urgency of her appeal. But as he heard her light footsteps retreating through the next gallery towards the door he *did* look back.

Mignon was out of sight.

Three minutes later Gregory was on the Embankment in front of the gallery, staring right and left. Dusk had drawn in, and the opposite bank of the Thames was curtained in mist. And then in the direction of Millbank, under the light of a street lamp, he had a glimpse of the scarlet cape.

As he set out to follow, another figure passed under the lamp, close behind Mignon—the white-coated figure of the dark man.

Gregory hurried on. Mignon was being covered. But if he could find out where she was going, Nayland Smith could do the rest. For Gregory was determined now to get Mignon away from Fu-Manchu even if he had to kidnap her.

The cape disappeared around a corner not far from the Gallery. The white coat closed up and disappeared also.

Gregory raced to the corner. He was just in time to see Mignon turn into one of the many narrow streets which abounded in this district The white-coated man followed no farther. He went straight ahead.

Gregory ran on to the head of the street where she had turned. He could see no sign of the scarlet cloak. It was dark in the opening, but there were some lighted windows beyond. He stood listening for the sound of an opening or closing door. He heard nothing—then moved in cautiously.

No sound warned him of his danger. No blow was struck. He suffered a sudden sharp pain—and remembered no more...

Except for a slight headache, he felt no discomfort when he woke up. He took one look around, then closed his eyes again. This must be a dream!

He lay on a divan in an Oriental room. The walls were decorated with a number of beautiful lacquer panels. The ceiling consisted of silk tapestry, and in and out of its intricate pattern gold dragons crept. The appointments were mainly Chinese. Rugs covered the floor. There was a faint smell resembling that of stale incense. At a long, narrow desk facing the divan a man sat writing. He wore a yellow robe and a black cap topped with a coral bead.

This man's face possessed a sort of satanic beauty. The features were those of an aristocrat, an intellectual aristocrat. And an aura of assured power seemed to radiate from the whole figure.

It was Dr Fu-Manchu.

"Good evening, Dr Allen," he said, without looking up. "I am happy to have you as my guest. I anticipate a long and mutually satisfactory association." Gregory swung his legs off the divan. Fu-Manchu didn't stir. "I beg you to attempt no vulgar violence. Even if it succeeded, you would be strangled thirty seconds later."

Gregory sat upright, his fists clenched, watching, fascinated.

"To all intents and purposes, Dr Allen, you find yourself in China—although this room, which has several remarkable qualities, was designed by a clever Japanese artist; for you must not fall into the error of supposing that my organisation is purely Chinese in character. I assure you that I have enthusiastic workers of all races in the Order of the Si-Fan, of which I am president."

This statement Dr Fu-Manchu made without once glancing up from the folio volume in which he was writing marginal notes. Gregory sat still, watching and waiting.

"For instance," the strange voice continued, "this room is soundproof. It was formerly a studio. The Chinese silk conceals top lights. The seven lacquer panels are in fact seven doors. I use the place as a *pied-à-terre* when my affairs detain me in London. I am much sought after, Dr Allen—particularly by officials of Scotland Yard. And, this apartment has useful features. Will you take tea with me?"

"No, thank you."

"As you please. Your unusual researches into the means of increasing vigorous life prove of great value to my own. I am no longer young, my dear doctor, but your unexpected visit here inspired me to hope that in addition to securing your services, I may induce a mutual friend to call upon us."

Dr Fu-Manchu laid his pen down, and for the first time looked up. Gregory found himself subjected to the fixed regard of the strangest human eyes he had ever seen. They were long, narrow, only slightly oblique, and were brilliantly green. Their gaze threatened to take command of his will and he averted his glance.

"When you followed a member of my staff, Dr Allen, whom you know as Mignon, I was informed of this—at the time that you left the Tate Gallery—and took suitable steps. A judo expert awaited your arrival and dealt with you by a simple nerve pressure with which, as a physician, you may be familiar. I am aware that Mignon made a secret appointment to meet you. She awaits her punishment. What it shall be rests with you."

Gregory experienced an unpleasant fluttering in the stomach. He sensed what was coming, and wondered how he should face up to the ordeal. He said nothing.

"There is a telephone on the small table beside you," Fu-Manchu told him, softly. "Be good enough to call Sir Denis Nayland Smith. Tell him that you have met with an accident on Chelsea Embankment and are lying in the house of a neighbouring doctor who was passing at the time. This apartment is rented by a certain Dr Steiner. His plate is outside. His surgery adjoins this room. One of the seven doors leads to it. The address is Ruskin Mews. Request Sir Denis to bring his car here for you at once."

Gregory stood up. "I refuse."

Lacquer doors to the left and right of him opened silently, as if motivated by his sudden movement. Two short, thickset Asiatics came in. They carried knives. Holding them poised in their hands for a throw, they watched him—waited.

"I deplore this barbarous behaviour, Dr Allen. At my headquarters I have more subtle measures available."

"To hell with your measures! You can kill me, but you can't make me obey your orders."

Fu-Manchu sighed. One long yellow finger moved onto his desk; and a third door, almost facing Gregory, opened. Mignon came in. Another member of the gang, who presumably acted as a bodyguard, grasped her by the wrist. In his other hand the man carried a whip.

Beret and scarlet cape were gone. Mignon wore a black skirt and a white blouse. Her auburn hair framed her pale face. One glance of entreaty she flashed at him, then lowered her head.

"You daren't do it!" Gregory blazed in a white fury. "You may consider yourself to be in China, but if you attempt this outrage, you'll find you're still in England. We'll rouse the neighbourhood."

The point of a knife touched his throat. One of the pair guarding him had moved closer. Fu-Manchu shook his head.

"You forget, Dr Allen, that this room is soundproof. Be so wise as to call Sir Denis. I am advised that he is at home at present and Whitehall Court, where he resides, is no great distance away. But he may be going out to dine. We are wasting time. I think you'll find the number is written by the 'phone."

Gregory cast a last glance round the room, then took up the 'phone and dialled the number. Nayland Smith's man answered, and immediately brought Nayland Smith.

"Smith here. What's up, Allen?" came the crisp voice.

The words nearly choked him, but Gregory gave the message which Dr Fu-Manchu had directed. His eyes remained fixed upon Mignon as he spoke, and he knew that he dared not risk any hint of warning.

"Good enough. Bad luck. Be with you in ten minutes." Nayland Smith hung up.

Fu-Manchu uttered a guttural order; the knife was removed; Gregory's guards retired; Mignon without a glance in his direction was led away. The doors closed. He found himself alone again with Dr Fu-Manchu. He dropped back on the divan.

He had done a thing with which he would reproach himself to his last day. To save a woman who had never truly meant anything in his life from suffering, he had betrayed an old, tried friend, into the power of a cruel and relentless enemy.

Fu-Manchu had resumed his annotations. He spoke without looking up.

"To do that which is unavoidable merits neither praise nor blame, Dr Allen. That curious superstition, the sanctity of woman which is, no doubt, a part of your American heritage, left you no alternative. I am transferring Mignon to another post, where I trust you will no longer be able to interfere with her normal efficiency."

Gregory was reaching boiling point, but knew that he was helpless to avert the evil he had brought about. If he could have killed Fu-Manchu with his bare hands he would gladly have done it. But he knew, now, that he couldn't hope to get within reach of him.

Nayland Smith was racing into a trap. In a matter of minutes he would be here.

A curious, high bell note broke the complete silence of the room.

Dr Fu-Manchu stood up, put the folio volume under his arm and, opening one of the doors, went out.

As the door closed behind the Chinese doctor, Gregory, risking everything, grabbed the phone and dialled Nayland Smith's number.

There was no reply.

But no one had disturbed him; none of the doors had opened. He went to one at random, could find no means of opening it. He tried another, worked on it frantically. It was immovable. He stepped back and put his shoulder to the lacquer. Nothing happened.

Then, with a tearing crash, the silence was broken. The door by which Dr Fu-Manchu had gone out burst open, and the dark man in the white raincoat stared into the room.

Gregory counted himself lost, when the man turned and shouted back over his shoulder: "This way, sir! Here he is!" He stepped into the room. "Glad to see you still alive, Doctor."

And Nayland Smith ran in behind him.

"You caught me only just in time, Allen," Nayland Smith assured him. "Sergeant Ridley here—" he nodded to the man in the white coat—"has been shadowing you for nearly a week. You see, I knew you were trying to get in touch with the little redhead, and his orders were, if you succeeded, to transfer all his attention to the girl when she left you. He did so tonight and had no idea you were somewhere behind. He reported to me that Mignon had just gone into Ruskin Street."

Gregory forced a smile. "Thank you, Sergeant," he said.

"Scotland Yard's crime map has a red ring drawn around this area," Nayland Smith explained. "We have suspected that Fu-Manchu had a hideaway here. The Japanese artist who reconstructed this place disappeared six months ago, and a certain Dr Gottfeld took it over, though the name of Dr Steiner appears on the plate."

"Of course," Gregory broke in. "Gottfeld was the name the hotel manager called Fu-Manchu when they came to my suite. Have you got him?"

Nayland Smith shook his head. "I'm afraid he has done another of his vanishing tricks. The raid squad I brought along is searching. But my guess is that Fu-Manchu has slipped away to one of his old haunts near Limehouse."

He motioned to the Sergeant, who brought in a man of perhaps fifty whose eyes had the peculiar glaze which showed he had been under Fu-Manchu's hypnotic spell. "But at least we've rescued a man who may be able to give us a great deal of information about Fu-Manchu's operations. Dr Allen, this is Dr Gaston Breon. Besides being a famous French entomologist, he is Mignon's father."

"Thank God you've saved him!" Gregory said, as he gripped the scientist's limp hand. "But Smith, have you rescued Mignon?"

Nayland Smith slapped him on the shoulder. "We got her with two of Fu-Manchu's henchmen who were trying to force her into a motor launch. I had her taken to my place." As Gregory looked at him gratefully, he smiled that boyish grin. "She's your responsibility now."

Ten minutes later Gregory walked past a guard and into Nayland Smith's large booklined study. Mignon sprang up from a chair near the window and ran to him, her eyes wild with terror.

"Gregory! You must compel them to let me go!" she cried "Fu-Manchu will kill my father if I do not return to him."

She stared at Gregory in bewilderment. "Why do you smile?"

But Gregory was looking beyond her to the door, and Mignon turned. A sigh of joy escaped her as she ran to her father. "My child, my child," Dr Breon muttered, awkwardly patting her shoulder. "The nightmare is finished, Mignon."

"Oh, what they've done to you these past two years, my father," she whispered.

Gregory crossed the room and stood at her side, his arm around her shoulders. "We'll have him right in no time," he promised. "All he needs is rest and the care we'll give him."

Mignon's head came back, and the tears were gone. What was more, the look of infinite sadness he remembered from their first meeting was gone, too. In its place there was a sparkle that danced in the light of the lamps with swift invitation.

"I think it is quite safe for you now to love me, Gregory," she said.

He took her into his arms.

THE WORD OF FU-MANCHU

Malcolm glanced aside at his companion, who drove the Jaguar both deftly and quickly. He studied the tall, lean man at the wheel, a clean shaven man, whose tanned skin and crisp, dark hair gave startling emphasis to the silver at his temples: he was sucking a briar pipe.

"I know what you're thinking, Forbes." The words were rapped out. "When I was a Commissioner at Scotland Yard, speed limits never troubled me. I formed bad habits."

"Is there so much hurry, Sir Denis?"

Sir Denis Nayland Smith grunted and swung out to pass a taxi, then:

"There is!" he snapped. "I asked you to join me tonight because I want someone with me where we're going. Also, as a young freelance journalist, you may be on the big story Fleet Street is waiting for."

"What's the story?"

"Dr Fu-Manchu. We're going to see Sergeant Jack Kenealy, of the CID. He's been on the case best part of the year. We have kept in touch. He called me an hour ago; said he had things to tell me which

97

he couldn't put on paper. Rather alarming. Hence the speed."

"You think—"

"Nothing to think about until we get there."

And Malcolm knew that Sir Denis didn't want any further conversation to interfere with his urgent journey.

Ten minutes later they were skirting the north side of Clapham Common, a place of mysterious shadows this moonless night. He became aware of bottled-up excitement as Nayland Smith parked the car at a garage and took Malcolm's arm.

"This is where we walk," he announced.

They set out on the side opposite the Common. Sir Denis was silent, but Malcolm noted that he often glanced across at the shadowy expanse, as if, during his long battle against the Chinese genius who dreamed of becoming master of the world, he had learned that Fu-Manchu was a superman who might materialise from space anywhere, at any time. Malcolm's excitement increased. They came to the next corner.

At which moment Nayland Smith, in the act of turning in, grabbed his arm again in a grip that hurt.

"Forbes, we're too late. Look!"

They had not passed a single pedestrian so far. But now—this side street was crowded.

The crowd had assembled in front of a house not far from the corner. Malcolm recognised the magnet which had drawn it together—two police cars, an ambulance, and uniformed men on duty before the door.

"Is that where Kenealy lives, Sir Denis?"

Nayland Smith nodded grimly, and began to hurry.

They forced a path through the group of curious onlookers. Then, a police sergeant barred the way.

"No one can go in, sir."

"Who's in charge?" Nayland Smith snapped.

"Inspector Wensley is here. But—"

"Wensley? *My* name is Nayland Smith—Sir Denis Nayland Smith."

"Sorry, Sir Denis," the sergeant answered. "I didn't recognise you, sir. Go ahead."

Sir Denis and Malcolm went up the short path to the open front door. Inside an elderly woman was trying to pacify a girl who was weeping in her arms: "There, there dear, I know how you feel. But orders are orders, and they have orders to let nobody see him."

"I shall die if I came too late!" the girl moaned.

Nayland Smith pulled up. "Madame—" he addressed the older woman—"please tell me, is this your house?"

"It is, sir. Mrs Sefton is my name; and my top floor was let to Mr Kenealy—as nice a young man as I'd wish to meet. Even now, I can't believe it's happened."

"What *did* happen, Mrs Sefton?"

"I was sitting sewing, not more than half an hour ago, when I heard him cry out. It echoed through the place. It was terrible. It was more of a scream than a cry. I knew he had nobody with him but I was alone in the house and so frightened I had to force myself to go up to his sitting-room. I called to him. But he didn't answer. So I tried to open the door. It was locked."

"Then what did you do?"

"I ran downstairs and out to the street meaning to ask the first man who came along to force Mr Kenealy's door. As luck would have it, the first one was a policeman."

While this conversation went on, Malcolm was watching the girl. She had persistently kept her face pressed to Mrs Sefton's shoulder.

SAX ROHMER

But now she turned suddenly, and cast a swift glance of amber eyes at himself and Nayland Smith. She was a strikingly pretty brunette and appeared to be in a state of terror rather than sorrow.

"The door was forced by the policeman and you found Kenealy," Nayland Smith said. "Tell me—"

"He was dead, sir!"

The dark girl turned and faced Sir Denis.

"So I understand," he said. "Details I'll gather for myself. And now, Mrs Sefton, who is this young lady?"

The girl fixed her strange, but beautiful eyes upon Nayland Smith as Mrs Sefton replied, "It's Miss Rostov, sir, a friend of Mr Kenealy's, who often called. She came to see him ten minutes ago, and the police wouldn't let her go up."

"Miss Rostov—" Sir Denis met the fixed regard of the girl's eyes—"how did you know Jack Kenealy was dead?"

"I didn't know!" she cried. "I didn't know! How could I know?"

"Was he expecting you?"

"Yes. But I was late."

"How long have you known him?"

"For a long time. Three or four months."

"When did you see him last?"

"The day before yesterday."

"Where?"

"At the restaurant."

"What restaurant?"

Momentarily, she hesitated, then: "The Café Stambul."

"And you haven't seen him or spoken to him since?"

"No."

Nayland Smith considered her for a while, and the amber eyes evaded him.

"Very well, Miss Rostov. You have all my sympathy. I'm afraid we shall want you as a witness." He turned to Mrs Sefton. "Please look after her. She mustn't leave at present. Just a moment, Forbes."

He went to the street door.

"I'm so sorry, my dear." Mrs Sefton put her arm round the girl, and included Malcolm in the invitation: "Come into my sitting-room and make yourselves comfortable."

Malcolm found himself seated in a small, cosy room, overcrowded with antique furniture, facing Miss Rostov, who reclined upon a couch which might have dated back to Queen Victoria. Mrs Sefton bustled out to "make a nice cup of tea". The girl's eyes, in which he read fear, were turned upon him.

"I don't know your name," she said softly; she had a slight, unfamiliar accent. "But I feel I can trust you. Why am I to be kept here? Please tell me. Are you of the police?"

"No." Malcolm felt embarrassed. "But I can only tell you what Sir Denis told you—that you'll be required as a witness."

"Sir Denis—who is he?"

"Sir Denis Nayland Smith, a former Commissioner of Scotland Yard."

"Oh! But shall I be allowed to go when he has talked to me again?"

"Of course."

She sighed, stretching out her slim body languorously. She had removed a black coat with a wide astrakhan collar; under it she wore a dark green dress. A striped silk scarf concealed nearly all her hair. Malcolm became uncomfortably conscious of her beauty.

"If I have to go to court," she murmured, "I hope you will come with me. I have, now, no friends in London."

Before he could think of a reply, Nayland Smith came in.

"Come along, Forbes."

Malcolm met a lingering glance of amber eyes and followed Sir Denis from the room. As they went upstairs:

"I gave her a chance," Nayland Smith said shortly. "Did she try the glamour treatment?"

Malcolm felt his colour rising. "I rather think," he confessed, "that she did. She's really a beauty, isn't she?"

"All Fu-Manchu's women are beauties."

"'Fu-Manchu's women'? You mean, you suspect this girl to be one?"

"We shall see… Hullo, Inspector! I had an appointment with Kenealy tonight, but unfortunately arrived too late…"

Sergeant Kenealy lay on a couch. Evidently a good-looking man in his early thirties, his present appearance made Malcolm shudder. This gruesome shell might be that of one dead, not for less than an hour, but for more than a week. The divisional surgeon, Dr Abel, was examining the body.

"We've ruled out the possibility of homicide, Sir Denis," Inspector Wensley declared. "The window, which overlooks the street, was fastened. The door was locked. I have checked every possibility, and I'll stake my job on it——no one else was in this room when he died."

A fire burned in a small grate, and the room was insufferably hot. Nayland Smith twitched the lobe of his ear, a trick of his when concentrating.

"Poor Kenealy had an enemy, Inspector, who uses strange allies—not necessarily human. You have searched the rooms, furniture closets—wherever any living thing could hide?"

Inspector Wensley looked troubled. "We've searched the place of course, sir. I don't think anything that moved could have escaped us."

"There seems to be a quantity of charred paper on the fire and in the hearth?"

"He had evidently been burning every bit of paper in his possession," the inspector told him. "In fact, we shouldn't have known his identity if West here—'" he indicated a plain clothes man talking to the doctor—"hadn't recognised him. I was shocked to learn that he was one of us."

Nayland Smith glanced at Malcolm. "We're in very deep waters." He crossed to the couch; Malcolm followed.

Dr Abel looked up at Sir Denis.

"Are there any marks on his body, Doctor, to suggest that he had been bitten by a reptile, for instance?"

"There are no such marks, sir. I cannot imagine why there should be."

"He was murdered. I'm here to find out how."

"Murdered! I disagree."

"Then what's the diagnosis?" Sir Denis demanded.

Able shook his head angrily. "A sudden seizure of some kind. But look at his colour. Feel the rigidity of the body."

Kenealy's features were of a uniform leaden grey, his limbs stiff as if he had been dead for hours. The features were frozen in an expression of horror.

"Cerebral haemorrhage?" Malcolm suggested.

"My dear sir!" Dr Abel snorted. "Look at his colour—look at his eyes."

"Heart?"

"What kind of heart? Only an autopsy can help us there. But I may add that I never knew a heart case, except angina, where the patient cried out at the moment of the attack. What's more, this muscular rigidity doesn't fit. A powerful electric shock might have accounted for it. But he was sitting in that easy chair when I arrived, and no contact was possible. This strange rigor had already set in. The man might have been struck by lightning…"

Nayland Smith turned away, his expression grim. "Show me what was found on him."

"Here you are, Sir Denis." Detective West drew his attention to a number of objects on a small table. "He must have had some other base he'd been working from. Mrs Sefton says he was often away for two or three days. There isn't a thing here to prove his identity."

"That doesn't surprise me," Nayland Smith said. "I see you have explored his bureau."

"Complete search, sir," Wensley assured him. "Nothing to help."

Sir Dennis glanced over the exhibits. "Where did you find this automatic?"

"Drawer in a bedside cabinet," West told him. "It's fully charged."

"H'm. And what about this?"

He was holding up a disc of some dull metal attached to a thin broken chain.

"That was fastened around his neck," Wensley explained. "I thought it was a religious emblem. We could find no way of unfastening it, so I had the chain filed. The loop was too small to go over his head."

Nayland Smith studied the disc with keen interest.

"There's some sort of hieroglyphic stamped on the metal," Malcolm pointed out. "I wonder what it means?"

"I think I know," Sir Denis answered. "With your permission, Inspector, I'll take this thing with me for expert examination. There's nothing more to be done here, Forbes. First score to Dr Fu-Manchu. A further chat with your charming acquaintance, Miss Rostov, might bring a little light on things."

* * *

In Mrs Sefton's sitting room the dark girl reclined on the sofa as they had left her. She was alone. A cup of tea stood on a table near her. She raised her eyelids languidly but otherwise did not move.

"I'm sorry to have detained you." Nayland Smith spoke drily. "But I thought you might be able to give me some information about this."

He extended the metal disc on his open palm.

The effect was electrical. The girl sprang up in one lithe movement, her remarkable eyes widely opened.

"Ah! It is mine! Thank you very much."

"Yours?" Nayland Smith snapped. "Then why was it chained about his neck?"

"There is a way to unfasten the chain. It is mine. Please give it to me."

"If that is the case, you shall have it—but not yet. What is it?"

"It is an Eastern charm. To me—" suddenly her eyes were brimming with tears— "it means so much. To you it can mean nothing."

"H'm, very interesting." He dropped the disc back into his pocket. "I should be obliged, Miss Rostov, if you would give Mr Forbes your address while I go and arrange for you to be driven home."

Nayland Smith went out, closing the door. And at the same moment that he did so, the girl moved forward and clutched Malcolm, raising tearful appealing eyes to him.

"Listen to me," she whispered. "You *must* listen to me! Persuade him to give me my amulet."

Malcolm tried, gently, to detach her hands. "I assure you, Sir Denis will do so. He—"

"My name is Nadia. Be my friend. I have no one but you to help me."

Malcolm's natural chivalry, and Nadia's beauty, might have conquered discretion if he had had it in his power to do as she asked. But she asked the impossible.

"I'd gladly help you, Nadia, but Sir Denis wouldn't listen to me."

She drooped against him, her head on his shoulder. Her hair had a subtle fragrance.

"I am sorry. I think you would help me, if you could."

Footsteps sounded on the stairs. Nadia drew back.

Malcolm pulled out a note-book awkwardly, and tried to force his mind back to normality.

"Please give me your address now, Nadia."

"Eighty-five Westbourne Terrace," she told him in a toneless voice.

The door opened and Nayland Smith came in, followed by West.

"Mr West will drive you home, Miss Rostov. You have the address, Forbes?"

On the way back from Clapham, Sir Denis said: "I hoped your friend, Nadia, might give something more away to you if I offered her the chance, but as a Don Juan you're fired, Forbes! She's some sort of Eurasian, and although devilishly attractive, I don't believe for a moment that there was any real attachment between her and Kenealy. We have what she came tonight to recover—the disc."

"That's clear, Sir Denis. But have you any idea what it is?"

"Except that it's stamped with the sign of the Si-Fan, none whatsoever"

"Sign of the Si-Fan? What is the Si-Fan?"

Nayland Smith laughed shortly. "It's a world-wide secret society of which Dr Fu-Manchu is president."

"Then why did Kenealy—?"

"The disc chained around his neck? Top marks to a brave man. He had joined the Si-Fan."

"Good heavens!"

"He had brains and nerve. But he must have slipped up. He was expecting another visitor tonight. And it wasn't Nadia. To the end, he hoped to bluff it out. Hence his destruction of all evidence against him. Is this clear to you, Forbes?"

"Yes—now it is. And it's horrible."

"The ways of Dr Fu-Manchu are always horrible."

The door of Nayland Smith's flat in Whitehall Court was opened by a manservant whose prominent jaw and grim expression inspired confidence.

"Good evening, Begby," Sir Denis said. "Any messages?"

"Yes, sir. A Mr West reported at ten-thirty-three."

"Good. Drinks in the study."

A moment later Malcolm was in a room which he could have recognised with his eyes shut from its overpowering smell of tobacco. As Sir Denis began to re-fill his hot pipe from a very large pouch, Begby came in with whisky and soda on a tray.

Begby put the drinks down, then:

"Going by way of Bayswater Road with this lady, Mr West got hit by a heavy truck that came out of a side-turning. He was knocked out, but not hurt, sir. The lady had vanished when he come round. They hung on to the truck driver."

"Thanks, Begby." Nayland Smith poured out drinks as his servant withdrew, and shrugged his shoulders. "You see, Forbes? We're dealing with Fu-Manchu."

He sat at his large, orderly desk, putting the mysterious disc on the blotting-pad; began to study it through a powerful lens.

Malcolm crossed and bent over his shoulder.

"Might I take a look, Sir Denis?"

Nayland Smith handed the lens to Malcolm and presently: "The hieroglyphic means nothing to me," Malcolm confessed; "but what metal is this thing made of?"

He picked the disc up, weighing it in his hand, when Begby rapped on the study door, came in and announced in a queerly muffled voice:

"Dr Fu-Manchu, sir!"

"What!"

Nayland Smith sprang up. Malcolm slipped the disc into his pocket. "At last you have him!" he whispered.

"Show Dr Fu-Manchu in here," Sir Denis said quietly, sat down and opened a desk drawer.

A tall figure came into the study, that of a man who wore a black overcoat with a heavy astrakhan collar and who carried a black hat. Begby retired and closed the door.

Malcolm became lost in fascination at the most wonderful face he had ever seen. The high, scholarly brow, the incredibly long, green eyes, the lined, intellectual features, the tremendous aura of power of Dr Fu-Manchu. He stood, stock-still, watching him.

"Good evening, Sir Denis." It was a high, metallic voice, the words precisely spoken. "This gentleman I assume to be Mr Malcolm Forbes, in whose career you take an interest. You may close the desk drawer. There will be no need for the revolver you keep there. I have taken the liberty of calling upon you only for the purpose of recovering a small metal disc which I believe you have in your possession."

Nayland Smith, his face set like a mask, watched him but did not speak.

"As I note a hand-lens there, perhaps the disc you have been examining is in your desk. Would you be good enough to let me see it?"

Malcolm, uneasily, slipped his hand into his coat pocket. The terrifying green eyes were flashed in his direction at the very instant that Nayland Smith, his elbow resting on his desk, covered Dr Fu-Manchu with a Service revolver.

"Dr Fu-Manchu, you are under arrest."

But Dr Fu-Manchu, his manner unperturbed, dropped the soft, black hat on the carpet and raised his hand. He held a small dial studded with several buttons.

"Take your hand from your pocket, Mr Forbes," he said sibilantly. "I know that the disc is there. I have my finger on the button which will connect it with the power centre. Your shot would come too late, Sir Denis, to save Mr Forbes. You have seen tonight how enemies of the Si-Fan die."

Malcolm, seeing again the grey face of Sergeant Kenealy, obeyed. His forehead was damp. Nayland Smith still covered Fu-Manchu.

"Put away your obsolete weapon, Sir Denis," the mocking voice went on, "unless you really believe my death to be worth the life of your friend. I have conquered a new vibration. The disc in Mr Forbes' pocket is tuned to it. A recruit to our order carries such a disc. If he proves unworthy, he is removed."

Nayland Smith grew pale under his tan. "What are your terms?" he demanded.

"Make no terms," Malcolm cried out. "I'll take a chance if you will!"

"I admire your courage," Dr Fu-Manchu spoke softly. "I need such men."

"What are your terms?" Sir Denis repeated tensely.

"Your word, which I respect, as you have learned to respect mine, that you will order your man, directly as I leave here, to take the disc, carefully packed, to André Messina, a guest at the Savoy hotel, and that you will take no further action until your man reports that it is delivered. I give you my word that I will take none."

Nayland Smith's grey eyes were angry, but he said, "Agreed," and pressed a bell. Begby came in. "Show Dr Fu-Manchu to the door, Begby."

Dr Fu-Manchu picked up his black hat, bowed formally and went out. Before the door had closed, Malcolm had snatched the disc from his pocket and dashed it on the floor.

Smiling wryly, Nayland Smith stooped to pick it up.

"Don't touch it, Sir Denis!" Malcolm's voice quivered. "For God's sake don't touch it!"

But Nayland Smith picked it up without hesitation.

"Forbes, you are new to the wiles and ways of Dr Fu-Manchu. Cunning and ruthless to all who stand in his way. Treacherous in all but one thing. He never breaks his word—for good or evil. In this, Forbes, lies his great strength…

THE MIND OF FU-MANCHU

She woke in completely incomprehensible surroundings. There was a vague smell of what she thought might be incense, a strange heaviness of all her limbs. "Where am I? Who am I?"—were questions which danced mockingly across her brain. Then came helpless fear, fear of the silence, the void around her. Had she been abducted? An accident? Was she suffering from amnesia? She lost control, wanted to cry out—but couldn't utter a sound.

And then, to crown growing panic, she became conscious of a presence. Softly came a voice, a sibilant, commanding voice: "You are quite safe, Miss Merton. There is no danger."

That voice! Its strange tones magically awakened her memory. She knew herself. She was Pat Merton. She knew the voice and where she had heard it before. Clearly, as though a veil had been raised, she remembered the crowded room in the Mayflower Hotel. A reception for Bruce Garfield and some of his colleagues was being held there. But his old friend Nayland Smith was arriving from Hong Kong and had wired him to meet his plane on a matter of vital importance, and so Bruce had phoned, asking her to rush over to the hotel and apologise for his unavoidable delay.

Bruce's colleagues assembled at the reception knew Pat and introduced her to some of the dignitaries in the throng. One of them was a Swiss scientist whose name she now failed to remember. But she recalled that he wore tinted glasses. Feeling rather uncomfortable as his voice droned on she had decided to leave, and then—this memory was crystal clear—the Swiss gentleman had removed his glasses, and a stare of long, narrow emerald-green eyes was fixed upon her. Apart from a hazy impression that he saw her from the hotel to a cab or car, the rest was a blank. But this was his voice. And then almost silently a tall figure appeared beside her.

Pat's inclination, as she looked up, was to scream. But a sense of horror, or, rather, of supernatural dread, reduced her to passive submission. This was the man she had met at the hotel, but he had changed. As the Swiss scientist, he must have worn a wig, for now his massive skull was only sparsely covered by hair. It was a wonderful face, the face of a genius, but of a genius inspired by hell.

He spoke softly, watching her, and his words soothed her terror strangely.

"I regret that you were overcome by the heat of the room at the Mayflower, Miss Merton. I took the liberty of bringing you here and restoring you." His eyes seemed to grow larger, to absorb her in their green depth; but she recovered in time to hear the words, "My. car is at your service."

The cool night breeze outside refreshed her as a courteous chauffeur in smart uniform made her comfortable in a limousine.

Numbly, she began to study her surroundings. The chauffeur had navigated several narrow, sordid streets. From one dark alleyway she had seen Chinese faces peering out in the gleam of the headlights. Over the low roofs there was a glow of night labour; she heard the hoarse minor note of a steamer's whistle. This was the East End dock area, of which she knew nothing.

Now they were speeding along a wide, straight thoroughfare, almost deserted, toward a part of the city with which she was acquainted. She had a glimpse of the Mansion House. There was Ludgate Hill… They were in the Strand… Charing Cross… Piccadilly.

The car pulled up. The chauffeur opened the door. Pat stepped out and found herself at the entrance to the Mayflower Hotel.

"Two o'clock!" Pat said in astonishment, when the night-doorman told her the time.

"Yes, miss." He looked at her in an odd way. "You are staying here?"

"No, I'm not. Will you please call a taxi?" Bruce will be frantic. She must get to him.

Pat opened her handbag, momentarily wondering if her money was still there. Everything was in order. She tipped the doorman and gave the taxi driver the address of Bruce's flat in Knightsbridge. As there were frequent occasions when she had to go there while Bruce was working, she had a key.

Bruce occupied a mews flat which Pat had helped to furnish and decorate. When the taxi pulled up, she saw that the windows were lighted; there were sounds of excited conversation coming through an open window. She hesitated for a moment, rang the bell.

The voices ceased. Then came footsteps on the short stair.

The door opened.

"Pat! Pat, darling! Thank God you're safe." Pat went into Bruce's arms.

She was so emotionally exhausted that he had almost to carry her up to the living room. The first person she saw, a tall lean man with sunburned skin, white streaks on dark hair above his temples, and grey eyes, she knew and welcomed: Sir Denis Nayland Smith, former Scotland Yard Commissioner and one of Bruce's oldest friends. The very man she had hoped would be there.

"A nice fright you have given us, young lady," he rapped in his crisp fashion. "Four divisions of the Metropolitan Police are combing London for you. This is Inspector Haredale of Scotland Yard"—indicating the third man—"who has been directing the search."

The inspector was so typical a police officer—fresh-coloured, frank blue eyes and a grey toothbrush moustache—that Pat could have guessed his profession. When the excitement of her unheralded, dramatic appearance had calmed down, Nayland Smith spoke.

"Before you attempt to explain your disappearance, let me bring you up to date about what has happened since you vanished from the Mayflower Hotel. Garfield found nothing remarkable in your leaving after giving his message of apology. After the reception, I went to my flat in Whitehall Court and Garfield came here. He made an unpleasant discovery."

He paused to relight his pipe which had gone out. Bruce crossed to Pat's chair and sat on the arm, his hand resting on her shoulder. "Don't let what has happened bother you, Pat. You're in no way responsible."

But Pat, looking from face to face, sensed that whatever had happened during those lost hours was intimately tied in with Bruce's flat.

"A report of a paper read by Garfield before a group of scientists a week ago," Nayland Smith went on, "had reached me in Hong Kong. It outlined his revolutionary theory of travel in outer space without rocket propulsion. He spoke of a scale model on which he was still working—and I knew he was in deadly danger."

"Why?" Pat whispered.

"Because I knew that Dr Fu-Manchu was in London. Scientists all over the world have been disappearing. What they had in common was that each one was working in the problem of anti-gravity." He sighed. "You don't know Dr Fu-Manchu, Pat—"

"Oh, but I do!" Pat burst out. "He's horrible. I don't think he's quite human—"

Nayland Smith checked her words with upraised hand and boyish smile which belied his greying hair. "I have often thought the same, Pat. You see, Dr Fu-Manchu claims to have solved the puzzle of anti-gravity, though we still don't know whether that is true. I knew he would want to see Garfield's model. And so I flew home at the earliest possible moment. But I was too late."

"What do you mean, Sir Denis, you were too late?"

"He means," Bruce told her gently, "that while he and I were at the reception, this flat was burgled. I discovered it on my return from the Mayflower and called you at once. There was no reply. Ten minutes' enquiry convinced me that you had disappeared from the moment you left the hotel with some unidentified man."

"*I* have identified him," Nayland Smith rapped. "Dr Fu-Manchu. Pat, the scale model of Garfield's interplanetary vehicle has been stolen. Only he and you knew where it was hidden. And you alone may be able to give us a clue leading to Fu-Manchu's London base."

Pat had got no further than her misty recollections of leaving the hotel when Nayland Smith broke in: "You hadn't been gone an hour before your description was known to most of the Metropolitan police."

Pat looked up at Bruce and went ahead with her story. Her awakening in the silent room, the smell of incense, the complete inertia of brain and body, seemed to convey some message to

Nayland Smith, for she saw him nod significantly to Bruce.

"As I thought, Garfield," he said. "And now Pat, please be very detailed about your return from this place—if you can. Do you remember anything at all?"

Pat described the midnight drive, the narrow streets, the Asiatic faces, the wide, deserted thoroughfare, the steamer whistles…

"The picture is clear. You agree, Inspector?"

"Entirely, Sir Denis. When your signal from Hong Kong reached us last week saying that Dr Fu-Manchu had left for London, I got busy. Every known or suspected hideaway of Dr Fu-Manchu was combed quietly. The only report that seemed at all warm came from K Division, Limehouse, as I have already told you. I have drawn a ring around a small area down there. I think the place where Miss Merton found herself tonight is inside that ring."

"Then let's not waste a moment," Nayland Smith said, getting to his feet. "We may be too late, Inspector, but we'll have a go at capturing Fu-Manchu. He has an inordinately high opinion of his hypnotic powers and may think himself quite safe. But my guess is that Pat came out of her trance sooner than he intended."

As they drove toward Limehouse in a police car, Nayland Smith explained the rest of the story to Pat. "Dr Fu-Manchu had learned that you had a key to this flat, that you knew where the model was hidden. The door in the panelling which only you and Bruce know how to open is closed. But the model has gone. To be sure the plans are locked up in the War Office, but to a man of Fu-Manchu's genius, the model would be enough. He brought you here from the Mayflower under hypnosis. You opened the panel and were taken to some hideaway where he could examine the model at leisure."

"I'll never, forgive myself," Pat said sadly.

"Nonsense," Bruce said quickly, "There was nothing you could do about it…"

Their police car raced on through the dark, still streets. Pat remembered the route, began to recognise certain landmarks. A man standing on the corner of a narrow street flashed a light three times as the car approached. "We're inside the cordon," Inspector Haredale reported.

And suddenly, "I remember that alleyway!" Pat exclaimed.

"Pull in on the right here," Haredale directed the driver. "This is where the hard work begins."

The car swung into a dead-end alley and, as they all got out, a man half hidden in its shadows saluted the inspector.

"Any movement, Elkin?"

"Not a thing, sir. If there was anybody in there, he's in there now."

A riverside warehouse, boarded up and marked for demolition, was suspected to be secretly used by Dr Fu-Manchu as a temporary base. One of K Division's detectives had found a way into it from a neighbouring building.

"We're in for some climbing, Pat," Nayland Smith warned grimly. "We need you or I wouldn't drag you along. Lead the way, Inspector."

The way was through a building which had an exit on the blind alley. Pat found herself climbing a narrow stair, guided by the beam of a flashlight held by Inspector Haredale. The climb continued until they came to the seventh and final landing. Pat saw an iron ladder leading to a trap in the roof.

"I'll go first, miss," the local detective told her. "It's a darkish night, but I don't want to show a light."

He went up, opened the trap, and stretched his hand down. Pat mounted, Bruce following, Nayland Smith and Haredale bringing up the rear. They stood in a narrow gutter, a sloping slate roof on one side and a sheer drop to the street on the other. An iron ladder to the top of a higher building adjoining led to a flat roof. A few yards away, in fleeting moonlight, Pat saw an oblong skylight.

"I must ask for silence now, sir," Inspector Haredale said. "Elkin, our guide, has managed to open a section of this skylight."

Elkin hauled a rope-ladder-from its hiding place, raised part of the skylight, hooked the ladder to the frame and climbed down. From below he flashed a light. "I'm holding the ladder fast," he whispered. "Would you come next, Mr Garfield, and hang on to Miss Merton?"

The ladder was successfully negotiated, and the members of the party found themselves in a stuffy loft impregnated with stifling exotic odours. The warehouse had belonged to a firm of spice importers.

Stairs led down to a series of galleries surrounding a lofty, echoing place where even their cautious footsteps sounded like the tramp of a platoon.

"No use going tiptoe," snapped Nayland Smith. "If there's anyone here, he knows we're here, too. The room you were in was on the ground floor, Pat. So let's get a move on. A little more light, Sergeant."

They descended from gallery to gallery until they reached the bottom. Then they stood still, listening. There was no sound. The place had the odour of a perfume bazaar.

"It was your mention of incense, miss," Inspector Haredale told Pat, "that convinced me you had been here. Now, Elkin, what's the lay of the land?"

"There's an inner office, and a main office beyond which opens right on to the street."

"Stand by for anything," Nayland Smith directed. "If we're

lucky, Fu-Manchu will be in there. If the door is locked, we'll break it down."

The door was not locked. As it swung open, they saw a lighted room.

"Stay with Pat for a moment, Garfield," Nayland Smith said tersely. "I want to make sure what's ahead."

He stepped in, followed by Haredale and Elkin. There was no one in the room. But as Pat strained forward to peer in, she saw a long couch illuminated by a tall pedestal lamp which shed a peculiar green light. "This is the room I was in!" she cried out.

She and Bruce joined Nayland Smith and, "Good God!" Bruce spoke almost in a whisper. "Can it be true?"

On a table beside the couch a curious object lay gleaming in the rays of the lamp. It was composed of some silver-like metal moulded in the form of two saucers, one inverted above the other and upheld by four squat columns apparently of vulcanite.

"My model!" Bruce shouted, and sprang forward.

"One moment, sir!" Inspector Haredale grasped his arm. "It may be booby-trapped. Elkin, make sure there's no wiring under the table."

As the detective dropped to his knees and began searching, Nayland Smith stepped to the door of the main office. It was locked.

"No wires, sir," Elkin reported. "All clear."

And almost before he had got to his feet Bruce had snatched up the model and was examining it.

"Bruce!" Pat spoke breathless. "Has it been tampered with?"

"I assure you, Miss Merton, it has not!" a sibilant, mocking voice replied.

"*Fu-Manchu!*" Nayland Smith snapped. "He's in the next room. Come on, Haredale. We have him!" He fired three revolver shots in quick order. It was the signal for the raid.

There came a quiet laugh. "Ah, there you are Sir Denis Nayland Smith. Before you start the raiding party, I have a few words to say. I assume that you are there, Mr Garfield? I could not resist the temptation of telling you myself that you have far to go in the field of gravity. After inspecting your model, I saw no harm in sharing a few facts. So I laid a trail, with the assistance of your charming friend, Miss Merton, which I felt sure you could easily follow."

Bruce, feeling like a man in a dream, said, "Very good of you!"

The wail of police whistles sounded, the roar of a racing engine, the screech as brakes were jammed on in the near-by street.

"Your model, Mr Garfield, is elementary," the strangely sinister voice went on. "But I was interested to examine it. You have advanced only a short way in the science of anti-gravity. But you are on the right route. Listen." The sibilant voice droned on as Dr Fu-Manchu became more explicit. Bruce listened, fascinated and rapidly made notes. Finally the voice concluded with this astonishing revelation.

"You may recall the sensation once created by the appearance of so-called flying saucers? Some of these—but not all—were test flights of my anti-gravity machine, which I have since perfected. The others, I assume, were from distant planets."

The door of the outer office was being battered down. A voice shouted, "Inspector Haredale! Are you there?"

"You may call off your raiders," the calm voice continued. "As I know you have already realised—I am not in the other office. I am fifty miles away. When you opened the door of the room in which you stand, you connected me with an amplifying device on a short-wave receiver, which, if you are patient, you may find in the main office. I installed it some time ago to enable me to give orders to subordinates assembled there."

A crash announced the collapse of the street door. Men could be heard running down the stairs from the entrance on the roof. Pat was trembling. There were tears in her voice when she turned to Bruce, who was holding the model. "Bruce, darling, is it true? Have you failed?"

Bruce put the model down, hugged Pat—and laughed. "This is the first model I ever made, and I should have hated to lose it. I suppose I feel about it the way a sculptor feels about a rough clay study for a statue. But it doesn't tell Fu-Manchu a thing. What's more, his boastfulness has made him tell *me* more than I think he meant to. But no one—not even you Pat—knows how far I have gone since that first model. Dr Fu-Manchu isn't the only man who has solved the riddle of gravity. The other saucers he mentioned don't come from outer space. And so he's in for a surprise. One of the greatest firms in the world has financed, and is now flight-testing, my own anti-gravity machine. That is the real secret of the flying saucers!"

NIGHTMARE HOUSE

"That's Low Fennel, sir."

My guide clambered out of the ditch, the withdrawing of his boots from the soupy mire involving an effort marked by successive reports like muffled pistol shots. Old Ord, my expert in the topography and lore of this uninviting stretch of Cornish lowland, reached me a gnarled paw and assisted me to the top of the small weedy hummock which gave us something more solid underfoot than the mud-porridge through which we had been wading for the last hour.

He pointed out an agglomeration of roofs, visible beyond the deep notch in the skyline made by the sides of the broad gully in which we were standing. I saw the heavy turrets of a Norman structure which seemed to constitute a left wing of a straggling house, and the more graceful corniced roof of a lower structure of later and more livable style (Jacobean, I judged) and this distant and restricted view of the House of the Drurocks was cut off here. There is a further wing of the place, modern brick enclosing plumbing and wiring of our century, but this part of the abode I came to know only later, when we got to the heart of that horror which hung in the air of those rooms, and most particularly the apartments of Margery, wife of Henry Drurock, major of the Cornish Guards, retired.

I looked and waited for John Ord's inevitable gloomy tale. The old fellow had some fearsome legend to fit every landmark, and his manner in pointing out the house in Low Fennel warned me that I was in for another number from my dour companion's repertory of the grey and grisly local lore.

"When the Drurocks die, their bodies don't die like other men's," began old Ord, and waited for me to react to the staggering and fanciful statement, which I did with the proper grimace of interest and awe.

"It's true," protested the old peasant. He lowered his voice. "Four generations of 'em were dug up when they sold the slope south of the church and those that saw them while they were above ground tell that they were as whole as when they were buried."

"And how is the phenomenon explained?" I asked, keeping levity out of my tone.

Old Ord looked at me sharply, but was either reassured by my blank expression or so well launched upon his tale that he could not stop.

"The brimstone preserves 'em," he said, hollowly. "Their house is built over a hole that goes straight down, forever and forever, and they breathe the fumes, sleeping and waking, all their lives."

"In short," I commented, "they're just devils without tails and they have their own private stairway down to Hades."

"Don't laugh," beseeched the credulous old gossip.

I scolded him mildly.

"After all, you live off the Drurocks one way or another, every blessed soul of you around here. It isn't good form or good policy for you to be telling a stranger that your landlord is—what? A ghoul sitting on the mouth of a chimney of the inferno, I gather."

Ord shook his head. "Nevertheless, if you meet him sir, if you go into his house and eat at his table, let me tell you, don't face him when you talk to him. Stay at his side and don't let him breathe on you."

Idly, I plied the gaffer with further questions, but some flavour of irreverence about my response to his tale shut him up. He became obstinately dumb, and finally set me in my place by setting himself in his—a paid guide to a foolish scientific Londoner whose incredible hobby was the uncomfortable and unhealthy one of exploring the ditches of the region, day after day, and assembling, in accumulating jars and vials, the ill-smelling fauna and flora of these stagnant pools.

In the comatose village of Upper Fennel, the inn stood at the head of a single village street, customarily so devoid of any signs of life that it was a distinct shock to find the widow Crowley's boy clattering toward us as we came out of the fields onto the road. My landlady's son was running toward us for all he was worth, waving a bit of paper and piping my name. I recognised the fold of a telegraph blank before it was handed to me.

"The telegram got here before the gentleman," gasped the boy.

"What gentleman?" I asked, pausing in the act of opening the message.

"Him which sent the telegram," panted the messenger. "He's in your room now."

The explanation scarcely made sense, and I was about to identify what I gathered was a visitor down from London by the simple expedient of opening the telegram when I was saved the trouble by Aubrey Wales himself.

Though I had not seen my schoolmate in five years, I recognised his voice at once as it called my name. I looked up to see him waving to me from the balcony of the inn. He had not changed much. Aubrey was still the fellow he had been at that period, the patrician among us studious clods, the Greek among us barbarians——a darling of the gods who carried his gifts so graciously that he inspired no envy. I know of nobody who begrudged him his money; his beauty, his good temper and his luck with women. We were all under his sway as undergraduates and I promptly fell under it again now, as I joined him in the low-ceilinged inn room and opened a bottle of the harsh local ale by way of making him welcome.

I still held the unopened telegram, and I thought I detected a note of constraint or embarrassment in his manner as he referred me to the message.

"You haven't looked at my telegram? Then you don't know what brings me down here," he said, with a seriousness which marked the end of the interlude of hilarious back-slapping.

"Anything grave and earnest?" I inquired. "My guess was that you were down here to set up your easel. I guessed wrong?"

He nodded. I was surprised to find him flushed and tongue-tied.

"If I had no better excuse for living than the bit of rotten painting I do from time to time, I might as well blow my brains out—if any," he said, with a bad attempt at lightness. The concealed bitterness was something so novel in him that I probably looked up sharply. He became more embarrassed than ever, a fact which he betrayed by speaking with a sign of irritation.

"Why don't you read the telegram?" he demanded, brusquely,

and got up to pace the room while I obeyed the hint. I gave the reading due seriousness.

"Have you met the Drurocks?" read the extraordinary message. "What do you know about him? Is she seen about in public? Is there any gossip? Please learn what you can, but do not reply. Coming at once.—WALES."

I put down the sheet and looked up at him.

"Sounds completely balmy, doesn't it?" he challenged. "Well, I'm not off my nut. Never more earnest in my life."

"In that case—" I began.

He leaped down my throat. "You *have* heard something!" he cried. "What? Is he mistreating her? What's this about their being locked up in that house and all the servants leaving? What do you know? If he's harmed her, Mac, I tell you I'll finish him. I'll cut his throat—with pleasure."

The outburst subsided. I think I must have worn the expression of my utter amazement, for he was brought up short.

"You don't know what I'm talking about!" It was an indictment. He was incredulous. "You mean you haven't heard about it? I had all London pitying me—and grinning when I wasn't looking." He shrugged. "Oh well, I suppose a disappointed lover is a comical object. I didn't feel comical, though, I can tell you. Of course, if you don't know what I'm talking about—" He had another one of his sudden changes of mood and subject. "You know, you're an irritating sort, Mac. You never know or hear anything. Where do you keep yourself? Don't you even read the papers? The tabloids got hold of it and smeared me with ink. You know the sort of thing. My picture and hers and one of those blurbs hinting scandal: 'Engagement

Mysteriously Broken.' That sort of thing! I could have wrung her neck at the time, but now, if she's in trouble—" He trailed off into silence and sent up a thick screen of cigarette smoke.

I took my opportunity to be heard. "Who's neck?" I demanded.

The answer was some more of his disconnected and excitable ramblings. But, out of his incoherence came eventually the coherent story, which I had complete before I got him off to bed far after midnight, bribed with a promise that we should look over the house at Low Fennel promptly after breakfast the following morning.

As a matter of fact, I did have some vague knowledge of his misadventure with a London girl who had gone off to marry some country squire, leaving Wales in the rather awkward predicament of being left waiting at the church. He did not gloss over his own humiliation in telling me of the circumstances. In view of his unheralded arrival in this blighted and inaccessible corner of Cornwall, all in a chivalric ferment and ready on any pretext to slaughter the husband, he did not need to add that he had recovered badly from the love affair and was ready to pick it up again at any sign from the lady.

She had been Margery Perth, daughter of Capt. Ronald Perth, VC, DSO, etc., etc.—more medals than shillings. Even before she got to be a newspaper darling by reason of her engagement to a London catch and the subsequent sudden marriage to an obscure Cornishman, one saw Margery's face in the illustrateds. The press snap-shots hardly did her justice, I was soon to discover.

I offended Aubrey by failing to be properly impressed by the origins of his love affair with the girl. It seemed to be the usual sort of thing, a house-party, an afternoon on the river, a walk back to the hall by summer moonlight and there you have it, all tied and delivered, ready for the parson. At that, I suppose a love affair is as good as its best moment, and even Romeo and Juliet must have been a common pair of moonstruck nonentities before they rose to tragedy. Aubrey and Margery had their splendid interlude, as I am ready to testify, so let us gloss over the humdrum beginnings.

They led up to an engagement in due form, with a public announcement. Then her father took her to the continent. A tour of the casinos was his regular annual custom and he saw no reason why his daughter's engagement should interfere with his habits. He was that kind of selfish pensioned Britisher, a fellow with his half-pay and a few extra pounds from somewhere and a liking for his ease.

"They left last June," Aubrey told me. "I saw Margery down to the boat-train. I'll swear she had no thought then, but to have the separation over with. It was to be an Autumn wedding. I never heard another word from her until early September, and then it was the news I read in my morning paper: 'Married: Margery Perth, daughter of Capt. Ronald. Perth—and all the letters—to Maj. Henry Drurock. Maj. and Mrs Drurock will return to England within the month, and to Cornwall to open Low Fennel, where Maj. Drurock has mining interests."

He quoted every line of the announcement. You could tell the bit of print had burned into his memory.

"She wasn't that sort," he protested, earnestly. "There must have been something wrong." He went on in a more subdued manner, as if a bit ashamed of what he was saying. "There were lots of rumours. I don't say they were anything but rumours, mind. But people came back from Biarritz with stories of cheating in the casino. Her father was an unconscionable gambler, you know, and on his half-pay. Anyway, they talked about his being headed for a French jail and this Drurock fellow buying off the authorities. Melodrama, isn't it? I daresay untrue, every bit of it. It was just the sort of thing my fool friends might concoct to salve my wounded pride." He questioned me. "What do you think?"

"How can I think anything?" I retorted. "I only know what you're telling me. Pretty daughters do marry bounders to keep their daddies in funds. It's been done. I've heard of cases. Perhaps only in books, but it's been heard of. What then? You say you never heard from her again and here you are in her village. This is Drurock's land, you know—the village, and everything you see for miles around. Though I wouldn't give a week's pay for the whole of it. It's hopeless terrain. It has no crop but leeches and toads, no climate but a poisonous fog."

"Poisonous?" His utterance of the word was a shout. "Did you say 'poisonous fog'?"

"Merely a figure of speech," I hastened to assure him; betraying, I hoped, no sign of my startled recognition of this reiteration, by an apparently sane Londoner, of the notion which obsessed old Ord. "What's the matter, Aubrey? What about a 'poisonous fog'?"

"I don't know." He shrugged, hopelessly. "It's something hellish, but I can't say what it is." On the last of his breath, he mumbled: "Poor Margery," and then leapt to his feet. "We've got to do something, Mac. We've got to get her out of it. I didn't know what her letter meant—poor child. I thought the poison fumes were something she had imagined, some obsession of her unhappiness."

"Oh, then you *have* heard from the lady?" I put in.

"Indirectly, yes." He brought out his bill-fold and extracted a written sheet from it. "It's a letter to her father. The old scoundrel popped off last week. They found him in his room at the club. He had been reading this. Maybe he had enough decency left in him to die of the shock of what's in the letter, but I doubt it. It was the drinking finished him off. The club people turned over his few effects to his solicitor, who happens to be mine, too. The lawyer had enough sense to be a bit alarmed about Margery's letter and he thought I might be the proper person to come to in the absence of any relative who would take the trouble to attend the funeral. In short, he turned the letter over to me and I'm asking you now. What do you think?"

I studied the pathetic scrawl, apparently dashed off in haste and under considerable emotional stress, for the taller letters all leaned like trees in a hurricane and half the lines ran off the page.

"Please, papa," the girl had written, "you *must* come now—at once—and take me away from him. He won't let me go alone. I know you don't believe about the poison fumes, but it's literally, awfully, devilishly true, papa, and I swear that I am not sick or anything and I haven't got hallucinations and this is *not a* trick to get away. If it happens *once more,* it will kill me. Get me out of this now, papa! Haven't I done enough? Margery."

"Well?" he demanded as I finished the reading.

"It's a perfect riddle," I ventured. "I should say, though, that the writer thinks she is in some kind of danger."

"*Thinks* she is!" he cried. "You don't know her. She isn't the kind that's afraid of a twig scratching against a pane. No—there's something wrong." He got up and stormed about the room. "Come on, Mac. We've got to act at once."

"Do what?" I reasoned with him. "Go up to the chateau at this hour, drag this Drurock, whom we do not know, out of his bed and tell him we are taking his wife away because she doesn't like the weather? Be reasonable. Sleep on it."

"And do nothing?"

"We'll do something, but we'll do it tomorrow. My suggestion would be to have breakfast, hire a car, and go over to call like civilised people. Drurock can hardly pull up a portcullis and drop hot lead on us. The chances are we'll get a fair sort of reception and you'll get a chance to talk to the lady in private for a moment and clear up the whole thing."

He calmed sufficiently to consider the programme.

"I mustn't go as myself," he said. "If there's anything really wrong, my turning up would give the show away. Drurock must know me by name. He must have seen those London papers." He warmed to my proposal and his own somewhat melodramatic revision of it. "I'll be an artist, sketching around, loafing in the. neighbourhood with you. As for you, you're quite unimpeachably explained. A frog-catcher come to where frogs are caught. That's it. Peter McAllister, RA, FRGS, subcurator of his Majesty's pollywogs and his artist friend, dropping in for some scientific chit-chat and a cup of tea. If that's a bargain, I'll get to bed."

"It's a bargain."

Old Ord's mumblings about Drurock came to my mind as I tucked myself in and bade my room-mate goodnight. I was on the point of telling Aubrey the tale, but soon thought better of it. The excitable fellow's suspicions and dreads already were feeding on too much food. I slept.

The day was steaming hot. Aubrey complained that his paints ran on the palette. However, he was obviously complaining for the sake of talking, for he was no more interested in the daub he was perpetrating than I, and that was not at all. We were established on a little hump of ground overlooking Low Fennel and Aubrey's composition on canvas took in the old tower which I had previously seen and the modern section which I now saw for the first time. This brick wing of the venerable pile of buildings had been carefully designed not to clash with the rest but it was plainly of recent date, and a materialistic eye, such as my own, could pick out the exterior indications of modern fittings within. A pair of telephone wires, branching off from the overland line up to the village, ended near what I took to be library windows in this modern wing. The grounds, to this side of the house, had been made as attractive as gardening skill could accomplish.

We had come on our expedition loaded like pack mules. Our equipment was principally painter's gear and included a ridiculous garden parasol which was set up on the knoll to give the artist shade.

"Certainly, it's ridiculous," agreed Aubrey when I complained. "But it's excellent advertising. I want to be noticed. Do you think we can be seen from the windows of Low Fennel?"

The question was redundant. The extravagant parasol would be seen and talked about for miles around. I pulled on my gloves. I was interested in a brambly gully which sloped down from this highland toward the bog behind the chateau.

"I'll do a bit of self-advertising, too," I informed him. "We meet at lunch hour and beg bread at Low Fennel; is that the programme?"

He nodded and I went about my affairs. I carried net and pail, but these tools of my much ridiculed profession remained idle. An interest other than scientific urged me on. I rebelled against it, but the sum of the extravagant talk I had heard in the last twenty-four hours was beginning to have its effect on the more unreliable and romantic sections of my brain. What was at the bottom of all this fantastic nonsense about an air-poisoned castle, prison for a London girl who cried desperately for rescue from something which, if it happened *once again,* would kill her? Scientific dispassionateness deserted me. I confess I stumbled down the gully, prey to an excitement which had nothing to do with the peculiar professional interests of Peter McAllister, zoologist.

The sides of the gully became steeper. It was turning in fact into a ravine. I had not judged the depression on this side of Low Fennel to be so deep. I approached a turn in the gorge and found myself face to face with—the master of Low Fennel!

I knew it was he the moment I saw him. For one thing, the man was London tailored and I knew that there was no other man of wealth living in the neighbourhood. For another, a portrait photograph of the landlord of the countryside hung in the parlour of the inn up in the village and I recognised the striking features at once. For a rough picture of the man as a whole, he was a fairly average sample of the genus, country gentleman. The tweeds were the suitable costume of the heavy-set man, strong-jawed and choleric, who first looked up in surprise and then advanced cordially toward me.

"You are the Londoner, the scientist staying at the inn?" He groped for and found my name. "Mr McAllister, isn't it?" He did not wait for my affirmation, but continued. "You must forgive my not having dug you up earlier. Mrs Drurock and I planned to make you welcome, but some other matters intervened. You must forgive us— and come up for lunch. Today? Now? Certainly. Let's make it now."

"I have a guest down from London." I embarked on Aubrey's arranged lie, stammeringly. I felt at a disadvantage, exchanging for this courteous and candid hospitality my discourteous guile. "He's a painter—Alfred Hume."

He nodded sagely. I could not guess him. I never quite did. Whether he had us identified from the start, or whether he caught on to Aubrey later; this is a puzzle without solution. He never gave any sign. I could assume that my whopper had gone down with ease.

"Alfred Hume—" he echoed the name and professed to have heard it before. "Though I am not as well acquainted with our English artists as I should wish," he apologised. "Your Mr Hume— do you think he will risk provincial hospitality—or is he a growling bear, like so many artists?"

"Not in the least," I hastened to assure him. "He's back on the hill, up there, and half-starved by this time, probably."

"Shall I make the bid personally, or shall I go ahead and announce you to my wife?"

"Don't bother to come with me," I said. "I'll bring him along. He'll come like a lamb."

Aubrey did. He packed up his parasol and kit and tossed them, together with the uncompleted masterpiece, under the nearest bush.

"We have to work this thing right." He was voluble and dictatorial as we marched down the slope toward the gates of Low Fennel. "You have to get a word with Margery first and tell her not to let on. A word will do.

"So you think that fellow, Drurock, is a decent sort, do you? Well, you're wrong. You may be a great judge of fauna, my dear fellow, but you're no judge of men. Don't worry, though. I'll be on my best behaviour. I'm Alfred Hume, overcome with the honour of a bid to a gentleman's home. I won't forget. I may sell him a sketch before I'm through. Tell Margery to patronise me. We'll wangle it so I do a portrait of her."

Margery was admirably quick in the emergency we presented to her. I succeeded in having my word with her alone and announced the arrival of Aubrey. She took my news calmly.

"I thought so," she murmured. "I saw him from the window and I was sure it was he." We were walking across the cobbled courtyard in front of the middle-house and Drurock was some fifty paces behind us, waiting for Aubrey, who had invented a pretext to run back for his kit on the hill.

Margery paused. To others, it might seem that she was pointing out to her guest the few scrubby flowers in the border before which we stood. She spoke without turning her face to me. Her deep, musical voice was husky with her suppressed vehemence.

"You must take him away again, Mr McAllister. Aubrey must not stay here," she commanded.

"Why?"

She hesitated for an instant. "I can't lend myself to what will surely seem to be the lowest sort of intrigue," she said, and I knew she was giving the false answer.

"Of course, it isn't anything of the kind," I insisted. "I can vouch for Aubrey. He hasn't turned up to capitalise any former relation."

I was on thin ice and deemed it best to go straight to the truth. I told her how Aubrey had become the final recipient of her letter to her father. She trembled a bit. She spoke hastily, as we heard Drurock raise his voice down at the gate and Aubrey call out a reply.

"Because he'll be in danger?" I asked.

My only answer was a fleeting nod. As I looked into the beautiful and disturbed face a conventional mask was drawn over it. The terror-stricken girl became the mistress of Low Fennel receiving her husband's guests with just the proper mixture of warmth and reserve. It was beautifully done, and I silently applauded Aubrey, too, who was bending deferentially over his hostess's hand.

A man appeared at a little door in the high wall which concealed the small formal garden before the new wing. Lunch was served. It was eaten on the brick terrace before the row of french-windows opening out on a comfortable living-room. We had come, Aubrey and I, full of indefinable expectations of we knew not what outward signs of the trouble afflicting this house. We were completely thrown off our guard by that lunch, an innocent country repast, served in charming surroundings, washed down with a palatable light wine.

The conversation around the table, starting at a low point of constraint, actually rose to something like gaiety before we rose from coffee that was poured at the table. It was the host who had accomplished the lightening of the common mood. He had talked almost incessantly, lightly, amiably. It was impossible to oppose glowering conspiratorial masks to all of this indefatigable good humour: impossible and scarcely politic. I responded first to our host's geniality, but Aubrey had laughed aloud before the meal was over and even Margery dropped some of her defences of quiet reserve before the liqueur glasses were set down.

"And now," suggested Drurock as we rose, "I think, my dear, you might show Mr Hume the old wing." He patted Aubrey's shoulder amicably. "As a painter, Hume, I think you'll relish the old tower. One look at it and I think you'll give in and have your stuff brought over from the inn."

The proposal that we move into Low Fennel had been suggested passingly during lunch. This reiteration of it informed me that it was a genuine invitation. I consulted Aubrey with a glance and saw that he proposed to accept. I looked to Margery. She shook her head. The movement was next to imperceptible but definite. Drurock did not wait for his answer, but took my arm.

"As for the two of us, we'll go poison ourselves with brandy and tobacco, as becomes our grey hairs. I think I can amuse our scientist with some of the fearsome local legends. Come along, McAllister. I'll chill your blood with tales of ghosts and warm it with some pretty good Napoleon I've got hidden away."

Drurock's study was on the ground floor of the new wing. The outlook here was pleasant enough, with roses growing up to an open window which commanded the savage stretchy of badland behind the house. Seen from this pleasant point of vantage, the evil countryside was not without its wild appeal. The heat was really oppressive, and Drurock invited me to remove my coat, setting the example himself.

We were comfortably ensconced, my host taking his lolling ease on a hard leather couch, myself deep in a saddle-back chair, our glasses to hand.

"You know," he began on a note of casual conversation, although I thought I sensed some latent emotion, an undertone. "You know, I think you might be amused by some of the tales of the district. You may already have heard some of them from the country-folk?"

He darted an inquisitive look at me.

"Oh, nothing that makes sense," I replied, evasively.

He chuckled. "I can see you've heard the best one of all—that the Drurocks breathe out sulphur. Is that the way it goes?"

I coughed.

"Yes, that's the tale," he laughed aloud. "Rather, it's only part of it." He refilled his glass and tossed off the contents.

"You've heard of the slithering ghost of Low Fennel? No?" His voice settled down to a drone. "It's an amusing legend. The strange part of it is that some rather level-headed people here-about will swear to its truth—have seen it, in fact.

"I first ran into the thing last year, when we came here and opened up the chateau. That was just after the marriage, you know. We got here to find the new wing still uncompleted. I was furious.

The building should have been finished well before our arrival. It was a fine mess to walk into with a new bride. We had to put up in the inn. I called for the local contractor—a fellow named Seager—whom I had left in charge of the work. The answer to the call was the information that he was dead—died on the job. You know, I could never worm the particulars of his death out of these workmen. They shuffled and lied.

"All I could learn was that the local officials had made inquiry and had brought in a finding that the man died of natural causes. Therefore I couldn't understand why there should be such an undercurrent of hard feeling about the matter. In short, I couldn't get the building finished. No one would return to the job."

"Someone did the work, though," I prompted.

"Yes, John Ord. You may have run into him?"

"He's been my guide around the district," I said.

"And has told you some tall tales, likely! Well, old Ord rose to the bait of extra pay and came up with his wife and son, a big lout of a boy who could help his father hoist a beam. The two of them finished up the structural work and I had city workmen up for the decorating. When the work was done, I made Ord and his wife an offer—to stay on as caretakers, the year round. He took me on, and fixed the family quarters in the old tower, in that part which juts out and touches the new wing at the Tear, over on the badlands side. They stayed on until last September—a dam' hot September it was, too. Then he rose up and gave notice."

"On what grounds?"

"He told me a cock-and-bull story about his wife having seen an apparition, or some sort of fearsomely deformed creature of flesh and blood slithering along the walk outside her bedroom window. I read all the evidence—Ord's story and his wife's. She stuck to her 'apparition'. She was circumstantial about it. The thing—whatever it was—had the body of a man—a nude man who wriggled along on the ground and showed a repulsively contorted face. Well, I came to a prosaic explanation of the whole affair. The 'apparition' was simply Ord himself, coming home in the night from some drunken spree, making a disgusting spectacle of himself and preferring now to subscribe to his wife's superstitious fancies rather than confess his delinquency. I let them go.

"It's one thing to have a story like that from a local but—"

"Ah," I cut in, "you've had some sort of confirmation from a more credible source. Seen the thing yourself?"

"Thanks for not laughing at me," he replied, "though I shouldn't blame you if you concluded that I'd lapsed into the state of bigoted ignorance that rules the district.

"About our apparition and its second appearance," he resumed, with animation. "No, I did not see it myself. I just missed it. But Mrs Alson saw it as plainly as I see you. Mrs Alson is my wife's maid. She's Yorkshire. She's placid. She's literal. She's a teetotaller. Her eyes are excellent. In short I accept her account of what she saw as if I had seen it myself. It was about two months ago."

My brain made a swift calculation. The date he named would correspond to the period of the writing of Margery's letter to her father. Once again I recalled the outstanding phrase: "If it happens *once again*, papa, it will kill me." I listened to Drurock with sharpened attention.

"It was infernally hot that night," he was saying.

I interrupted him. "That's the second time you have mentioned the heat. I gather you trace some connection between the— phenomenon, and the thermometer."

"Excellent!" He purred applause. "You are right up with me." He approved me with a warm glance of something like affection.

"Let's have Mrs Alson's tale," I said.

"She came down from her room on an upper floor about two a.m.," he obliged. "She was suffocating, she told me later, and the idea came into her head to go down into the cellar and draw herself a glass of cider. She was coming down the stairs and she reached the bend. There is a landing—or a wider step—at this point, and on this step stood the man—or thing. He was coming up. Moonlight was streaming in through the oriel and he stood fully revealed. Mrs Alson suffered grave shock, both to her nerves and to her English sense of the proprieties. The creature was stark naked. It had the body of a man, she says. The face! Well, she can only describe it as that of a demon, a contorted and devilish caricature of a human face, the eyes crossed and glaring like a mad dog's!

"Of course, she fainted on the spot. I really think she might have died there of shock if I hadn't awakened about that hour. I awoke parched and dripping out of the kind of stupor that sleep becomes in excessive heat and I also was driven downstairs in search of something to drink. I nearly fell over Mrs Alson's prostrate form. I got her into the room of one of the maids and we revived her. I sent the maid out while Mrs Alson whimpered her tale. That was a precaution. You'll understand."

I nodded. "You didn't want the story disrupting the whole household, naturally."

"And specifically," he said, "I didn't want it— don't want it to get to my wife."

"Oh," I asked, somewhat disingenuously, "then Mrs Drurock knows nothing of all this?"

"Absolutely nothing," he affirmed. "And she must know nothing of it. My wife is rather finely strung. She is delicate. It's a matter of both breeding and health. If she should hear of our visitant, the effect on her system might be grave." He shook his head deploringly. "And if, by any chance, she were ever to encounter the thing itself, I shudder to think of the possible consequences."

"Why don't you close up the house and move away?"

He scowled. "The Drurocks belong here. A patrimony must not be renounced. If you do not understand the force which keeps me here, surely you will follow me when I say I can't go away from here with the mystery unsolved."

"Yes," I agreed, "as a scientist I can understand that."

He brightened again. "You must stay here and solve it with me. We'll compare notes."

"You have no further data?" I asked.

He hesitated. "In a way, I have. There's the miasma."

"Miasma?"

"Yes. A sort of thick vapour. Sometimes it becomes dense enough to form an opaque column, rather definite in outline. I've seen it. So have others. That's the source of another legend, of course. The house is haunted, in the approved manner, by a wraith that walks in white."

"It rises, then, *within* the house?"

He nodded.

"Where?"

He was evasive. I was certain of that and that he was withholding some definite knowledge he had. "Oh, here and there," he said, vaguely. "I'm not sure about the exact spot."

"Then that's all?"'

Again he hesitated. "There's a document," he slowly said, and then leaped to his feet briskly. "But you've had enough for one sitting. You've got—" He counted off the elements of his account on his fingers. "You've got: the slithering visitant—"

"A naked man with a contorted face," I checked.

"—the heat—"

"Seen when the thermometer is high."

"—and the miasma," he concluded.

I waited, studying my own thoughts. When I looked over to him I caught him observing me from under lowered eyelids.

On impulse, I said, "Why do you tell me all this?"

"Isn't it what you came here to find out?" he retorted, quietly.

I digested the import of his words, which meant that he knew of our reasons for entering his home, that we were not the casual visitors in the neighbourhood that we professed to be—that he knew or guessed all this; and how much more?

I traded boldness for boldness, frankness for frankness.

"Yes," I said. "I do want to get at the explanation for some curious things I've observed."

"There speaks the scientist," he cried, with undisguised irony. "And your friend, Mr Alfred—or was it Aubrey? Hume—or is it Wales? Is his interest—zoological, too?"

I stood up. "Shall we leave?" I inquired.

"With curiosity unsatisfied?" he cried. "No, certainly not." And then he became earnest. "For some time, I've expected that outsiders would become interested in us down here. It was inevitable, with all the tales being spread around. I welcome investigation, Mr McAllister. I welcome having it conducted by one so competent as yourself, a fellow with 'RA' and 'FRGS' after his name. And—" he gave me a courteous nod—"I like its being done by a gentleman."

"And Aubrey Wales—" I began.

"—my wife's former fiancé," he put in.

"Is he a welcome guest, too?"

"Why not? Why not?" he chuckled.

He gave my shoulder a friendly pat of dismissal. "Don't hurry your solution, Mr McAllister," he said, a light of mocking complacency dancing in his eyes. "Let's make it last. You can't imagine how this visit relieves the monotony which is the *other* disadvantage of Low Fennel."

I turned and went up the hall. My foot was on the lower stair when I heard his low call behind me, and turned around. He had his head stuck through the study door and a smile of chummy complicity was on the large face.

"And—another thing, Mr McAllister," he whispered, loudly. "I propose a trade. Don't you tell young Mr Wales about this and I shan't bother Mrs Drurock with it. Have you ever noticed that young and beautiful people are entirely devoid of brains?"

He winked at me and closed his door.

I did not like the looks of things.

I was being left severely alone. Drurock either slept through the whole of the stiffing afternoon or was gone somewhere on his own business. I saw nothing of him.

I saw something of Aubrey and our hostess, and wished I hadn't. I had no intention of so doing, but it came about that I spied on what gave every evidence of developing into a clandestine affair. Under my breath I roundly cursed Aubrey for his utter folly. So this was what his Galahadian mission had come to! Kissing another man's wife behind doors! I decided to subscribe to Drurock's proposal, and leave my fool in blissful ignorance.

Towards Margery I extended a more charitable feeling. I could begin to guess at her horrible adventure in this noxious place, where she was tied to a thing immeasurably loathsome and impure. The return of healthy young Aubrey into her existence must have been like a letting of sunshine into a foul dungeon. Her reaching out to him must have been pure instinct, irresistible, as urgent a gesture as breathing.

I came upon them when I probed my way into the ancient wing. I wished to view the quarters deserted by the family of John Ord, this being the only place which, in my host's account of the resident spectre, was precisely located with reference to the phenomena described. I found my way through a servants' yard and to a fine old kitchen suggestive of days when earlier roasting was done on a royal scale. A cook startled from sleep gave me the directions I needed, and I was soon stumbling over the rotten flooring of one level of the old tower. The dank odour of a mushroom bed below came up through the generous floorcracks.

I discovered a partition and, behind it, a little hive of rooms showing shreds of wallpaper still upon the walls. This would be the erstwhile Ord habitat. Seeking to fix the location with reference to the general plan of the rambling pile, I put my head out of a paneless window and looked around. I was instantly aware of a murmuring of low voices close at hand. I recognised Aubrey's at once. I looked down.

The precious pair of love-sick fools were directly under my eyes. She was seated on a little hummock. Her hands lay in her lap and he was bending over to kiss them. Whatever he was saying had an imploring sound. I could guess the import—"Come, fly with me." She drew away from him, but it was plain that simple instinct would have bent her the other way.

I turned to find a little frisking dog dancing at my heels. I made friends. Then I made a discovery. In one of the inner rooms of the deserted Ord abode there was a deep embrasure with a door. This wall was obviously the outer shell of the tower, immensely thick, and the opening in it was either an egress to the outdoors or a means of communication with another part of the structure. I tried the door. It resisted. While I tugged at it, the little dog began to whine at my back and presently darted over and seized my trouser leg in his teeth. He tugged with all his little strength. I desisted from my vain efforts at the door, and the dog was at once reassured and began to frisk again.

The dog continued to yap at my heels all the way back to the new wing, to which I returned by covering, roughly, the arc of a circle around both of the older sections of the chateau. I was doing a small problem in geometry as I walked and I reached the conclusion that I had all but closed a complete circle by the time I reached the library doors. Unless my rough calculations had misled me, this meant that the door in the deserted Ord apartment gave communication into the modern wing. I was about to take one of my longest steps forward toward solution of the problem of Low Fennel at this juncture and, in the next moment, I took it. As I crossed the sill into the library, the little dog which had pestered me suddenly dropped back with a low whine and lay shivering on the gravel path outside the room. Nor would he budge to rejoin me when I emitted a coaxing whistle and snapped my fingers.

I suddenly darted back and, seizing the dog by the collar, dragged him into the study with me. The result was extraordinarily encouraging to the hypothesis forming in my mind. The brute whimpered and whined piteously. At the door he struggled furiously and even tried to snap at my hand. I got him inside and imprisoned him by closing the french-window. Then only did I release him. What followed was immensely suggestive, in fact conclusive. The dog began circling about the room in a frenzy, seeking a way of escape. His neck-hairs stood out like a bottle-brush. He no longer barked, he roared. Finally, ending a dizzy circuit of the room, the small animal hurled himself like a projectile at the closed window and smashed his way to the open through sash and pane.

I did not need to make further inquiry into the geographical confines of the problem. It lay here, in the modern wing!

Dinner was a disastrous affair. The various causes of disunion which lay among us all were coming too close to reckless action and utterance to permit a flow of small talk. We nibbled at tasteless viands and were all ready enough for the signal to rise from the table. Each made a pretext to be alone.

I passed an inner door to the library as I started for my room, wanting nothing but a chance to lie on my back and puff on a pipe and think this thing out. Drurock intercepted me at the library door. He was in a listless, beaten mood.

"I spoke about a document I wanted you to see," he said, but I knew that this was a pretext to draw me into the room. I saw nothing for it but to join him in a cigar. He handed me a small bound volume, which I slipped into my pocket.

"I'll read it in bed," I said.

I sat, but he paced before me. His first question took me right in my wind by its brutal unexpectedness.

"Am I utterly repulsive?" he cried.

It was not the sort of thing that required answer and I held my tongue. He made another restless crossing of the room and stopped before me again.

"A man has a right to protect his home—even if it's not such a very happy one, hasn't he?" His manner bordered on complete loss of self-control and I was on my guard against feeding his state with any badly chosen comment. I elected to make none at all.

He pounded his palm with his fist and harangued the walls.

"Even in law, he has the right, hasn't he?"

I-made some inconsequential comment and rose for a leave-taking which was flight.

"Sleep soundly," he recommended with an especial emphasis. "And don't leave your room."

The heat was intolerable. I discarded everything but a shirt and stretched out on the bed. Sleep was out of the question. I left my bed lamp burning, lit a pipe, and drew out the volume Drurock had given me. It was a piece of bound handwriting. The ink was very old and pale. There was no date anywhere to be found, but the script was Elizabethan.

"In the reign of Mary accursed," began the reading, "a Duroque of Bas-Fenelle in Cornwall came to be martyred for his faith the manner of execution being the ministration of a lethal draught which was handed him duly in his cell in the Tower and, which drinking, he did sit down upon his pallett showing no sign, nor yet suffering any discomfort, and this for two whole days and nights, until the warden, accounting it a miracle and being afraid, did privately release the prisoner for fear of offending heaven by detaining him.

"Truly it was a miracle, even as the warden supposed but not one of heaven but rather of hell, and this has become known, to wit:

"The Duroques of Bas-Fenelle in Cornwall are immune to all lethal matters, such as the poxes and the potions and even the bite of the serpent and this not because of a virtue of their blood but because of a foulness of it which is fouler than any poison. This is the true account of how this comes to be.

"This was in the time of the first Plantagenet and the first Duroque of England built his house then close to the mouth of the rich mine of Fennel, granted him by his King. Having built, the first Duroque turned against his King and refused tribute, wherefor Plantagenet did send forces against him, but the King's soldiers never came to attack Bas-Fenelle, having all sickened or died long ere they could come to its walls and this by reason of the waters in the country about Duroque's house, which were fatal and accounted for all who drank.

"The first Duroque died and his son, Henry, followed him and made peace with the King. The second Duroque took a wife from the Court, but the lady sickened in the house of Bas-Fenelle and complained and said to her husband that she was wasted by the poison waters and air of the countryside where the house of Bas-Fenelle stood. And being a young and delightsome lady her plaint had weight with the second Duroque, who resolved to drain his lands and make them sweet and, seeing that the mine stood beside his house, a great hole in the ground, gave orders that his serfs should divert all the pools to this catch-pit and also drive all the foul life of the waters into this place. And the serfs were loathe to obey, knowing that to go into the foul ditches and breathe the vapours there was death, but they were forced by Duroque's armed men.

"And Duroque's soldiery came behind the serfs, advancing only when the ground was dried and made sweet by their labours, but keeping the circle at all times closed, so that no man could desist from the labour. And he who paused or turned away was shot down by the arquebusiers. And the master of Bas-Fenelle sat upon his wall in a great chair and drank wine and gave this order and that and witnessed the cleansing of his land.

"At the end of many days, those of his serfs which were still alive, having survived both the pestilential waters and the arrows of the arquebusiers came close to the mouth of the mine and made sluices and the last of the poisoned waters ran down into the mine and Duroque's steward came to the master upon the wall and said: 'Messire, are you satisfied? Shall we close the pit now and send these men home?' And Duroque shook his head and said: 'No. These men are all tainted. They are no better than receptacles of the foulness which is otherwise gone. Have them slain and thrown into, the pit.' Which was done, and the men were slain and thrown into the pit to the number of more than forty score and there was no male of the people left over the age of ten. The pit was sealed then by the men-at-arms and when the earth was firm Duroque came down off the wall and stamped upon it and beat the air with his arms and cried: 'For the first time a Duroque may walk on his own soil and breathe his own air and be in health!' And even as he cried out in pride, he fell prone, stricken by a curse for what he had done in the slaying of forty-score souls, and he lay upon the ground a full night in torment and was carried then into his house and put upon his bed as one dead...

"Then there came a physician, who had knowledge of many things and he saw and declared that the curse upon Duroque was that what was sweet to other men was foul to him and what was foul to other men was the breath of life to him, and, even, that the mine must be opened up again to let him breathe the vapours and revive. The mine was opened as the physician did recommend and a stench issued from the hole and everyone fled from the foul place, but Duroque, upon his bed, breathed of the foulness and was awakened from his. stupor and was filled with strength, for his blood had taken on the foulness of his deed and of the fruits of it sealed in the mine, and this blood is the blood of the Duroques, generation after generation.

"And the Duroques must live in their ancestral home above the lake of poison which lingers underground, being the liquid of the pestilential waters and of toads and of forty-score dead men. They must live there and replenish the foul blood in their veins always from the vapours which rise out of the accursed ground. And other penalties put upon them are that they are friends of no men but only of crawling and swimming things and that no woman of warm blood will willingly mate with them and perpetuate the breed but must be constrained or bought, nor never give her consent nor show a Duroque amiability."

I finished the reading in a cold sweat. The credulous and ghastly legend cast a numbing spell over my brain. Try as I would, I could not evoke the smile of tolerant disbelief in a witch's tale which the effusion merited.

In the end I was forced to leap out of bed and switch on the lights in the room. Hurriedly dressing, I decided to take a walk in the gardens. I was shaking like a child awake from nightmare. I went to the wash-hand-stand and dashed cold water over my face and neck. I was ashamed to look at my reflection in the mirror and when I did, I saw a livid caricature of myself staring back at me. I saw more. I saw the *contorted face*, as Drurock had described it. In the glass it was reflected beside my own. The horrible apparition to whom it belonged was standing, I judged, just outside my open bedroom door, in the low-lit hall. As I stared, the creature seemed to lose its strength to stand erect, and it sank to the floor, collapsing slowly and clawing at the doorpost as it sank.

I had to straighten up to see the floor in the mirror. No power could have turned me to face the thing direct.

The landing lights were low and remote so the area beyond my door lay in comparative darkness. But there, crawling slowly into the lighted area within my room, progressing serpent-fashion, inch by inch, silently, intently, so that the head, throat and hands were actually across the threshold, came a creature out of hideous nightmare. It had the form of a man and so much of it as I could see was naked. The dreadful head was being pushed slowly across the carpet, held sideways, so that one ear all but touched the floor. Then the face came into the light. But this was not a face—not within the ordinary meaning of the word, although it had the elements of a face and was the fleshy covering of the frontal surface of the skull.

The chin and lower lip seemed to be drawn up to meet the nose, entirely covering the upper lip. The nostrils were distended to an incredible and wholly unnatural degree. The skin had a kind of purple iridescent sheen unlike anything I have ever seen. The effect was grotesque in the truest sense of the word, for the thing was clearly grinning at me, though God knows there was nothing in the situation to provoke that grin.

Nearer it came, and nearer. I could hear the heavy body being drawn across the floor. I could hear the beating of my own heart. At the moment when the awful thing seemed to *coil* for a spring, there suddenly intruded on the ghastly silence the sound of whispered conversation rising from the garden below.

In the same instant, the sound seemed to impinge on the monster's hearing likewise. The hideous mask became bloated with a grimace that was legibly rage. The protruding eyes twisted in the head. Even in this dreadful moment, a monitor section of my brain registered an outside impression. I identified the source of the whispered conversation in the garden and the whispers—Aubrey and Margery. In that moment I believe I guessed the truth. The thought was but a flash, and then it was gone, dispelled by the necessity for action. By a backward slithering movement the thing which had been in my room was gone and swallowed up in the darkness of the hall. I turned and sprang. I had my nerves fairly in hand again and a fear for those two below galvanised me.

On the landing I paused and listened intently. No sound came up from the darkened stair and when, stepping quietly forward and leaning over the rail, I peered into the hall below, nothing stirred.

Again I heard the whispers in the garden. I crept back to my window and leaned out. Over to my left and on a level with me, a shaft of light shone out from our host's bedroom. Otherwise there was no light except the ghostly faint one falling from a moon veiled by racing clouds.

Between my window and the. new wing and on a level with my eyes, was the window of Mrs Drurock's room; and in the bright moonlight I could see her leaning out, her elbows on the ledge. Her bare arms gleamed like marble in the cold light, and she looked statuesquely beautiful. Wales I could not see, for a thick, square-clipped hedge obstructed my view...but I saw something else.

Lizard fashion, a hideous unclad shape crawled past beneath me amongst the tangle of ivy and low plants. The moonlight touched it for a moment, and then it was gone into denser shadows.

A consciousness of impending disaster came to me, but, because of its very vagueness, found me unprepared. Then suddenly I saw young Wales. He sprang into view above the hedge, against which, I presume, he had been crouching; he leapt high in the air as though from some menace on the ground beneath him. I have never heard a more horrifying scream than that which he uttered.

"My God!" he cried. "Margery! Margery!" and yet again: "Margery! Help!"

Then he was down, still screaming horribly, and calling for aid. The crawling thing made no sound, but the dreadful screams of Wales sank slowly into a sort of sobbing, and then into a significant panting which told of his agony.

I snatched up my kit, raced out of the room and down the stairs. I was held a moment at the door by the heavy and numerous bolts, but fumbled my way to the open at last. I almost fell over Aubrey where he lay inert upon the ground. I wasted no time in futilities, but busied myself with my restoratives at once. I found the wound quickly, having an inkling of where it would be—upon the neck. I got a terrific dose of ammonia down his throat and went about the cauterising. Margery came rushing out of the house over to us.

"Be quiet!" I commanded her. She had started to sob. "What did you see?"

"I don't know," she quavered. "What was it?"

I was instantly put at rest on one subject. She had not had time to glimpse the horrible thing which had attacked her lover. "It's a snake-bite," I said at random. "He'll be all right. He's coming to now," I told her and gave her no time to collapse. "You must get back to your room at once. People will come. Your husband will have heard. Do you understand?"

For answer, she turned and fled. I breathed relief. I had spoken true. Aubrey was stirring. I would have him out of this, with another stiff dose of the ammonia and a poultice. His life was safe, though he might carry a scar on his neck for the rest of his days. It was Drurock, turning up fully dressed, but dishevelled and red-eyed from sleep, who helped me carry Aubrey to his room. We deposited our six-foot burden on the bed. I faced our host across the unconscious form of my friend.

"I'll have a few more minutes with him and then he can sleep it off," I told him, levelly. "That's fortunate, for I think I could have proved a murder charge."

He blinked and said nothing.

"When I'm through here," I said with authority, "I think you and I may as well talk it out. Will you wait for me in the library?"

He nodded imperceptibly and turned to go. I thought it just as well to add:

"I shall be very much on the alert—and armed."

"To be specific, Drurock, I mean to maintain that these phenomena are conjured out of the soil beneath this house."

"Conjured?"

"And I think we know the conjuror," I retorted, and went on: "What stumps me is your having put so many of the clues in my hands. It's as if you wanted me to smoke you out."

"I have still to be convinced that you *have* 'smoked me out' as you put it," he said, equably, and then added, on a dote of self-communion: "If the secret *is* out—well, maybe it was time at last."

"Do I have to prove my reasoning?"

"Well," he shrugged, "isn't that the scientific method?"

"If I could stage a demonstration," I retorted, "would that be more convincing than words?"

He nodded.

"May I have an axe?"

He was taken aback for a moment. Then a slow smile spread over his face.

"Mr McAllister," he said, "it was due me."

"Due?"

"That I should finally encounter another man with a brain as good as my own. I shall bring you the axe."

Although Drurock had agreed to act exactly as I might direct, he stared in almost comic surprise when he learned the nature of the directions.

Placing two large silk handkerchiefs upon the table, I saturated them with the contents of a bottle which I had brought with me in my kit. I handed my host one of the handkerchiefs.

"Tie that over your mouth and nostrils," I said. "Whatever happens, don't remove it unless I tell you." I significantly tapped the revolver which lay in my pocket. "I'm taking you at your word. It is time for the secret to be out."

I rose, finally, perspiring from the task I set myself. The hole I had chopped down through parquetry and under-flooring was about a foot in diameter. It was really disgustingly hot. Despite the hour, which was one for dawn breezes to stir and cool the air, the wall thermometer stuck at high level. If anything, the mercury rose. Ensconced in his favourite sprawling pose on the couch against the wall Drurock made no move either to deter or assist me.

I opened windows and doors. A little ventilator near the ceiling worked by a hanging wire caught my eye and I opened, that, too.

"And now," I explained, when I had finished my preparations, "we have opened all the avenues. The thing can come through the door. It can enter through a window or it may—as I expect it will— ooze up through that hole in the floor—ooze up from the arsenious mass, that buried store of poison beneath our feet. So far, am I right?"

"I am audience," he purred. "I make no comment. I only applaud."

An hour passed. I had an impression that Drurock dozed off and on. I read the thermometer. The temperature had not abated a fraction of a point since sunset and, sitting immobile as I was, I found myself bathed in sweat. Despite the open doors and windows, not a breath of air stirred in the place.

Then, of a sudden, I thought I sensed a change in temperature. I shot a glance at the thermometer. It was falling with a rapidity that was visible. The conditions favourable to condensation were at work. My senses became more than ever alert. I glanced across at Henry Drurock. I believe that his eyes were keener organs of vision than the normal human pair. He had come half erect and was staring at the hole in the floor.

I followed his gaze. I was some minutes before I too perceived the very thin miasmic vapour which was rising—rising, ever rising from the aperture.

Now the column rising from the hole became thicker. A credulous observer of the ghostly phenomenon might well have expected it to progress on to some sort of materialisation into ectoplasmic form. Becoming more dense, it rose more rapidly, although it remained from start to finish a vapour not much lighter than air. It rose like a column of oily smoke until it touched the ceiling, where it mushroomed out among the rafters. I saw wisps of it sucked into the little ventilator and drawn away.

I looked to Drurock. He shrugged.

I thought I heard a door open somewhere overhead. I glanced at my companion but he, apparently, had heard nothing. He made no sign, though I thought he held his head cocked in the position of one intensely expectant of a sound or a sight. Again I thought I heard a movement, was sure some one had stirred. The sound resembled the rustling of silk and I thought it came from the stair. And then, as in a flash, I connected little bits of evidence together and knew what I had done.

"Where does that ventilator lead?" I cried, leaping to close it even as I exclaimed.

"I am under the impression it communicates with my wife's room," he said banteringly, through the handkerchief.

And now the sounds upon the stair became plainly audible. Some one was breathing stertorously out there and that some one was coming down on hands and knees or—or—I uttered an oath as I recalled the vision of the horrible thing which had slithered serpent-wise into my room a few hours back. That—and Margery?"

Another sound came from overhead. A second person was moving without concealment. A door slammed. I heard Aubrey's voice lifted in shrill dismay.

"Margery!" he cried. "What are you doing, Margery?" And then: "My God, Margery, don't look at me!"

I sprang to the door. Major Henry Drurock, retired, tenth of the Duroque line, was close behind me.

Almost at our feet the vile thing appeared, the head first, slipping, thrusting, crawling, from dark toward light. The ghastly contorted face, one cheek brushing the floor, came into the zone of illumination, the lower lip and chin drawn up as though they were of rubber, touching the tip of the nose. The visible eye glared balefully up at me and the hair hung a dishevelled mass about the face. But the horror was to be more fully revealed. After the face came the body, and what we glimpsed of that alabaster flesh was symmetrically beautiful. If anything, this apparition was more horrible than the last. The contrast of the hideous twisted demoniacal face with the fair body was intolerable.

Suddenly, springing to its feet, the apparition stood, framed in the doorway, a slim figure, seeming like a black silhouette upon a silver background, or a wondrous statue in ebony. Elfin, dishevelled locks crowned the head; the pose of the form was as that of a startled dryad or a young Bacchante poised for a joyous leap.

For an instant, like some exquisite dream of Phidias, the figure stood…then crumpled!

I heard Aubrey's heavy invalid step upon the stair. He came into view, carrying a flimsy garment.

"I found this in the passage," he babbled. His face was as white as the bandage around his neck. "What's wrong? I thought I saw Margery and—oh, my God!"

"Go back!" I shouted at him. "You're delirious. Go back!"

"No, come on!"

Drurock's cry rose above my own, wild and imperative, more shriek than cry. "Come on down, you damned, healthy school-boy! Come down and see her. See what you wanted to steal. Do you want her now? Come and take her! All her loveliness—all that rose-white English beauty—that perfection—they're yours. Look! Look! Look!"

I could not prevent it. Aubrey found use of his legs and was with us before I could stop him. He stooped over the white form on the floor. He had not yet seen the face a second time. He lifted the demented thing tenderly and wrapped her in her discarded robe.

And then she turned her face to him. Aubrey cried out, but he did not release her from his supporting embrace. And in that moment I decided that he loved her, well and true.

"Don't you want to kiss those lips?" screamed Drurock. "By the way, where *are* those lips—those sweet honeysuckle lips?"

His breath rasped in his throat; his chest rose and fell visibly with the effort of his breathing. Suddenly he tore the handkerchief from his face and stumbled toward the column of vapour which still coiled upward from the hole in the floor. I may have cried out. For, before I could move to intercept him, Henry Drurock thrust his face into that noisome emanation, and inhaled!

He drew back, and slowly turned to face us. He seemed to have grown taller, and a light of mocking triumph shone in his eyes. Then, in an instant, it was supplanted by a look of surprise and horror. His mouth fell open and his hands pawed ineffectually at his throat. I saw his face begin to change.

"Wales!" I called over my shoulder. "Get Margery out of here! Now! Out of the house!"

He did not stop to protest. Drawing upon some unsuspected source of strength, he gathered Margery Drurock's slight form in his arms and staggered from the room.

I turned again to Drurock, just in time to see him fall against a small table and topple it as he crashed to the floor.

Back and forth he writhed, clawing at the air, his hideous face upraised toward the grey cloud which seemed to stoop above him.

I could watch no longer. I turned and fled from that room above the ghastly pit, that room where now the line of the Duroques was coming to an end…

I was with my London friend, a medical research man. He had accepted my specimens from the ditches of Low Fennel with curt thanks, and was proving more interested in my tale of the humans of the locality than my report on its other fauna.

"Moreover," I went on, "that old Norman pillager, the first mad Drurock, was your precursor in the matter of volatilised arsenic as a preventative against the fits, by a longish bit—nine generations."

"Yes," mused my medical friend, the nerve and brain research specialist. "We do have to go back to some of that old lore of the medieval healers."'

"I guess the whole history of the Drurocks, victims of the inherited taint, one after the other, all along the line, proves the case of arsenic," I said.

"Provided you can get it in that particular gaseous form, and at the proper degree of temperature, I suppose," nodded my medical friend, then shook his head regretfully. "Too bad I can't dump a thousand dying men into a vat lined with the natural ore and get the Drurock prescription duplicated. What a lot of drudgery I'm going to have to go through before I duplicate it."

"Have you accounted for the failure of the Drurock prescription in the recent years?" he asked me. "It's fairly obvious that the force of the emanations was either diminished or the source polluted. Else why the emergence of Major Drurock's convulsive symptoms toward the end?"

"Pollution is the answer," I stated, sure of my ground. "You mustn't forget that the tetanic convulsions attacked three normal persons that we know of—Seager, the contractor, Ord, the handyman, and lastly, Margery."

"How is Mrs Wales?" asked my friend. "No recurrence of the trouble?"

"Oh," I laughed, "they're honeymooning in Sweden, and Aubrey writes me she's put on five pounds and is taking a reducing diet."

"Then," my friend went back to the discussion, "you account for the outbreak of these epileptiform attacks by something known?" ·

"Rather by something guessed," I countered. "We didn't linger long in Low Fennel after Drurock's death, I can tell you—not long enough for research. But I assume that those corroding waters down in the mine finally ate down to a hitherto sealed stratum, probably one of barium. That busy, underground chemical plant tried an experiment in barium compounds, and you know what some of those do to the central nervous system!"

"Crawled like reptiles!" mused my friend. "Now, I should have liked to see that. Poor old Drurock. You've got to pity the tortured soul. His old reliable remedy played out on him; worse—reversed itself. He must have suffered damnably. Quite ready for you or any one to find him out. Why don't you write up a paper on all this?"

I shook my head. "I don't pretend to have worked the whole thing out and I rather think I never shall."

"Too bad," deplored my medical friend, the research specialist. "An autopsy might be rarely instructive."

"Don't be scientifically obscene," I protested.

"Don't be unscientifically romantic," he retorted.

THE LEOPARD-COUCH

My name first became associated with that of Dr Maurice Bode upon the publication of a small treatise dealing with a certain phase of the complex religion of ancient Egypt. In the preparation of *The Worship of Apis at Memphis* he was good enough to collaborate with me; and although this little work was designed solely for the use of students, it nevertheless had a fairly large sale, undoubtedly owing to its containing accounts of many unique investigations conducted by Bode in Egypt.

Since its appearance in 1895 we have regularly worked in concert; and it is my intention to here set forth the broad facts connected with a very remarkable experiment which took place at my own rooms during the autumn of last year, and to give some account of the circumstances that led up to it. Occult students who were in London at the time will already be familiar with the matter, which formed the subject of a paper read by Maurice Bode before one of the leading research societies. As the affair seemed to open up an entirely new field, it has been suggested to Bode that a more popular account thereof might serve to promote inquiry into a subject which has but latterly begun to arouse anything approaching general interest. It is, therefore, at his request that the following is penned.

Early in August I received a note from a well-known dealer in antiques to the effect that an ancient couch of Egyptian workmanship had come into his possession. As I have myself a small collection of Egyptian curios—though insignificant beside that of Maurice Bode—and, as such antiquities are always of interest to me, I called at the shop to examine the specimen. I must confess that I was anticipating comparatively modern workmanship, probably evincing indications of the Roman influence; it was, therefore, a welcome surprise to find that the couch alluded to was of much earlier design. It was constructed to grotesquely resemble a leopard, the feet and claws being of copper. The body of the couch and a part of the legs were of acacia-wood, heavily gilded. The head and shoulders of the leopard were so contrived as to furnish a hollow, presumably for the reception of a large cushion, and along the framework of this singular piece ran a line of partially defaced hieroglyphics. The execution throughout was magnificent, and, though fantastic, betrayed considerable artistic taste. The wood had in many places decayed, and of the hieroglyphics I could make neither head nor tail. Nevertheless, I would have given much to possess it; but the figure mentioned by the dealer placed it beyond the reach of my somewhat slender purse.

"The price I'm asking leaves me very little profit, sir," he assured me. "It was one of the lots put up at Northbie's last Friday, and there were buyers from three big museums to bid against."

"Who was the previous owner?" I inquired.

"Professor Bayton, who died at the beginning of the year. It was the last item he ever added to his collection."

"How did they describe it at Northbie's?"

"Antique Egyptian couch—later Theban."

"No further particulars?"

"No, sir," said the dealer, with a smile.

I determined to draw the attention of Bode to this very peculiar piece of furniture, and, mentioning my intention, I left the shop. It so happened, however, that the doctor was out of town at the time, and nearly a week elapsed before I saw him. At the earliest opportunity I called at his place, and proceeded to describe what I had seen, intending to ask him to accompany me upon a second visit. There was no need for me to make the request: I saw from the first that he was interested; and when I endeavoured to explain the unusual formation of the leopard's head he sprang up excitedly.

Seizing a sheet of paper and a pencil, he executed a rapid sketch. "Like that?" he said eagerly.

"Exactly!" I replied, in astonishment.

"We'll go now," was his next remark; and clapping his hat on his head, he clutched me by the arm and hurried from the house.

On the way I endeavoured to elicit from him some explanation of his sudden enthusiasm; but he declined to gratify my curiosity, promising to explain more fully later. Upon our arrival at the dealer's a disappointment awaited us. The couch had been sold two days before to a wealthy amateur collector, and was only that morning removed from the shop.

I have rarely seen Bode so keenly annoyed. "I'd have willingly given twice the price," he declared. "The thing is of no earthly use to M'Quown; to me it is of vital importance."

We were both acquainted with the purchaser, and I suggested that we should call upon him and examine the antique. My friend, however, opposed this. "M'Quown has wanted a certain uraeus from my collection for a long time," he said. "I shall endeavour to arrange an exchange."

As I knew that Maurice Bode numbered this uraeus to which he alluded—the earliest example extant—among the three most valuable items of his museum, I wondered more and more why he was so eager to gain possession of the leopard-couch. I was about to press him for an explanation, when he began abruptly:

"You are no doubt wondering what peculiar attraction this object has for me? Well, then, let me explain. I need not point out to you that I regard Egyptology from a different standpoint to that of previous and most contemporary inquirers, principally in that I look upon the period between the reign of Mena (once termed the first historic Pharaoh) and the Christian era merely as the latter end of Egyptian history. You are familiar with the results of my investigations upon the site of Heliopolis, and you know that I have definitely established the existence of dynasties earlier than the Theban. The secret of that synonym for mystery, the Sphinx of Gizeh, seemed almost within my grasp when an essential datum eluded me."

"You refer, of course, to the nature of the creed professed by the leopard-worshippers?"

"Precisely! At that point my investigations failed utterly. We both know that a mystic cult, the emblem of whose doctrine was some extinct or mythical species of white leopard, actually existed up to the reign of Tehutimes III; but subsequently, as you are aware, this ancient and mysterious priesthood, probably founded before the carving of the great sphinx, totally disappears. I take it that this leopard-couch which has fallen into the hands of M'Quown was used in their temple—probably about the time of Hatshepsu."

Bode had no immediate opportunity to further pursue the matter, for on the following day he again left London in response to an urgent appeal from the Continent, where he was engaged in some matter connected with one of the principal museums. He was still absent at the end of August, and it was upon the last day of the month that I observed the following paragraph in a well-known scientific journal:

"The extensive collection of antiquities made by the late Mr Edward M'Quown, who died suddenly this month, will be sold by auction tomorrow by Messrs. Northbie, at their house in Wellington Street. The sale will commence at 11 a.m. when a large attendance may be expected."

I had known M'Quown slightly, and, as he was barely forty, was shocked to learn of his death. I saw, however, that I must act with promptitude, and without a moment's delay I sent off a wire to Bode:

"M'Quown dead. Auction tomorrow. Am I to secure the couch?"

The reply was brief but definite:

"At all costs—Bode."

Accordingly, at the hour of eleven on the following morning, I duly presented myself at the auction-rooms. I found the couch to be catalogued as Lot 13, and a mournful man who stood immediately beside me commented upon this circumstance.

"Between ourselves, I am inclined to think that the bidding for Lot 13 will be rather slow," he confided. "An unlucky number to an unlucky article."

"I am afraid I don't quite follow," said I.

"Well, does any one know where Professor Bayton got the thing? No, nobody does. Did he or did he not die three weeks after it came into his possession? He died. How long did M'Quown have the couch? *Four days!* Then *he* died. Now it's up as Lot 13; and if you're thinking of bidding, it's my personal opinion that you'll get it cheap."

Whatever the reason, it was an undoubted fact that the bids for Lot 13 were few and cautious. It was ultimately knocked down to me at one-third of the price that poor M'Quown had paid for it. There were no other lots in which I was interested, so, having made arrangements for the conveying of the couch to my rooms, I wired Bode of my success, and spent the remainder of the day delving among Babylonian records in the British Museum. I returned home about half-past six, to find that the purchase had just arrived; and hastening through my dinner, I lit a cigarette and began a methodical examination of this latest acquisition.

I had hoped to find something that would serve to confirm Bode's theory; but beyond the fact that the work was of undoubted antiquity, I could establish nothing. The hieroglyphics might possibly contain a clue to the matter, but they were peculiarly complicated and difficult, and I felt too weary after my day's labours to attempt their immediate translation. Being seized with a desire to learn whether any degree of comfort could be enjoyed upon so strangely shaped a piece of furniture, I placed a large cushion in the hollow behind the leopard's head, and, lighting a fresh cigarette, stretched myself upon the couch.

The result was surprising. A more delicious sense of restfulness stole over me than I had ever before experienced. I had only to close my eyes to believe that I was suspended in space. The aroma of the Turkish tobacco seemed to gain an added fragrance, and almost unconsciously I abandoned myself to the seductive languor that grew upon me. At what point I slept I am unable to state; but I recollect feeling the cigarette drop from my listless fingers. It must have been some little time after this that I began to wonder, or to dream that I wondered, why the odour was still in my nostrils. Without opening my eyes I made up my mind that the cigarette lay smouldering upon the floor just beneath the head of the couch. This reflection would seem to indicate that I was not really asleep; yet no other theory can cover the extraordinary facts of my subsequent experience.

Realising that this sweet, heavy perfume was dissimilar to anything I had ever known to arise from a cigarette, I reached down, still keeping my eyes drowsily closed, to find if it were really still burning. My hand failed to touch the floor!

As the mysterious nature of this circumstance came home to me, I sprang up into full wakefulness. Good heavens! What was this? I am not an exceptionally nervous man; but I can say with all truthfulness that my heart seemed to cease beating!

The familiar room was no longer there, nor did I recline upon a couch. I was upon a long, narrow balcony, having a low parapet, with pillars at frequent intervals supporting the roof. It was constructed entirely of marble and overhung a garden. Brilliant moonlight threw into bold relief arbours of strange design and vines trained over artistic trellis-work. Beds of many-hued flowers, tastefully blended and arranged in groups intersected by paths, extended to the bank of a river. In the distance, apparently rising out of the water, could be seen a huge white temple, significant and majestic even beneath the great vault of the gleaming heavens. The real origin of the heavy aroma now became evident. It was wafted from the flowers but six feet below me.

I will not attempt to give an analysis of my feeling, save to state that I seemed to be a bodiless entity, enjoying all my faculties but two—the sense of touch and of hearing. Try how I would, I could hear no sound, nor was I conscious of being in contact with anything palpable; in short, I was myself impalpable! I seemed to feel my heart throbbing, yet realised in some strange way that, being but an immaterial mind, I could have no heart.

At this moment, I discerned a boat upon the water, and, becoming conscious of an ability to change my location by merely willing it, passed without perceptible effort from the marble balcony to the brink of the river.

A man and woman were in the boat, which was rowed from the bow in the manner of a gondola by a gigantic Nubian. The woman was robed in white, and as she lay, with her head upon the man's shoulder, and the moonlight fell upon her upturned face, I saw her to be as beautiful as a nymph of classic lore. A strange resentment, such as Zeus might have experienced toward a mortal lover of Io or Dana, possessed me; and when a shaft gleamed through the air and the man in the boat sprang up, to fall dead into the river, an incredible satisfaction took the place of my former resentment.

An eight-oared galley shot out from the dense shadows of a huge bed of rushes, and then ensued a scene such as should have moved the heart of a stone; yet I observed it to its close without being conscious of any emotion whatever.

The white-clad form of the girl rose up in the boat, and in another instant would have plunged into the river beside the dead man; but the huge Nubian seized her in one muscular arm and restrained her. A moment afterwards the galley came alongside, and she apparently lost consciousness as her body was roughly hauled on board. I saw her lying upon the deck as still and white as though death had claimed her too. I have no recollection of being actually on board the galley, but I remember vividly the silent journey across the calm bosom of the river, and can recollect that there seemed to be something familiar in it all. I even noticed the infinitely cooler air out there upon the water, and the scene of the arrival at the great temple shall be with me to my dying day.

At the foot of a flight of marble steps the galley was moored, and I saw a number of men clad in long black robes descending slowly. Two of them carried a kind of bier, and as they reached the edge of the water the death-like form was lifted from the galley's deck and placed upon it. Solemnly raising their beautiful burden, they mounted again to the top, and, passing between two tall towers, advanced along an avenue lined upon either side by the figures of sphinxes. I witnessed all this quite clearly without knowing by what means I was enabled to follow; and when the bearers reached the propylaeum of the temple and passed within I still accompanied them.

Across an area surrounded by high walls they proceeded, and through a doorway that was either gold or gold-plated, into a vast hall, dimly illuminated, and seeming to be a very forest of pillars. At this juncture, I experienced an unaccountable difficulty in following, and, though I made a great effort, soon lost myself amid the innumerable pillars. Like some wandering spirit, I drifted about in that wondrous hall of shadows for what seemed like several hours. I had now apparently lost the power to control my own movements, and how I came to find myself where I ultimately did I do not know.

Since, after all, the whole was nothing but a vivid dream, I will not endeavour to explain. Suffice that I was in a small, rectangular apartment, fitfully lighted by a fire in a tall tripod. A man in a long robe of dull red was standing by a niche in the wall, and before him, ranged on narrow shelves, were rows of phials, apparently of blue glass. In the centre of the place stood an object that I had good cause to remember. It was the leopard-couch! Upon it was stretched the motionless form of the beautiful girl I had seen on the river. Her dark eyes were open now, and fixed in a changeless stare upon a brass vessel suspended above the fire. Her head rested, not upon a cushion, but upon a great crystal sphere which occupied the hollow in the couch.

The man took from the niche in the wall a long metal rod, and, dipping it in the pendent vessel, withdrew it again with what looked like a globule of liquid flame adhering to the end. Advancing to the couch, he thrust the rod into the open jaws of the leopard, and almost immediately the crystal globe beneath appeared to be illuminated by an internal light. I became conscious of a sensation as though an irresistible power were carrying me to destruction; the scene grew dim, and a great despair possessed me. Then I felt myself to be borne away into darkness as by the mighty wind, and a voice was in my ears. Two conflicting wills seemed to be striving for the mastery of my derelict spirit. I struggled madly against some subtle force that sought to overpower me, and awoke—to find Dr Maurice Bode, supporting my head whilst he held a glass to my lips.

"Thank Heaven!" he exclaimed. "You were beginning to frighten me."

I felt strangely dazed, and stared at him so blankly that he smiled. "I came away as soon after receiving your first message as possible," he explained, "and learning at Northbie's that the couch had been sent on to you, I called here immediately, to find you sound asleep upon the identical article. Without disturbing you, I took the liberty to examine it; and I am pleased to say that I have made two highly interesting discoveries. A couple of minutes ago you became so deadly pale that I grew alarmed. Were you dreaming?"

I rose to my feet as unsteadily as though leaving a bed of long illness. "Before I answer your question, what have you discovered?" I asked, sinking into a comfortable arm-chair.

"In the first place, I have partially translated the hieroglyphics, and, in the second place, I have removed the top of the leopard's head."

"How could you possibly translate the hieroglyphics in so short a time?" was my incredulous inquiry.

"Well, you have slept for over four hours, and I have, moreover, been engaged upon the inscriptions of this particular period for nearly a year now."

"You don't mean to state that this couch dates back to the time of Hatshepsu?"

"There can be little doubt of it. The inscription contains as romantic a love-story as the heart of a modern novelist could desire."

"Wait a moment, Bode!" I cried. "Does it correspond to the following?" And I related the incidents of my extraordinary dream as I have already set them forth.

He remained silent for a moment at the end of my narrative, his eyes dreamily closed. Then, rising to his feet, he bent over the head of the couch. "Yes," he said slowly, "there is a narrow channel from the mouth of the leopard that presumably communicates with the hollow at the base."

He paused, then added irrelevantly: "The rock temple at Deir-el-Bahari."

"Right, Bode!" I cried, in sudden excitement. "It *was* the temple at Deir-el-Bahari! I understand now why the scene seemed vaguely familiar. But how do you account for the leopard-priesthood being established there?"

"A secret cult, consisting of priests ostensibly following other creeds. You have undoubtedly witnessed the punishment of Neothys, a beautiful priestess of the mystic goddess, who is never named in the inscriptions, but of whom the white leopard is emblematic. This Neothys had a lover, one Neremid, a captain of the warriors, and their trysting-place was in the very shadows of Hatshepsu's temple at Deir-el-Bahari. He used to await her coming in a boat upon the river. But one night she was followed. Neremid died by the hand of Thi, chief of the temple-guard, and Neothys was dealt with by the high-priest."

"What was the meaning of the extraordinary experiment I witnessed in my dream?"

"The man in the red robe was undoubtedly Karpusa, whom I believe to have been the last high-priest of the cult. I have previously encountered this singular personality in the course of my investigations; and his knowledge of the 'unknown' appears to have exceeded the credible. According to the inscription upon the couch, Karpusa wrecked vengeance upon Neothys by denying her immortality for all ages."

"I fail to follow."

Maurice Bode manipulated the head of the leopard in some way so that the top came off in his hand. Inserting a finger and a thumb into the aperture, he drew forth a small ball of sparkling crystal. "Examine that," he said, handing it to me.

It was no larger than a full-sized walnut, but had all the brilliancy of a precious gem. I was gazing into its changeful depths when an idea occurred to me—an idea that caused me to return the thing with a shudder of revulsion.

"You do not, surely, suggest—" I began.

"I suggest nothing," said Bode; "but by way of an experiment I propose acting thus."

Raising the crystal above his head, he dashed it with all his force on to the marble hearth. I had just time to observe that it was shattered, when the electric light went out.

Dense fumes seemed to fill the room, and there was a buzzing in my ears. Then suddenly I caught my breath and listened; for it appeared to me that I had detected the sound of a low, clear voice—singing. Before I could determine whether it were imaginary or otherwise, the sound died away and the electric lamps became relighted.

There was a faint blue vapour in the air. Bode was standing on the other side of the room, and his tense attitude betrayed him.

"You heard it?" I inquired.

"I heard *something*," he replied. "The extinction of the electric light was highly instructive." Seeing me about to speak again, "I have no theory," he said. "The only one that can cover all the facts is too incredible to be entertained."

"I wanted to ask you what you make of the sudden death of Professor Bayton and M'Quown."

"Again I have no theory. We should, however, remember that the incidents you mention, though singular, do not justify us—with our present inadequate knowledge of the circumstances under which they occurred—in placing them outside the province of coincidence. But I may mention that when I endeavoured to arouse you this evening, I at first failed to do so. It was not until I treated you as a hypnotised subject, and employed the usual means of restoring consciousness after hypnosis, that you revived."

THE MYSTERY OF THE FABULOUS LAMP

They lived in what had been, described as an "artistic apartment". Bram always referred to it as a "walk down". Lorna was delighted with it.

If you happened to be passing a reconstructed New York brownstone house between Lexington and Third Avenue, at night, and if the shades weren't drawn, looking down you had a glimpse of the living-room, lit by a lamp with a square shade of plaited straw which gave out a pleasant glow.

You saw chairs upholstered in golden brown, an olive-green bookcase, painted by Lorna and well-stocked with books. Some modern light maple furniture. A small buffet of English walnut, decorated with a Wedgwood salad bowl (wedding present), displayed a few pieces of good crystal.

Four steps led down to a tiny forecourt and a blue door, with bright brass fittings. Two sky-blue window boxes were filled with geraniums. Bram had always suspected that the blue door stood for $10 a month on the rent. The boxes Lorna had decorated.

But a sense of happy contentment crept over him when he halted

at the top of the steps that evening and surveyed this little home—
his and Lorna's…

He had his key ready, but Lorna had heard his footsteps. The blue
door opened as if by magic.

"Darling!" she cried, as she broke away from his arms. "I bought
a lamp, second-hand. It cost $20."

Bram stifled a groan. He adored his pretty wife. She was a gay
companion and a practical housekeeper; but two months of marriage
had proved her to be, also, a fanatical interior decorator.

"Our budget's getting low, honey."

"I know, Bram. But I simply couldn't stand the flying saucer any longer!"

The flying saucer was a standard ceiling fixture—a dull glass
bowl—supplied by the landlord in the entrance foyer of their
apartment, and Lorna hated it.

"Oh, Bram." she said, clinging to him. "You've never regretted
what we did?"

Bram grabbed her, held her hard.

At the time Lorna came alone and changed his way of life, Bram
had saved up $2,000 and had planned to put it into the publishing
business where he was a promising junior editor. This would have
meant postponing their marriage for at least a year, and Bram hadn't
hesitated for a moment. He had chosen Lorna, and the $2,000 had
gone to set them up in their little apartment.

"Don't be cross with me, darling!" Lorna drew back, turned his
gaze. "Look!"

Bram looked.

An Arab brass lamp with panels of coloured glass hung where the
living saucer had been.

The effect was remarkable. Their nine-foot square hall, walls and ceiling bathed in subdued coloured rays, resembled the end of a rainbow. An enlarged snap of Bram in uniform on a camel in front of the Sphinx had taken on the violet hue of an Egyptian afterglow. The coffee table was bathed in mysterious golden light. The long, narrow settee lurked in deep shadows.

Lo`a was explaining eagerly: "I had Stobell fix it, Bram. I knew you'd be tired when you got home, and superintendents are used to fixing lights. Don't you think it's cute?"

"Certainly is. Marvellous."

Lorna was standing right under the lamp, pointing up.

Bram caught his breath, shut his eyes, looked again, and then: "Lorna—" he spoke quietly—"come over here, honey. I want to find out if you see what I've seen."

"What?" Lorna was anxious. "Is something wrong?"

"Nothing to worry about. Just come over here, and let me stand under the light." He crossed and stood under the lamp, facing Lorna. "Do you notice anything?"

"Oh!" Lorna's hands stole up to her face in a helpless sort of gesture. "Bram—you look simply terrible! Pale green; and—well, I can almost see your bones! Come away. You frighten me."

Bram came over and gave her what she called his "trust-me grin" .He put his arms round her. "You frightened me when you stood there. Don't let it bother you."

"But it does, Bram. It's uncanny."

"It's just some sort of effect, produced by all the coloured glass being reflected directly downward. What we want to do is cover the holes at the bottom. Maybe you could think something up that would do it."

After dinner had been cleared away, Bram settled himself at the desk in the corner with some work he had brought home from the office. Lorna was painting tiny coloured designs on cellulose tape, which she intended to cut out with nail scissors and fix over the perforations at the base of the lamp.

The doorbell rang. Bram crossed the rainbow lobby, opened the blue door. A tall man stood there, his heavy features oddly lighted by the rays of the lamp. He wore a tan coat and a black Homburg hat. His eyes, which were dark also, looked past Bram. Their gaze was fixed on the lamp. He lowered them and bowed stiffly.

"Mr Bramwell Barton?"

"That's my name."

"Pardon me if I disturb you." He spoke with a marked accent. "My name is Ramoulian. I have called to make a proposition, Mr Barton, which I hope you will think it profitable to accept."

Mr Ramoulian removed his Homburg, uncovering glossy black hair. Lorna was standing up when they came in.

"Mr Ramoulian has called on business, Lorna," Bram explained. "This is my wife. Please sit down."

Mr Ramoulian repeated his stiff bow and sat down.

"You are a business man, Mr Barton—yes?"

"Not exactly." Bram dropped back into his chair. "I'm an editor in a publishing house."

"I see. And, perhaps, also an author?"

"In a modest way."

"Good. You have the artistic conscience. You will understand— and sympathise. I am here tonight, Mr Barton, and madame, on the instruction of the Sherif of Mecca."

"The Sherif of Mecca!"

"But exactly. Let me try to explain. Some months ago, while the holy places were crowded with pilgrims, a great sacrilege was committed in the tomb of the Prophet at Ab-Madinen. One of the lamps which for generations had lighted the tomb was stolen—"

Lorna started to speak, but Mr Ramoulian raised his hand, a quiet, but impressive command. "Apart from its history, the lamp was not of sufficient value to justify so great a risk. It was reported to be in Mecca. By one hour the custodians were too late to recover it. Again, it vanished. Then I was assigned to trace the lamp."

"Do I understand you're a detective?" Bram wanted to know.

"I am an antiquarian expert. I could identify the lamp of the Prophet among 1,000 other lamps. One of my agents traced it to Cairo. It was in the possession of an American tourist, who refused to part with it. I followed her here. She had died before I arrived. All her property had been sold at auction. I interviewed the auctioneers today. The lamp, with a number of other articles, had been bought in one lot, cheaply, by a small dealer on Third Avenue—"

"Mr Lincke!" Lorna spoke the name on a high key.

"But exactly. Late this evening I called on Mr Lincke. And again I was too late. Once more, the lamp had been sold. But, fortunately, he knew the name and address of the purchaser. You were the purchaser, Mrs Barton, and there"—he turned, pointed—"hangs the lamp of the Prophet!"

Stupefied silence fell like a curtain on those last words. It was Bram who broke the spell.

"I suppose you want us to re-sell the lamp?"

"But exactly." The dark eyes became focused on him. "Mrs Barton paid $20 for it. I offer you $100."

Bram said: "I'm afraid I can't accept your offer. The recovery of a thing so highly valued that you're sent half around the world to trace it is worth more than $100. If you'd started the bidding at $1,000, we might have talked business."

Mr Ramoulian sighed. "And I thought I was dealing with an artist."

Bram laughed. Mr Ramoulian took out a cheque book and a pen. "Very well. A thousand dollars, you say?"

"I said I'd consider a bid of $1,000, Mr Ramoulian. I need time to think this thing out."

"As you wish."

Mr Ramoulian replaced pen and cheque book and stood up. He bowed to Lorna, bowed to Bram, and took up his black hat. "I shall leave you, Mr Barton, and your charming wife to discuss this matter. I shall return."

Bram closed the door. Lorna heard heavy footsteps mounting to the street.

"Bram!" She ran to him as he turned. "Why ever did you let him go? A thousand dollars! Oh, Bram!"

Bram's long repressed excitement burst. He grasped Lorna, held her so tightly that she winced.

"Don't you see, honey—don't you see? Whether the tale about the Prophet's tomb is the truth or not this lamp is a treasure of some sort. I want another opinion—"

"But we don't know Ramoulian's address!"

"Don't worry. He'll be back. I'm going to call Jim Crowley. He's one of the Spink and Barrett's experts, and he lives only a few blocks away. He'll come when I ask him."

Jim Crowley came, but he was in a furious hurry. He mounted a chair and inspected the lamp.

"Have you a flashlight, Bram?"

"Yes, I'll get it."

"Then switch this thing off."

"Right."

The rainbow lobby became plunged in shadow. Using the

flashlight handed him by Bram, Jim examined the lamp minutely.

"What did you pay for it?"

"Twenty dollars," Bram told him.

"You were scalped! Except for the bits of glass, which are good, it's worth not a cent more than five bucks. The glass might fetch another five. So say ten. We wouldn't touch it at Spink and Barrett's. Imitation Arab stuff, mass-produced in Europe. Sorry."

Jim dashed off.

"So much for the experts!" Bram laughed when the door closed.

Lorna said: "Mr Lincke's been in the business a long time. He didn't think it was worth much. We have only Mr Ramoulian's word that it's old. There's something very strange about all this. I'm beginning to hope Mr Ramoulian doesn't come back!"

"I'm beginning to wish I hadn't let him go! But Jim just has to be wrong. A sane man doesn't offer $1,000 for a brass lamp worth $10."

"But he's a strange-looking man, Bram. He may not be sane."

Bram shook his head. "It could be the original Aladdin's Lamp!"

"It couldn't." Lorna sat down. "I should know. I spent an hour this morning polishing it—and no genie appeared! Nothing happened, except to my fingernails."

"I have a hunch he'll come back."

Two hours later he came. He bowed and walked across the alcove with that noiseless, dignified step which vaguely alarmed Lorna. He glanced back to where Bram was reclosing the blue door. "You have extinguished the lamp, I see."

"Just while I gave it a careful check-up," Bram explained, joining them.

'That was prudent. But tell me—you have decided?"

Bram sat down facing him. "I have decided, Mr Ramoulian, that if you'll raise your bid to $2,000 the lamp is yours."

Mr Ramoulian's expression didn't change in the slightest degree. He merely shrugged.

"Your artistic conscience is dead, Mr Barton. But I am not accustomed to commercial haggling. May I use your desk?"

"Sure, with pleasure."

Bram jumped up, placed a chair. Mr Ramoulian took out his cheque book and pen and drew a cheque on a Manhattan bank for $2,000, payable to Bramwell Barton. Then, on a sheet of Bram's notepaper, he wrote a brief form of receipt and stood up.

"Will you be good enough to sign this, Mr Barton? As you don't know me, no doubt you will want to make inquiries through your own bank. If I call here at, say eleven in the morning, to remove the lamp—which I wish to do personally—will that be convenient?"

Bram nodded, and Mr Ramoulian took his leave.

"It's hard to believe, Bram, that it all happened a year ago."

It was hard to believe, on that sunny afternoon, as Bram and Lorna crossed Fifth Avenue, she holding his hand as she had always done at street crossings. Yet ten months had passed since the strange sale of the Prophet's' lamp to Mr Ramoulian.

They had been ten eventful and happy months. Bram had invested their $2,000 windfall in the business, as originally planned, and the publisher had promoted him.

"I have a sort of hunch," Bram declared as they went through revolving doors into one of Manhattan's more expensive stores, "that we're going to buy another lamp!"

"We're not!" Lorna laughed at him. "We're only going to look at one. I'm quite glad about the one we have. But the advertisements for the Magus lamps intrigue me. You know how interested I am in lighting effects."

Bram knew. He said no more.

The demonstration which Lorna was set on attending took place on the ninth floor. When they got, there they found themselves in a small room fitted up as a typical living room. It had neutral walls, modern light wood furniture, a few books and non-classic ornaments. A demonstrator welcomed them. Ten or more inquirers were there already.

"Magus lamps," she explained, "operate on an entirely new principle of lighting. The one I am using is a medium-price lamp—$100—but it has the full range. By adjusting panels, 21 changes can be made."

Lorna drew closer. She saw a graceful silver lamp on a silver pedestal, standing on a table. It had panels of varicoloured glass.

The demonstrator moved a knob on top of the lamp. A murmur of almost incredulous surprise swept around the audience. The walls had become olive-green. The furniture looked like Spanish mahogany. Every book had changed colour. A white vase was black. And the shapely demonstrator appeared now to be sheathed in scarlet!

"But you will notice," the modulated voice went on, "that no change has taken place in our faces." People began looking at one. another. "The special bulb supplied by Magus prevents distortion. Suppose we make another change. You are tired of a green-walled room. Very well."

She moved the knob. The walls became russet-brown, the furniture silver-grey, the vase rose-pink—and the demonstrator was revealed in deep violet. Lorna looked at Bram. He had been wearing a light-coloured suit. It was brown. Lorna laughed. So did Bram. Lorna's blue dress was red!

The musical voice followed them as Lorna grabbed Bram's hand and led him into an adjoining room: "Sales department next door. There you can see the many attractive models."

"Have a heart, honey! You're not planning to buy one of these crazy things? We don't want to turn our apartment into—"

"I just want to look, Bram. I get ideas sometimes."

A smart young salesman who prided himself on recognising possible buyers attached himself to Lorna.

"If you're interested in acquiring a Magus lamp, I shall be glad to advise you. Those large models—I sold one recently to Mrs Partington Perkins for her Park Avenue apartment—are more suited to ballrooms, restaurants and so on, than to the ordinary home. The model you have seen demonstrated—it comes in three styles—is the most popular for…"

But Lorna lost the rest of the sales talk. Her gaze was fixed, hypnotically, upon one lamp which hung in a comer of that lamp-laden room. The salesman noted her look.

"You are surprised to see such a commonplace model in our collection?" he suggested.

Bram looked where Lorna was looking. Bram, also, became rigid.

"It isn't for sale, of course. It's our special museum piece. The original lamp which Dr Fechter, inventor of the Magus process, used in his experiments… I'll be right back. Pardon me."

He moved away, intercepting another pair of potential buyers.

Lorna clutched Bram's hand. "Bram, it's our lamp!"

"Was our lamp, honey."

The salesman dashed back. "Interesting, isn't it, when you consider what it developed into? A common brass lamp, of eastern design but perfectly suited to Dr Fechter's purpose. He had completed his experiments at the time of his sudden death. The results were contained in this lamp. His widow auctioned all the property and returned to Europe.

"Dr Fechter's financial partner was abroad. The news took some time to reach him. He hurried back—-to find the vital lamp sold. He traced it, though, bought it from the other buyer, who had no idea of its importance, and so recovered the secret. Quite a drama, isn't it?"

"Quite." Lorna spoke like a sleepwalker. "What was this financial partner's name? Do you remember?'

"Of course. Mr Ramoulian, president of the Magus Lamp Corp…"

Out on Fifth Avenue Bram let himself go. "The Prophet's tomb! The Sherif of Mecca!" He spoke between clenched teeth. "What an inspired liar! The man's a swindler!"

Lorna held his arm lightly. "Don't be cross, Bram. Just think calmly. We might have had the lamp for years if Mr Ramoulian hadn't traced it, and never even guessed it was anything more than just an old lamp. It meant a lot to him. But I don't know what you'd have said if he'd told you the truth about it—"

"He didn't have to tell such a big, bad lie!" Bram grumbled. He hailed a taxi. They got in.

"I don't think I blame him altogether, Bram. Don't forget, he paid us $2,000. He could have told a smaller lie and got it cheaper. That $2,000 put us on our feet," Lorna reminded him.

Bram slipped his arm around Lorna. "Maybe you're right, honey."

"So it was really Aladdin's Lamp, after all."

A DATE AT SHEPHEARD'S

The streets of Cairo looked dirty, shadow-haunted, vaguely sinister, as Cartaret walked back from the garage where he had parked his Buick. Dusk had fallen, and he thought, as he came to the steps of Shepheard's Hotel, that once the terrace would have been crowded at this hour. Now it was almost deserted. He had heard no sunset gun boom out from the Citadel, and he wondered if the custom had been abandoned.

He walked through to the reception desk to ask for messages.

The hotel register lay open, and he saw that only one name had been added below his own: "Mrs Parradine—Alexandria."

A woman was writing a radiogram, and a boy stood behind her guarding some baggage. Presumably the lady was Mrs Parradine. She wore a smart, tailored suit, a beret crushed down on well-groomed hair. She had not removed her sunglasses. Something in the profile struck Cartaret as familiar; but he was sure he had never met Mrs Parradine.

There were no messages, and Cartaret walked into the bar. As a once familiar figure in Shepheard's, old Abdûl, the bartender, greeted him, and the greeting was returned.

"It is good to see you in Cairo again, *bimbâshi.*"

Abdûl was mistaken in addressing him as *bimbâshi,* a rank he had never held, but Cartaret didn't trouble to correct him. Abdûl was nearly as old as the sphinx, and even his fabulous memory couldn't last forever.

"Six years since I was here last, Abdûl."

Abdûl set a tall glass before him.

"You have not changed, sir. But—" he shook his red-capped head—"Cairo has changed."

"It seems unfriendly in some way."

"It is all different, *bimbâshi.* Everything is different. All Egypt is different. We have gone back to the days when I was a boy, the days of the *harêm* and the eunuchs."

Cartaret made a rapid mental calculation, but was unable to decide whether those were the days of the Turks or of the Pharaohs.

"You mean business is slack?"

"Not at all. It is just different. Some of those we used to call the pasha class have much power now. They do things they would not have dared to do. Who is to stop them?"

"I don't know. What sort of things?"

Abdul glanced suspiciously around the nearly empty bar and then bent forward across the counter.

"For visitors who like adventure," he whispered, "this is the time to come to Egypt. Let me tell you something that happened not long ago. You remember the young Syrian Aswami Pasha used to bring in?"

Cartaret recalled her quite well, for Military Intelligence had posted him to Cairo during the latter part of the war. Aswami, a handsome fellow of Turco-Egyptian vintage, had a nice taste in girl friends. The Syrian Abdûl referred to was a beauty in her sullen, Oriental fashion, and at that time probably no more than fifteen or sixteen years old. He had once heard Aswami call her Sirena, but never knew her other name.

She had passed by his table one night, as she and Aswami went out together. Unseen by her escort, Sirena had favoured Cartaret with the age-old smile of Eastern women. Her darkly fringed eyes were of a strange amber colour, speckled with green like the eyes of a tigress...

He nodded. "I remember her, Abdûl."

Abdûl's voice dropped still lower. As Cartaret had greeted him in Arabic, he continued in that language.

"Aswami surprised her with another man! In the garden of the villa."

Picturesque, and obscene, details followed in true Arab style. But, as Abdûl whispered on, Cartaret drew back, horrified—

"They were dragged into the villa, *bimbâshi,* and they..."

"Stop, Abdûl! Such a thing is impossible—today! There are still police in Cairo."

Abdûl extended brown palms which spoke a universal language.

"Have I not said, *bimbâshi,* that it is all different? What I tell you is true. I have a grandson who works in the garden."

Cartaret passed his tumbler to be refilled. As ice tinkled in the glass:

"Who was the man?" he asked.

Abdul, back turned, shrugged heavy shoulders.

"I don't know. I only know that he has disappeared. The Syrian girl is still at the villa."

Cartaret suspected that Abdûl knew the man's name perfectly well. He knew, too, that when an Arab says "I don't know" it is sheer waste of breath to ask any more questions.

* * *

The dining room seemed fairly full when Cartaret went in to dinner. But there was no one there he knew. Although he took a good look around, he failed to see Mrs Parradine. He gave his mind over to memories—particularly to those associated with Aswami Pasha.

Aswami's luxurious villa at Bûlak contained many treasures, he had been told, feminine and otherwise, the latter including a collection of rubies made by Aswami's father and said to be the second finest in the world. Cartaret tried to recall the men he had known who had found Sirena attractive, and succeeded in compiling quite a list. Although unable to credit Abdûl's statement, entirely, he made up his mind to try again to learn the name of the man concerned. If the facts were as stated, he would be horribly disfigured for life.

The story had left a bad taste in his mouth, which a bottle of perfectly sound Bordeaux failed to remove. He went out into the lounge, with its fretwork pillars and arabesques. It reminded him of a *harêm,* and he began to glance suspiciously at his neighbours, wondering if those who looked like wealthy Egyptians favoured the medieval customs of Aswami Pasha.

He ordered brandy with his coffee.

Then he saw Mrs Parradine.

She was seated, alone, in an alcove. She had changed into a simple dinner frock but still wore the tinted glasses. Cartaret supposed that she suffered from eye strain. He began to study her. What was it about Mrs Parradine which seemed so familiar?

This vague memory irritated Cartaret. He got into that frame of mind everybody has known; when a name goes darting around the brain like a mad hare that can't be captured. He was watching her, as she sipped coffee, when a boy went across to her table and handed her a message.

She read it, and seemed to Cartaret to become suddenly restless. Once, he had an impression that she was considering him in a furtive way. And then, just as suddenly, she became passive again, bending over the table to pour more coffee.

An elderly Egyptian had entered.

Fat and hairless, he provided the missing link in Cartaret's uneasy imaginings of those days of the *harêm* and the eunuchs mentioned by Abdûl. Obviously, the Egyptian was looking for someone. His prominent eyes swept the lounge in a questing stare. But he was apparently disappointed. He turned slowly and went out again.

Cartaret saw Mrs Parradine's glance following the obese figure.

Then, she looked swiftly but unmistakably in his own direction. On a slip of paper taken from a large satchel purse which swung from her shoulder she scribbled something. She slipped the note under an ashtray, stood up and crossed to the elevator.

Cartaret continued to watch her. She was very graceful, well poised. As the boy opened the gate, she turned for a moment, stared directly at Cartaret, then back to the table she had just left, then at Cartaret again.

The elevator went up.

He took a quick look about the lounge. No one had seen what had happened, for Mrs Parradine had been screened by the alcove. He stood up, yawned—and changed his place.

The note under the ashtray said:

"Room 36 B at 10.30. I *must* see you. Don't disappoint me."

Cartaret walked into the bar.

It had filled up with men who looked like officials of some sort, but none of whom he knew; a totally different set from that to which he had been accustomed. He got himself a double Scotch and carried it to a seat in a corner where he could be alone.

What was he to make of this note?

That it was meant for a love tryst he dismissed as an idea too ridiculous to be considered. Without the glasses, Mrs Parradine might be a pretty woman. She had an exceptionally good figure. But grey hair and assignations with strangers didn't mix.

What, then, did it mean?

She *must* see him! What on earth about? And why couldn't she have spoken to him in the lounge, instead of inviting him to her room?

The whole thing was utterly incomprehensible. Cartaret decided that it must be linked with that elusive memory. Perhaps after all, they met at some time. Why the devil didn't she take off those tinted glasses?

Restlessly, he wandered out on to the terrace. A cool breeze had sprung up, but the sky was cloudless, the night lighted by a perfect crescent moon.

At the foot of the steps the head doorman was talking to a portly Egyptian.

Cartaret stared.

It was the man who had come into the lounge seeking someone…

Cartaret went back to the bar and ordered another double Scotch.

This business called for careful thought. He would have liked to ask Abdûl if he knew anything about Mrs Parradine, but Abdûl was too busy for conversations and he didn't care to make such an enquiry at the desk.

Was he right in supposing that the entrance of the fat Egyptian had alarmed Mrs Parradine? Cartaret believed he was. He finished his drink and went out to talk to the doorman, whom he knew slightly.

The doorman had gone off duty; another had taken his place.

And that fat Egyptian had disappeared.

Cartaret wandered back into the lounge. It was beginning to empty, and he sat down and lighted a cigarette. He had dined late, and ten-thirty was not far off. Even now, he remained undecided. Some queerly underhand game was afoot. Of this he had become certain. Where did *he* fit into the pattern?

He was far from a wealthy man, no bait for blackmailers. And he had never aspired to the cloak of Don Juan.

What should he do?

A clandestine visit to a woman's room might compromise both of them. And what was its object?

Cartaret, at this crucial hour, might have failed to keep his mysterious date, except that curiosity, perhaps, is the last instinct humanity loses. At twenty-seven minutes after ten he crossed to the elevator and stepped out on the third floor.

Not until that moment did he recognise the fact that his own room also was on the third.

His watch told him that he had two minutes in hand when he walked along the corridor to No. 36 B. Astonishment on receiving Mrs Parradine's note might have been responsible for his absent-mindedness. But No. 36 B proved to be next to No. 34 B and 34 B was Cartaret's room.

He paused, staring at the closed door.

Had she deliberately chosen this room because his own adjoined it? Was he being drawn blindly into some web of intrigue?

Again, he hesitated. No amorous urge drove him. There was nothing to excuse his walking into a trap.

But, on the stroke of ten-thirty, he rapped on Mrs Parradine's door. There was no reply.

He rapped again, louder, then rapped a third time.

Silence…

Man is a complex animal. Cartaret's hesitancy, doubts, fears, all were swept away now on a wave of angry disappointment. He had built up a mystery, the solution of which lay behind the door of No. 36 B. And the door of 36 B remained closed.

He looked at his watch again. Perhaps it was fast. There was no one about, and so he walked up and down the corridor, half expecting Mrs Parradine to appear from somewhere.

But she didn't.

Cartaret opened the door of his own room and went in, snapping the light up.

Shutters before the french-windows were closed, but Cartaret went across and irritably threw them open. He stood there, one foot on the balcony, looking down at the moon-bathed gardens. The trunk of a tall palm near the window split the picture like an ink stain on a water-colour. A frog was croaking in a pond below. From some place not far away came faint strains of reed pipe.

What should he do? Mrs Parradine's sense of humour must be peculiar if this was her idea of a practical joke. But there was that curious incident of the fat Egyptian.

He remembered something, for he knew Shepheard's well. These rooms formed part of a large suite. His balcony continued right past the window of No. 36.

Stubbing out a cigarette which he had lighted, Cartaret stepped onto the balcony and glanced to the left.

Light streamed from the window of No. 36. Mrs Parradine's shutters were open. He walked quietly along and looked into the room. It was in wild disorder—and a woman lay gagged and tied to the bed!

The shock was so great that Cartaret stood stock still for perhaps ten seconds, one hand on the partly opened windows. His ideas were thrown into chaotic confusion, not only by this scene of brutal violence but also by something else.

The woman on the bed was not Mrs Parradine!

This woman had raven black hair. The eyes glaring across at him were amber eyes flecked with green. As Cartaret ran to release her, he nearly stepped on tinted sun-glasses which lay on the floor.

Like a sudden revelation, the truth burst upon his mind.

Mrs Parradine had been a disguised Sirena, for this was Sirena!

He unfastened a silk scarf tied tightly over her mouth.

"I had one hand nearly free," she whispered, hoarsely. "Scissors—on the dresser."

Cartaret ran across, found the scissors and ran back. As he began to cut the cord with which she was trussed up, Sirena wrenched her right hand clear of the fastenings.

"Look! In another minute I should have been loose! Cut the cord from my ankles. It is hurting me."

When at last she sat up, stiffly, Sirena pointed.

"Fasten the shutters. The door is locked."

She dropped back weakly on the pillows, watching Cartaret as he bolted the shutters.

He turned to her.

"As the door is locked, how—"

"They climbed to the balcony." Sirena spoke wearily. "They went that way, too. Where are you going?"

She sat up.

"To call the manager."

Sirena smiled.

"Please sit down. I know you don't understand, and so just listen. Please."

"Let me get you some brandy."

"Not yet. I am all right. You can help me. You must help me. But you can only do it in my way. I escaped this evening from Aswami's villa."

"*Escaped?*"

"Yes, escaped!" Her eyes flashed. "It had been planned a long time. I had the grey wig made and hid it. I came to Shepheard's because I thought they would never look here. I hoped my friends would come for me. But I had word tonight that I must find some way of joining them."

"Was that the message you received in the lounge?"

Sirena nodded.

"I had seen your name in the book, I remembered you, and I thought I might need someone to help me. I managed to get a room near yours. You see, I dare not give myself away down there. That's why I asked you to come here."

Cartaret watched her. Six years had dealt lightly with Sirena. She was still beautiful, but had suffered. She told her strange story with the simplicity of a child.

"You really mean you have been a prisoner?"

"Yes. Ever since a terrible thing happened. But I knew I could trust you, for you were Rod's friend—"

"Rod? Do you mean Rod Fennick?"

"Yes."

"Then he was the man—"

"Yes. Rod was the man. Who told you?"

Rod Fennick had been a squadron-leader in the Royal Air Force. He wasn't a regular officer. He had joined up early and made great headway. Cartaret rather thought that in civil life he had been a sort of charming parasite; one of those ornamental but useless young men who used to haunt the Ritz bars in London and in Paris and who sometimes turned up at Cannes. But he was good company, and a brilliant and fearless fighter pilot. If Rod was a black sheep, it was plain that he had been thrown out of a sound flock…

"Abdûl told me," Cartaret said. "He mentioned no name, but I thought it might be Rod. Is it all true—all he told me?"

Sirena gave Cartaret an almost scornful glance. Unfastening the top of her dinner frock, she turned her back to him and let it drop to her waist.

"Look."

Cartaret looked. Sirena's shoulders and the creamy skin as far down as it was visible were wealed with lash marks, old and new!

"Good God! The dirty blackguard!"

Composedly, Sirena re-fastened her dress and turned to him.

"Didn't Abdûl tell you?"

Cartaret nodded grimly.

"Yes, Abdûl told me."

"And about Rod?"

"Yes. Is that—true?"

Again, the tigress eyes flashed, dangerously.

"It is true. You remember—" she swallowed—"how handsome he was? Now—" She paused for control. "He has been to a famous French specialist—and there is hope. But it will take a long time, and cost a lot of money."

"It's almost incredible! Surely, the authorities—"

Sirena's smile was openly scornful now.

"I told you you didn't understand. Everything here is different."

Almost an echo of old Abdûl's words!

"What happened tonight?"

"You saw Selim come in?"

"Selim? The fat Egyptian? Yes. Who is he?"

Sirena's full lips curled contemptuously.

"He is in charge of some of Aswami's treasures! I was afraid, although I didn't think he had recognised me. I was wrong. As I came out of the bathroom, a man who had climbed from the garden to the balcony and hidden in here, sprang on me from behind. They think I am safe until all the lights are out. Then, they are coming back for me!"

Cartaret was thinking that this fantastic affair belonged to the days of the Caliphs, not to the prosaic twentieth century. But all he said was:

"They'll have a surprise."

Sirena impulsively, threw her arms about him.

"You must get me away! You have a car. It was this I wanted you to do. But now—it is even more urgent I *must* be out of here before midnight…"

As Cartaret drove his Buick from the garage he was wondering to which particular variety of fool he belonged. The role of knight errant he had never fancied. In this particular case, the captive princess was far from a paragon of injured innocence, and her Prince Charming ranked pretty low.

But the atrocious behaviour of Aswami Pasha had fired his blood. Rod Fennick might be no model of an English gentleman, but he was, or had been, a gallant officer, and there are more civilised methods of dealing with fickle girl friends and their admirers than those once practised by the sultans of Turkey…

"Mrs Parradine", grey haired, bespectacled, and trapped in a mink coat, joined Cartaret as arranged at the corner of Sharia El-Maghrabi, below the Continental. With one swift backward glance, she jumped in beside him. The night air was chilly.

She carried no baggage other than her large satchel purse. She nestled up to Cartaret.

"I don't think I was followed. But drive quickly. I will tell you the way to go."

Cairo's streets were curiously deserted, except in one district through which their route lay, where discordant music and harsh female voices disturbed the night. They left the city by an unfamiliar gate and drove right out on to the fringe of the desert. Cartaret tried to imagine where they could be going.

He slowed down and glanced aside at his passenger.

She had discarded the grey wig and was combing her hair. Its blue-black waves gleamed in the moonlight.

"Which way?"

"Follow this road."

"Road? It's hardly even a track!"

"It is an old caravan road. But you will have to drive slowly."

In this, at least, Cartaret agreed with her. The path was more like a dry ditch than anything else, beaten out by generations of camels stepping in one another's foot-prints.

Cartaret had groped his way along several miles of this when Sirena directed him to turn east. He could see nothing vaguely resembling a surface, but all the same, as he obeyed, he found himself driving on a sandy but practicable road again.

He recalled, at this moment, that such a road had been made in those dark days when Rommel's Afrika Korps lay like hungry jackals watching the flesh-pots of Egypt. It led to an emergency landing strip long since abandoned.

Evidently, this was it.

Cartaret saw a few tumble-down buildings, desolate under the moon. Sirena had the key of one, at some time used as an office. She opened the door and they went in. Some papers were littered on a desk before which was placed an old cane-bottomed chair. An almanac and a map were pinned to the wall.

The night was diamond clear. Sirena had left the door open, and silver light poured right in, touching a dilapidated divan upon which she had thrown her mink coat and the leather satchel purse.

She sat there with the moon mirrored in her amber eyes and smiled at Cartaret.

"Safe at last," she said, "free! We have some time to wait."

Sirena opened a little cigarette case and offered him a cigarette.

He crossed, lighted one for her. She looked into his eyes all the time. Then he lighted his own. He went back and sat down in the broken cane chair.

There was a silent interval until:

"I'm sorry you won't make love to me," Sirena said softly. "It would make it so much easier."

"Make what easier?"

"To tell you the truth."

"Then all you told me was a lie?"

Sirena shook her head.

"Not all of it. You know I didn't lie about how I was treated. You have seen. And it's true what Abdul told you about Rod, and what I told you, too. I slipped away from Aswami's house while he was taking a siesta, and when Selim came into Shepheard's tonight I knew he was looking for me."

"Then I'm afraid I don't know what you mean."

"I mean that Selim didn't recognise me. But I knew, when I saw him, that I must get away at once."

"If he didn't recognize you—" Cartaret began.

"Then who tied me up, you mean? Well, that's what I think it only right to tell you. I tied myself—with some cord I got from the porters' office! You were so quick that you didn't notice my right hand was really free already."

Cartaret watched her in a new way. Either he had formed an entirely wrong impression of Sirena's character before, or she had changed. There was something ingenuous about this confession. She wanted to play fair. And there was an undercurrent of sadness.

"Whatever did you do it for?"

"I wanted to make you excited! I thought (because, you see, I know the Service mind) that if I didn't, you would try to call up consuls, and police—and that would have spoiled everything. I had seen Selim looking for me. I knew he would have been to the police already—"

"Aswami has no legal claim. He can't detain you."

Sirena sighed like a tired child.

"Truly, you don't understand. Please, believe it was the best way——and forgive me."

"I don't believe it was the best way, but say no more about it. What would have happened, if I hadn't walked along to your window?"

"I should have half untied myself and called out to you. You see—" a new expression came into the amber eyes—"you are still thinking about me as I used to be, before I knew Rod. I love him. I have never loved anyone else, and I never shall—even if…he stays as he is."

Sirena dropped her cigarette on the floor and crushed it out under her foot.

"Suppose I hadn't been staying at Shepheard's? What should you have done?"

Sirena shook her head.

"I don't know. Thank God you were. I wouldn't have dared to hire a car. Selim will have called up every garage."

"I always thought Rod had gone back home long ago."

"No." Sirena shook her head sadly. "Rod and a partner bought an old transport plane. They carry goods, and sometimes passengers, between Egypt and Persia."

Cartaret checked a question just before it could be spoken. He was listening intently, listening to the drone of an approaching engine.

Sirena stood up and threw the mink coat over her shoulders; she picked up her satchel purse.

"I must go," she said. "Do one more thing for me. Stay here until we have left. Just close the door. No one ever comes to this place."

Cartaret nodded.

"As you say."

Sirena moved close to him. She slipped her arm around his neck. "I am glad, now, you didn't try to make love to me. For what you have done I thank you with all my heart."

She kissed him. It was a kiss of pure affection…

When she went out and closed the door, Cartaret found that through a cracked window he had a partial view of the landing ground. He saw a plane touch down and a mechanic scramble out. Sirena was helped on board and the plane was away again in record time.

Cartaret stood there for several minutes, thinking it all over. The shouted instructions of the pilot had been clearly audible—and the voice was the voice of Rod Fennick.

He was awakened, early the following morning, by a disturbance in the next room. Then, followed a banging on his door.

An English assistant manager came in. He was accompanied by an Egyptian police officer in a field marshal's uniform.

"Sorry to bother you, Captain Cartaret," the manager said. "But this officer wants to know if you heard anything unusual taking place last night."

Cartaret collected his thoughts, and:

"At what time?" he asked.

"At about half past eleven."

"I was out then. I didn't return until after one. Why?"

"A certain Mrs Parradine had the next room. She was seen to go out at about eleven-thirty, and she hasn't come back. Her baggage contains the suit in which she arrived, toilet articles, and so on, and a lot of tissue paper and cord. The whole room is in a state of disorder."

"What do you suspect? Suicide?"

The manager glanced aside at the police officer.

"We don't know. I apologise again. Obviously, you can't help us as you weren't here."

They went out.

Cartaret had just come from the bath when the manager returned alone.

"I couldn't tell you while that damned policeman was standing by," he explained. "But this disappearance of the mysterious Mrs Parradine is probably linked up with something that happened out at Bûlak last night."

"What happened there?"

"One of Aswami's girl friends drugged him and got clear away with a haul of his priceless rubies! I wasn't on duty when Mrs Parradine arrived—but I wonder. Aswami's a nasty bit of work, and my own sympathy is entirely with the lady, even if she left without settling her account! Knew you'd be curious, so dropped in to tell you."

For a long time after he had gone, Cartaret sat smoking and trying to find out where *his* sympathy lay. He recalled the horror which Abdûl had whispered. He recalled Sirena's eyes when she had said, "You remember how handsome he was?...He has seen a famous French specialist. There is hope, but it will take a long time and cost a lot of money—"

These recollections settled the point.

But he changed his plans. He decided to leave Cairo that morning.

THE MARK OF MAAT

"What you say is true enough," Tom Borrodale admitted. "Most professional Egyptologists are unimaginative. Meant to be, I guess. You see, they come across queer things, things which just have to be written off for the good of a man's health. There's the Haunted Tomb in the Valley of the Kings where the unwrapped mummy of a strangled girl was found; there's the empty room in the Pyramid of Meydum; and there's the Woman of the Great Pyramid."

He rested bronzed and hairy legs on one chair, leaning back in another—six feet of sunbaked stolidity arrayed in shorts and a khaki shirt. It was the in-between hour, so that Shepheard's terrace showed as nearly deserted as I had seen it since my arrival in Cairo. There were inky shadows and dazzling high lights, and, save for rather more uniforms than usual, traffic in the Sharia Kâmel was much like the traffic I remembered ten years before.

"You look fit, but a trifle warworn, Tom."

"Yes." He nodded and began to fill his pipe. "I joined the infantry, like a mug—and any foot slogger who follows Montgomery wants iron feet as much as iron nerves. Enjoying a spot of leave at the moment."

We fell silent, until: "You are not one of those, I recall, who believe that Ancient Egypt holds no more mysteries for modern man?" I said.

"Not by long odds." He threw a worn pouch on the table and took a sip from his glass. "Those I have mentioned, for instance. Then, since your time, a case cropped up which eclipsed, for a while, the Tutankhamen legends. Something quite in your way."

"What was it?"

"Oh, a classic example! If we hadn't been in the middle of a number-one war, the home newspapers would have sent special reporters out on the job. It happened to a man we'll call Lake. You don't know him, and nothing would be served by using his other name. The second man—a fellow in my own line; experienced excavator and well up in Arab matters—we'll call Thomson. Then—there was a girl."

And this is the story which Tom Borrodale told me about Lake, Thomson, a girl, and the mark of Maat.

Thomson, before the war, had been employed by the Department of Antiquities, and was recognised as a sound Egyptologist. His last job (for which he had been "lent" by the department) was an attempt to complete an excavation begun by Schroeder, the American. Schroeder had sunk a shaft, at great cost, by means of which he had hoped to gain access to the tomb of a queen who was also a priestess of Maat (Maat is the Ancient Egyptian goddess of truth, a somewhat mysterious deity of whose rites little is known).

Funds failing or something of the kind, Schroeder went home and this shaft was never completed; but Thomson, who had followed the work with interest, decided to try to influence new capital and to carry Schroeder's shaft through. This was where Lake came into the scheme of things.

Lake and Thomson had been up at Oxford together; but Lake, who had inherited a considerable property, had blossomed into a fashionable dilettante, whereas Thomson had had to work hard for his living. Lake, latterly (this was just before the outbreak of war), had been pottering about Egypt and had developed a keen interest in Thomson's studies. Perhaps seeing himself as another Carnarvon, he agreed to put up the necessary funds and, Thomson in charge, they resumed the work.

It seems that Schroeder's calculations were accurate enough, and in rather a shorter time than Thomson had anticipated, they found their way into the antechamber of the tomb. Further progress was held up by a massive portcullis which offered every promise of a first-class nuisance. However, there were some objects of interest in the anteroom, including a great part of the regalia of a royal high priestess. An amethyst scarab set in a heavy-gold ring and inscribed with the sign of Maat, Thomson pronounced to be unique.

Much encouraged, they had just gone to work on the portcullis when war was declared—and once more Schroeder's shaft had to be abandoned. Lake, who already held a pilot's certificate, joined the R.A.F., and Thomson obtained an infantry commission. In due course, both drifted back to North Africa, and both became attached to the Eighth Army. It was during the lull before Montgomery's great advance that the girl stepped into the picture.

Moira (let's call her Moira) was an Irish-Australian and had come out as a nurse with a contingent from Melbourne. Her family had plenty of money, and she had been educated in England, and I gathered that she was by way of being a beauty.

Both Lake and Thomson met her socially in Cairo, and Thomson, who found her altogether too attractive for his peace of mind, seems to have resigned her to Lake, slightly the younger man, good-looking, and in every way more suitable; or so Thomson thought. "He didn't believe," as Tom Borrodale put it, "that mere brawn, a medium brain, and small prospects beyond five hundred a year could appeal to any sensible girl. Particularly, with a charming and wealthy man, who one day would inherit a baronetcy as competition."

Thomson was shifted first; and Moira saw him off. There were tears in her eyes, and he decided that she was sorry for him. Although he had tried hard to conceal his real sentiments, he gave her credit for knowing how he felt; he believed that women were like that. To Lake, on parting, he said simply, "Good luck, old man."

When the campaign really got going, Lake's squadron was right up in support. But the two men had seen little of each other up to the time that Thomson was sent over on a special job behind Rommel's lines. His intimate knowledge of Arabic and the Arabs was not wasted. Suitably dressed, he could pass for a member of any one of six or more orders without much risk of detection.

Attired in Senusi style, he was flown across by a roundabout route to be parachuted at a selected point; and the pilot allotted to him was Lake.

Well, they were unlucky. An unsuspected A.A. gun, hidden in a wadi, scored a beauty just as they were turning northward toward the coast. It developed into a race against leaking petrol and faltering engines—and they lost. Lake crash-landed in the middle of what Borrodale described as "God knows where."

Thomson had a splinter in one shoulder, and lost a quantity of blood; the wound was difficult to dress; but Lake escaped intact. Observations showed that they were about sixty miles west of the British lines. They had, and could carry, sufficient rations and water, sparingly shared, to last them for three days. Their radio had cracked up. It would have been grim enough under normal conditions: being in enemy country made it worse.

They started to trek back; "and," said Borrodale, "only those who know the gritty, shelterless hell called the Libyan desert can begin to imagine those days and nights."

Both were bitten by some unidentified crawling thing while they slept in the shadow of a wadi, and Thomson developed a high temperature. His injured arm swelled to nearly twice its normal size and he began to laugh out loud and talk nonsense. Lake, a man of slighter physique, was not in much better shape. But he did his best to drag Thomson along.

Just before dawn of the third day, Thomson fell into a sort of coma from which Lake was unable to rouse him. Weak as a kitten, himself, he waited until the end. It meant the loss of eighteen precious hours and of nearly all the water. Then, he scraped out a shallow pit and dragged the largest bits of stone which he could carry from a neighbouring mound to make a cairn over his dead companion. It was the best he could do to protect him from the jackals and the vultures.

Lake was picked up, a whole day later, by a reconnaissance party from an Indian unit and rushed to a hospital in Cairo.

"I may as well tell you," said Tom Borrodale, "that he was a pretty desperate case. He looked more like a mummy than a man; and for a long time he hovered on the border line."

No one followed the stages of his slow recovery with greater interest than Moira. You see, so far, he had been quite unable to tell the story of that dreadful march. Incoherent rambling formed his only conversation; and the grim facts were fearfully awaited.

When, at last, a sick man but a sane one, Lake told his story,

Moira was among the first to hear it Much to most people's surprise, she took the news of Thomson's death very badly. The thing that seemed to worry her, and it was a queer thing to worry about in the circumstances, was the possibility that Lake, in his weakened state, had made an inadequate cairn—the possibility that Thomson's body might become the prey of carrion birds and beasts. Lake did his best to reassure her, but he was not altogether successful, as will appear.

Whether the thought of the dead man lying out there in the Libyan desert preyed on her mind or whether overwork at the hospital where she was stationed was responsible has little to do with the matter; but Moira had a breakdown and became a patient herself.

However, she made a good recovery, and was given sick leave. This was the cool season, and she decided to go up to Luxor. Lake was still reporting to the MO when she left, but he had never failed to send flowers, fruit and such offerings to Moira throughout her illness. They lunched together at Shepheard's on the day she left, and Lake saw her off. About a week later he was given a clean bill, and he lost no time in heading upriver;,too. He, also, decided to spend his leave in Luxor.

"This brings me," explained Tom Borrodale, "to the mystery I promised; and here is the mystery."

"There is something I want you to do for me," Moira said to Lake one morning as they sat in the hotel garden.

Lake, stretched beside her in a long chair, looked at Moira smilingly. She was well worth looking at, too: one of those chestnut blondes with warm, creamy colouring whose production in the climate of Ireland seems so odd. With her deep violet eyes and her daintiness, she looked like a flower of the sunny south. Actually, of course, Moira was born in Australia, but both her parents came from Ireland. Lake was a goodlooker, also—a man of medium build, fairish, and always groomed perfectly, whether in uniform or out of it. He looked quite fit by this time, and so, for that matter, did Moira. They used to take long rides together on the other side of the Nile, Lake loving to act as her guide to the city of dead kings.

"You know I would do anything for you," he replied—and he meant it; his brown eyes glowed as he watched her. "What is it you want?"

That he was hopelessly, blindly in love with her no one who saw them together could doubt. She was his religion; for Lake there was no God—only Moira.

She hesitated a while before she answered, staring out over the river to where a native dahabeah moved slowly through morning haze like a giant hawk moth with lifted wings. Except for the clanking of an ancient water wheel near by, there was hardly a sound. The pair of them just lay there in a peaceful world that didn't seem to know that Hitler had ever been born. At last, Moira spoke.

"I want you to let me go down Schroeder's shaft," she said.

This was not the first time she had made that request. But Lake, gently, and evidently inspired by sincere anxiety to spare her pain, had always headed her off. In their many expeditions among the tombs and temples he had avoided showing her the spot upon which he and Thomson had been at work when war interrupted them. Moira didn't even know quite where it was located.

At first, thinking that she understood the motives of delicacy which prompted him, Moira had dropped the subject; but she had returned to it later; and now she made the request in a manner which invited no evasion.

"Very well," said Lake, "of course. It's not a pleasant business from any point of view, but if you are set on it we can go, say, on

Tuesday morning. The shaft has been closed up, of course, but not permanently. I'll go into the town and gather up a few men to prepare the way. Men who know the work are easy to find."

Moira just replied, "Thank you, Vernon," and didn't refer to the matter again.

"If you want to picture Schroeder's shaft to yourself," said Tom Borrodale, "don't confuse it in your mind with an elevator shaft. It wasn't straight and it wasn't smooth; it was more like the inside of a Swiss chimney. It went sheer down for about ten feet and then it had been cut in at a pretty sharp angle to avoid solid granite. That part was shored up. Beyond, it went straight down again, a rugged, rock-studded pit. At this point Schroeder had met more rock and had had to give the job up. Thomson, later, tunnelled around this obstruction and broke into the antechamber from the south."

Lake (so Borrodale told me), although a man of proved courage, had an almost morbid horror of snakes. So that when, early on the appointed Tuesday morning he and Moira arrived at the reopened shaft, Lake sent the Arabs down first to report if all was clear.

They were an experienced crew, one of whom had worked with Thomson and Lake before. "These fellows are born excavators," said Borrodale, "whose fathers dug for Flinders Petrie and Howard Carter. The ghafir of one of the Luxor temples, a white-haired veteran who remembered Maspero, was in charge, and although already he had assembled a gang of six, he had roped in an odd man who came from the Faiyûm, a big, bearded fellow, who seemed, for all his physique, since he kept well in the background, to be work-shy. I need not say that such a mob was unnecessary, but the old boy had jumped at the chance to employ all his friends and relations. It's their way."

Lines had been rigged and arrangements made for forming a sort of human escalator by means of which Moira and Lake could be passed down to the foot of the shaft. From the moment that they proceeded beyond the angle, daylight disappeared: but Lake had a big army flashlight which he housed in the hip pocket of his shorts.

They managed the descent successfully and then squeezed around that narrow semicircular cutting which gave access to the anteroom. It was very still down there, when the Arabs had been told to clear out, and it smelled of Ancient Egypt. "That smell of Ancient Egypt," said Tom Borrodale, "is something which no one has ever been able to define. But although it isn't strictly pleasant, it has some hypnotic quality which, even over a bridge of years, can call a man back to the Old Land."

A feature of the antechamber was a central pillar hewn out of the rock, and before this pillar, on the westward side, stood a sort of shrine, also of rock, upon which had rested a porphyry statuette of the goddess, Maat. The statuette had been taken to the Cairo Museum, but the rock altar was immovable, of course. There were some fine mural paintings in perfect preservation, and the floor of the square room was paved with black stone.

It is necessary to remember the shape of the entrance passage and the presence of this central pillar in order to understand why Moira, after the Arabs had gone, suddenly said, "Are you sure there's no one in the room?"

"No one but you and I," Lake, assured her, and shone his light all around from where they stood. "Why?"

"I thought, or perhaps I imagined, that someone else was here," Moira explained.

Lake was wearing a white silk shirt open front, and it seemed to Moira, in the reflected light, that he looked rather ghastly. He was of a naturally pale complexion, which illness had accentuated, but since leaving hospital he had enjoyed plenty of open-air exercise and had regained colour. All the same, as he stood there, Moira thought that his face looked almost as pale as his partly exposed chest. It must be borne in mind, however, that the air of the place was hot and oppressive. Lake laughed but not overconvincingly.

"Suppose we get the inspection through," he suggested, "and return to the outer air. Although I took up this business, once, I may as well admit that the atmosphere of tombs, or their lack of atmosphere, soon bowls me over."

Well, they walked right around the antechamber, examining its murals, which Lake did his best to explain. He showed Moira where the portcullis was hidden in the eastern wall beyond which lay the real tomb.

They had completed their tour and stood one on either side of the empty shrine before the central pillar when Moira whispered, "There it is again!"

She grabbed Lake's arm so suddenly that he dropped his flashlight. It fell on the black pavement with an awesome crash and immediately went out.

"Damn," he exclaimed; then, "Don't get frightened, Moira," he added. "Stand quite still until I strike a match."

"Please don't strike a match," she said—"at least, not for a moment."

Her voice was not entirely steady, but she spoke so quietly that it was evident that she had herself well in hand.

"Whatever do you mean?" Lake asked, and his tones were pretty husky.

"Oh, it's just an impulse—perhaps a silly one. It came to me as the light went out. When you asked me to marry you, Vernon, in Cairo, don't think that I refused lightly, or frivolously. Indeed, I was honoured, and very, very sorry to have to hurt you. But I told you, quite honestly, why it was impossible, and I respected you enough to tell you, when you asked me, the other man's name—although he didn't know."

"That's all true," said Lake, in a low voice. "But what has it to do with our remaining here in the dark?"

"Just that while we stand here, by this shrine of Maat, which you—and he—discovered, I want to ask you a question. Will you promise to answer truly—in the name of Maat?"

"In the name of *Maat!* That's a queer pagan oath."

"Perhaps it is. But will you?"

"Of course."

"Very well. Swear, by Maat, with your hand on her altar, that you buried him as well and as deeply as was in your power."

For the next few seconds there was that sort of silence which seems to throb, as though an astral dynamo vibrated near by. Then, Lake's voice came out of the darkness:

"I buried him as well, and as deeply, as was in my power. I swear this—in the name of Maat."

The thing that followed may never be satisfactorily explained. Conjecture is permissible, but proof unlikely. There was a blinding flash of light. It shone directly onto Lake's face, leaving everything else in utter blackness. Something shot toward him, something which Moira described as "a brown shadow". Lake uttered a choking sound and fell. There was utter blackness again.

Moira's shriek—the only sound that she uttered before collapsing, unconscious—was heard by the waiting Arabs. It had a curious (but by no means unusual) effect. For a number of reasons, Schroeder's shaft was reputed to be haunted by a powerful and evil spirit. In consequence, on hearing that wild cry, three of the gang promptly bolted and were seen no more.

It was the white-bearded ghafir who carried Moira up. Laying her in a shady place, he returned for Lake. And when they brought Lake out into morning sunshine, only the old Arab's holy reputation (he was a hadji who had five times kissed the black stone of the Kaaba), his fists, and his uncommonly fluent invective, prevented the others from deserting as well.

Imprinted on Lake's pale skin, right over the heart, and growing plainer every minute, was a reddish-blue mark, like a bruise. It was clearly defined, resembling a seal, and it represented the conventional Feather of Justice: the mark of Maat!

"This extraordinary story does not rest on the testimony of the Arabs alone," said Tom Borrodale. "By the time that Moira was in a fit state to see Lake (who was dead) the mark had faded into a sort of general contusion. But she could swear to its character, nevertheless: there were many similar inscriptions on the walls of the antechamber."

Medical evidence, when it could be obtained (they had to hold a post-mortem), showed that death had been from shock, apparently caused by a tremendous blow over the heart.

"So there's your mystery," Borrodale commented; "and I flatter myself it's a pretty deep one. Which brings me to Thomson's story."

"To Thomson's story?" I echoed.

"Yes. About a week later Thomson turned up in Cairo. He had a story to tell, also; but he told it (in full) to no one but Moira."

And this is Thomson's story:

Thomson came temporarily to his senses in that dreadful hour just before dawn of the third day in the desert. Hovering between sanity and delirium, he saw Lake creeping stealthily away over a neighbouring mound—taking with him their remaining stock of food and water!

He staggered to his feet and tried to run after Lake. He shouted—or he thought he was shouting: it may have been a husky whisper.

And Lake? Lake looked back and then began to run, also…away from Thomson! Thomson ran on until he fell.

His next recollection was one of lying in an Arab tent, raving. A man and an old woman were trying to soothe him. They forced him to swallow some bitter draught. A good Moslem respects insanity, looking upon it as a visitation of God and a thing to merit a True Believer's pity…

In time (Thomson had no idea if in days or in weeks) he recovered. He had been picked up and tended by a small party of wandering Bedawi; and he was his own man again.

Lake! The mere thought of Lake set Thomson's brain on fire. His first idea was how soon he could find his way back and expose Lake. Nothing else mattered until he had broken Lake, until he had shown him up for the cad and cur he thought him to be. Then—he fell to thinking about the thing from another angle.

"You will recall," said Borrodale, "that both had been bitten, or stung, by some unspecified reptile or insect. It occurred to Thomson that Lake might not have been in his right mind when he deserted, when he left a fellow man to almost certain death in the desert. This theory worried him so much that he determined to prove or disprove it before he acted."

"Thomson must have been a fellow of singular generosity—or simplicity."

"That's as may be. I merely state the facts. Anyway, he knew that he would be posted missing, perhaps dead, and he made up his mind to stay missing until he could find out if Lake had got back—and, if so, what Lake had said."

I gathered that, according to Thomson's explanation when he turned up in Cairo, he had been wandering about in Arab dress, bearded to the eyes (he was heavily hirsute), in Libya and Egypt for many weeks, still uncertain of his real identity. The fact was (or so Borrodale hinted) that Thomson was seeking news of Lake.

"It is probable," said Borrodale, "that he learned of Lake's illness, and it is possible that he made his way up to Luxor in order to confirm the reported facts. He might have reached Cairo, for instance, just after Lake left. It is even possible, if a little farfetched, that he was watching Lake and Moira. I hesitate to suggest so fantastic a theory, but he may have been one of the party recruited by the ghafir to reopen Schroeder's shaft. The blinding light described by Moira would not be inconsistent with someone suddenly turning on a flashlight—someone concealed behind the central pillar."

While Tom Borrodale had been talking, people had begun to drift onto the formerly deserted terrace, and now, from behind me, I heard a soft call: "Coo-ee, Tom!"

Tom Borrodale came to his feet at a jump; his eyes gleamed; his whole rugged face irradiated happiness. I turned and stared at a girl who had just come up the steps. She was well worth staring at: a petite chestnut blonde with that Irish rose complexion which has inspired so many songs, and widely spaced violet eyes. She wore nurse's uniform. A quick intake of breath drew my glance away. Tom Borrodale was grasping his left arm, which evidently pained him.

"Moved my chair too hurriedly," he explained. "Stopped a bit of shrapnel with this arm."

He had also grasped it too hurriedly; for a heavy gold ring which he wore with the bezel concealed had got twisted, and I saw that it was set with a large amethyst scarab.

"You don't know Sheila Asthore, do you?" he asked. "Sheila, one of my oldest friends has turned up in the nick of time—to act as best man." He turned to me. "We're to be married in three days."

THE TREASURE OF TAIA

B rian Desmond recognised that he was no more than a wretched interloper. Almost he regretted his own temerity. Camp life within the precincts of the Temple of Medinet Habu has many drawbacks, but at least one may stand where heaps of precious ingots once gleamed within the treasury of Rameses in Thebes, the city of the hundred gates; one may share the apartment over the great pylon with bats and creeping things, and, by the light of that same old moon which shone upon golden Pharaoh, watch painted ladies of the royal harem wave flabella before the mighty one, cast flowers at his feet, and receive the reward of his godlike caresses. According to the inscriptions, the queen was never present.

Oft times Desmond had spent his evenings thus, imagining how, in some earlier incarnation, he, too, might have worn the double crown of Egypt.

Tonight he felt less godlike. Luxor was crowded, and money could not obtain a room at the Winter Palace Hotel. The German representative of one of Europe's great Jewish families had secured twenty apartments for the accommodation of his dahabeah party.

Mr Jacob Goldberger, of Johannesburg, occupied three suites. Others, still more newly rich than Diamond Jake, made Egypt glad with their presence. Only for sentimental reasons had the great M. Pagnon granted Desmond the use of a chamber apparently designed for a hat box, top floor back—at the nominal rate of ninety piastres per day.

What is a distinguished Egyptologist, an MC, a BA, a Bsc, a member of numerous learned societies and one of the oldest families in Ireland, compared with a millionaire banker who is a director of numberless companies and a member of one of the oldest clans in the world? Small fry, indeed—and a beer-drinker withal, whose wine bill for the week would not total as much as Jacob Goldberger paid for a single postprandial cigar. One should not expect impossibilities!

Fashionable women of Europe and America moved about him, with black-coated manhood hovering in attendance. Desmond felt uncomfortable—as every public school man, even though he be Irish, and strive how he may to defy the conventionalities, must ever feel when he is conscious of not being "correct". Dress suits are unnecessary in the desert, and Desmond was arrayed in a serviceable outfit of washable linen. He concealed his discomfort, however, for in his secret heart he despised the sheeplike trooping of society equally with the gilded glory of Goldberger, and sought to crush that within him which was allied to the ways of the fold.

He turned to his companion, who sat beside him in the gayly lit lounge, and a slight smile disturbed the firm, straight line of his mouth.

Desmond's smile had once been described by an American lady as "worthwhile". He was one of those grim six-footers, prematurely grey, and straight as a mast. His short moustache was black, however. When he smiled, he revealed his lower teeth—small, even, strong-looking teeth—and his deep-set, rather sinister blue eyes lit up. The stern face became the face of a lovable schoolboy—and a bashful schoolboy, at that. With his fine appearance his romantic name, and his smile, he was fatal to women; but he didn't seem to know it.

"It is good of you to consent to be with me," he said, in his slow, hesitating fashion; "for, although I am neither distinguished nor wealthy, I dare to be shabby."

Mme. de Medicis dropped the cigarette from her tapered fingers into the little bowl upon the table at her side. Women were there to-night whose reputation for smartness was well deserved, and who, covertly watching *madame,* knew her to be dressed with a daring yet exquisite tastefulness which they might copy but could never equal. Women were there whom society called beautiful, but their beauty became very ordinary prettiness beside the dazzling loveliness of Desmond's companion.

She wore a gown of Delhi muslin with golden butterflies wrought upon its texture, and over it, as a cloud, floated that wondrous gauze which is known in the East as "the breath of Allah". No newest tenet of Paris was violated in its fashioning; no line of the wearer's exquisite shape was concealed by its softness.

Madame smiled dreamily, protruding one tiny foot cased in a shoe of old gold. Under her curved black lashes her eyes turned momentarily, glancing at Desmond. Those eyes were such as have never been bestowed by the gods upon woman save as a scourge to man. They possessed the hue seen in the eyes of a tigress, yet they could be as voluptuously soft as the shadows of some dim lagoon. Her carmine lips were curved with a high disdain, and, though her hair was black as the ebony pillars of the Hall of the Afreets, her lovely cheeks glowed like the petals of a newborn rose and her velvet skin was as fair as the almond blossom.

"You lack the courage of the *soi-disant* grand duke," she murmured.

Desmond turned languidly in his chair, fixing his queer, lingering regard upon the speaker.

"You refer to the eccentric royal personage who braves the wrath of Alexandria arrayed in a frock coat fastened by a piece of string? Poor fellow! His estates are confiscated, and he wears a pair of canvas shoes and a straw hat with a crown that permits the genial rays to caress his scalp."

Mme. de Medicis laughed softly.

"But he is so clever an artist!" she said.

Desmond shrugged cynically.

"There you are!" he protested. "An artist and a grand duke—all is forgiven!"

Madame laughed again, adjusting the filmy scarf that caressed her white shoulders as lightly as the amorous cloud which of old enveloped Io, the beauteous.

"You are so English!" she declared. "Oh, no—please forgive me! You are Irish—but so absurdly sensitive! You fly to the Winter Palace because you are weary of the Theban solitude, and here you find yourself more lonely than when you camp in wilderness!"

"But you have taken pity upon me," said Desmond, leaning toward her; "and now wild horses could not drag me back to my camp."

"Ah!" sighed *madame,* archly lowering fringes of black lashes. "So you are not so English that you cannot make love!"

"On the contrary," he replied, "I am so Irish that I cannot help it!"

She rose slowly to her feet. Her moving robe diffused a faint perfume. For a moment Desmond feared that he had offended her. Naïvely, he revealed his concern.

"Come, my desert man!" she said. "Walk with me beside holy Nile, and tell me that I am beautiful, in that deep, deceptive voice which has such tender notes! With what sweet English maids have you rehearsed the ballad of love, my friend! You strike its chords with rare proficiency!"

Many regarded Desmond's naïveté as a pose. It was not a conscious pose; yet he knew a certain sense of pagan triumph as he came out from the Winter Palace, past the bench upon which were seated the picturesque dragomans, and so on into the shadowed part of the street between the hotel entrance and the arcade of shops.

Beside him walked the most beautiful and elegant woman of all that gay gathering. An old *roué* whose name may be found in Debrett bowed to *madame in* mid-Victorian fashion, and eyed her cavalier unkindly. Lord Abbeyrock, said to be the handsomest man in Europe, who had been haunting the foyer for an hour past, bit savagely at his moustache and turned brusquely to re-enter the hotel. Quite a company of young cosmopolitan bloods followed with longing eyes the exquisite figure in the amazing cloak of flamingo red. With manifest reluctance, a stolid New York business magnate—whose wife was in Cairo—quitted his strategic post near the dragomans' bench, hitherto held against all comers.

Mystery is woman's supreme charm. It is the mystery of dark eyes peeping from a *mushrabiyeh* lattice that constitutes the love lure of the East. Mme. de Medicis was utterly mysterious—tempting, taunting, unfathomable—at once a Sibyl and a Cleopatra.

Who was she, and from whence did she come? She was steeped in mysticism, spoke intimately of the strange writings of Eliphas Levi, and quoted Pythagoras and Zarathustra with the same facility where with Desmond, of catholic literary sympathies, quoted Kipling and Yeats. She had tremendous intellectual fascination. At one moment she made him feel like a child; in the next, her wondrous eyes would look into his own, and they were the luresome eyes of a *ghaziyeh*, setting his blood more quickly coursing.

Groups of tourists lingered around the native shops, volubly chattering of their travels. Boatmen and donkey boys sat upon the low parapet, watching the idle throng and smiling their inscrutable Egyptian smiles. In the river lay the lighted dahabeahs. From one of them—that of Diamond Jake—came the softened tones of a sweet violin.

"Art lays its treasures at the feet of Mammon," murmured *madame*.

For a moment she paused, resting her slender hand upon Desmond's arm. The strains of a Spanish caprice of Sarasate's, played by one of Europe's greatest violinists, floated across the waters of the Nile.

It was Luxor reborn—Luxor, that has known so much of peace and war, of fashion and art; Luxor, that once was Thebes, beloved of Amen, the city of temples and palaces. And near them, beside them, cloaked in velvet night, swooned the deathless mystery of that historic land.

Desmond looked long and ardently at his companion, as she moved onward again. Only *she* had a true place in a picture of the greater city which now was rising up before him. The modern, empty Luxor was fading, and upon rich banks of the ancient river; looming shadowly, were the stately walls of the city of a hundred gates.

He seemed to be pacing beside the Nile with a Pharaoh's queen on a night of long, long ago.

"Tell me about your work in the temple," she said, breaking an eloquent silence. "You are looking for the sacred ornaments of the Princess Taia, are you not?"

"Yes," Desmond answered dreamily, "under the floor of what is sometimes called the Treasure Room."

"You know that the Egyptian government expedition, under. Van Kuyper, is similarly engaged at Biban el Muluk?"

"Van Kuyper is wrong," snapped Desmond, with sudden animation; for the enthusiast within him was awakened by the challenge in her words. "He confuses the princess with the queen, whereas they belonged to different families. I am glad he is wrong. He deserves to fail."

"Why do you say that?"

"Because," said Desmond grimly, "Van Kuyper is no true Egyptologist. He is an impostor and the so-called government expedition is no more than a marauding expedition. It is subsidised by a millionaire collector, and if the jewels were found by Van Kuyper they would mysteriously disappear and reappear in New York. It's a scandal! Such things belong neither to the Egyptian government nor to any purse-proud collector rich enough to pay to have them stolen. They belong to the world."

His enthusiasm was infectious. Covertly, Mme. De Medicis watched him; and in the dusk the man's strong, rugged profile resembled that of the great Rameses who holds eternal court amid the ruins of his great temple-palace.

"You, then, seek for love of seeking?" she asked softly.

"I revere the grandeur that was Egypt," he replied. "To commercialise such majesty is intolerable!"

"May it not also be dangerous?"

"Well!" Desmond laughed. "Princess Taia certainly had an odd reputation!"

"You refer to the fact that she was a sorceress?"

Desmond started, glancing aside at his lovely companion. Then he laughed again. "You seem to know everything!" he declared. "At times, when you question me on some point of Egyptology, I feel that you are amusing yourself. Yes—the princess was famous for her beauty and notorious for her witchcraft."

"Beware, then, that you are not playing with fire," said Mme. de Medicis softly. "Others have suffered—is it not so?"

Desmond pulled up suddenly. They had passed the shops, and passed the imitation temple gateway which marks the boundary of a hotel garden. They were alone with the night mystery of the Nile, upon a footpath leading to an old shadoof.

Something sombre, a new fascination, had come into the woman's silver voice. The moon poured its radiance quenchingly upon the flaming figure of this strange woman who warned him to beware of a sorceress dead twelve hundred years before the dawn of Christianity. Her tigress eyes looked fully into his own; and now—their glance chilled him coldly, as but a moment ago it had warmed him like wine.

"You speak in riddles," he said awkwardly, again become the boy who questions the Sibyl.

"Have you then heard and seen nothing strange in the temple?" she whispered, and looked about her fearfully.

"I have seen nothing," he replied, "but I have heard much. Some of the Arabs in these parts regard the ruins of Medinet Habu as haunted, I am aware; but if one listened to natives, one could not avoid the conclusion that the whole of Egypt is haunted. My headman and several others come from Suefee, in the Fayum, and are of different mettle."

"And so they camp in the temple?"

"Well," Desmond admitted, "not exactly. They sleep in the village, as a matter of fact—or have been doing so for some little time past."

"And you sleep in Luxor?"

He stared fully into the lovely, sombre face.

"You don't seriously believe that I am *afraid* to sleep in the temple?" he inquired slowly.

"Not at all; but I think you are wise to avoid doing so."

Awhile longer he watched her, betwixt anger and perplexity, until her carmine lips softened, parted, and hinted the gleam of pearly teeth. She dropped her heavy lashes, then raised them again; and her wonderful eyes were changed. They chilled no longer. Mme. de Medicis raised one slender, round ivory arm and laid her jewelled fingers caressingly upon Desmond's breast. The flaming cloak fell back, revealing a peeping shoulder wooed by the daring moon.

"How I love the English character!" she whispered, lending the words a bewitching little foreign intonation. "Ah, my Irish friend, forgive me—but you are so perfectly English! Look!" She moved her hand and pointed out across the silvery Nile. "There is my dahabeah!"

Desmond stared across the water toward where a vessel showing but few lights lay moored in the stream.

"Your dahabeah?" he said in surprise. "But I thought—"

"That I was one of the Goldberger party?" she suggested. "Oh no! I have my own dahabeah; but because I was lonely, too, I came, as you came, to the Winter Palace."

"I am grateful to the gods of Egypt!" said Desmond in a low voice.

She turned and laid her hand upon his breast again. He clasped his own tightly over the little jewelled fingers, crushing them against his heart, which was beating wildly, tumultuously.

Across the waters of the river of romance there came, faintly, magically, the sound of a throbbing *darabukkeh* and the wail of a reed pipe—that ancient music which the ages have not changed, and which accompanied the gliding of Cleopatra's golden barge down the mystic Nile to meet the great Roman soldier.

A man's voice—a light baritone, possessing in a marked degree the wild, yearning note peculiar to oriental vocalists—rose upon the night's silence. The song was a ghazal of that sweet-voiced singer of old Shiraz whom men called Chagarlab, "the sugar-lipped."

"If a cup of wine is spilled and I have spilled it, what of that? If ripe, tender lips be crushed and mine have crushed them, be it so!"

Transfixed by something compelling and magnetic in the vibrant tones, Desmond stood, tightly clasping *madame's* jewelled fingers. The final syllable of the verse died away, to ever diminishing beats of the dram and a softly sustained wailing note of the reed.

"You have Persians among your crew?" he said, and drew his lovely companion closer to him.

"But why?" she whispered, looking up into his eyes. "Do you recognise the words of Hafiz?"

"Perfectly! May I translate?"

Her reply was barely audible.

"If you wish!"

Desmond stooped and kissed her upon the lips.

Desmond always began working the temple at an early hour. His enthusiasm ran higher than ever, but his ideas had taken a strange twist. He began to study his men, to listen to their conversations with a new interest, and to interpret what he saw and what he heard from a different angle.

His excavators laboured with skill and good will; and, once

having penetrated the six or eight feet of tightly packed stone which closed the top of the opening, Desmond's task became a mere job of shovelling. Clearly enough, he had blundered upon a shaft opened in very early times, the lower part of which had apparently been filled up with sand. His only fear was that it might prove to be the work of early tomb robbers, and not of those who had hidden the sacred ornaments.

Medinet Habu affords a lively enough scene in the daytime during the Egyptian season, being visited by hundreds of tourists from Luxor. Hence Desmond's early starting of operations. There were many visitors to the temple during the day, and not a few penetrated to the barrier and read the notice posted there. None of them, however, had the necessary official permit to enter the closed Treasure Room of Rameses, and work proceeded without interruption.

Evening came, the labourers departed, and Desmond was left alone—save for the headman, Ali Mahmoud—in the wonder of Egypt's dusk. He watched the pale blue merge into exquisite pink, and the two colours, by some magical transmutation, form that profound violet which defies palette and brush. He became lost in reverie.

Not a sound came to disturb him, save a faint clatter of kitchen utensils from the tent under the ruins, where Ali Mahmoud was preparing dinner. A dog began to howl in the nearby village, but presently ceased. From the Nile, borne upon a slight breeze, came the plaintive note of a boatman's pipe. Presently the breeze died away, and silence claimed the great temple for its own.

Desmond bathed in the extemporised bath which the headman had filled. Then he shaved, changed into his best linen outfit, and dispatched his dinner.

"Ali Mahmoud!" he called, stepping to the tent door.

Out of deepening shadows the tall Egyptian appeared.

"I shall be away for some hours," said Desmond. "Keep a sharp lookout!"

"But you will return before morning?"

There was an odd note of anxiety—almost of reproach—in the man's voice. Desmond felt his cheeks flush.

"Of course I shall return before morning," he answered sharply. " 'For some hours,' I said. The temple ghafir will keep you company."

Ali Mahmoud shook his head.

"That Coptic robber has departed," he replied simply.

"What?" Desmond cried. "Since when?"

"Since the opening to the passage was made, he has departed each night at dusk."

"Then you have been here alone?"

"It is so."

"He had orders to remain!"

"It is true; but he is an unclean insect and an eater of pork."

"Has he been bribed?"

"How can I say, Desmond Effendi? But I will keep a sharp lookout, as you direct."

Ali Mahmoud saluted with graceful dignity, turned, and walked away.

For a long time Desmond stood looking after the headman, his mind filled with misgivings. From what he had overheard of the men's conversation he had been forced to conclude that superstition was working among them like a virus. The source of the strange rumours passing from man to man he had been unable to trace. He wondered if definite human enmity might not be at the bottom of the trouble. The desertion of the official watchman of the temple was significant.

Clearly, in the circumstances, it was unfair to leave Ali Mahmoud alone on guard. Desmond hesitated. A mental picture uprose before him, and he seemed to hear a soft voice whispering his name:

"Brian!"

"Damn!" he exclaimed.

Then, lighting his pipe, he set off briskly in the direction of the river, where he knew that a small boat awaited him. He would explain the position to *madame* and return immediately—so he determined.

Yet such is the way of things that more than four hours had elapsed when the boat brought Desmond back again to the bank of the Nile. He thought of Ali Mahmoud, and was remorseful. Furthermore, he despised himself.

He set out for the camp at a smart pace, wondering what had taken possession of the village dogs. From near and far came sounds of dismal howling.

Then, as he passed the village, and came at last in sight of the great ruin, he heard the sharp crack of a rifle.

"Ali Mahmoud!" he exclaimed.

Plunging his hand into his pocket, where latterly he had carried a pistol, he set out running.

"Good God!" he muttered, but never checked his steps. The pistol was missing!

Familiar with every foot of the way, he raced on through ebony shadows, making for the excavation. Out of the darkness he ran into the dazzling moonlight that bathed one side of the Treasure Room.

"Ali Mahmoud!" he shouted.

From a cavernous doorway, framed in deep-hewn hieroglyphics, the tall figure stepped out.

"Thank God!" Desmond panted. "I thought—"

He paused, staring at the headman, who carried his rifle, and whose strong, brown face betrayed some suppressed emotion.

"I am here, effendi!"

"I heard a shot."

"I fired that shot."

"Why? What did you see?"

Ali Mahmoud extended one of his small brown hands in a characteristic and eloquent gesture.

"Perhaps—hyena," he replied; "but it looked too big."

"It was some animal, then? I mean, it walked on four legs?"

Ali Mahmoud shook his head doubtfully.

"I thought," he answered slowly, "not *always* on four legs. I thought, *sometimes* on two. So I challenged. When *it* did not answer. I fired."

"Well?"

Ali Mahmoud repeated the gesture.

"Nothing," he explained simply. "All the men say they have seen this unknown thing. I am glad you have returned, Desmond Effendi!"

In the morning Desmond awakened early. The vague horror of the night, the mystery of the "thing" seen in the temple ruins, had fled.

Egyptian sunlight flooded the prospect, and he thought that moderate diligence on the part of the gang today should bring him within sight of his goal.

Ali Mahmoud, having performed his duty of awakening his chief, did not retire at once, but stood in the door of the tent, a tall, imposing figure, regarding Desmond strangely.

"Well?" Desmond asked.

"There is more trouble," the Egyptian answered simply. "Follow me, effendi, and you shall see!"

Desmond leaped out of bed immediately and followed the man to the excavation. The site was deserted. Not a labourer was there.

"Where are the men—?" he began.

Ali Mahmoud extended his palms.

"Deserted!" he replied. "Those Coptic mongrels, those shames of their mothers who foraged with their shoes on, have abandoned the work!"

Desmond clenched his fists, and for many moments was silent.

"You and I, Ali Mahmoud," he said at length, "will do the work ourselves!"

"It is agreed," the Egyptian replied; "but upon the condition, Desmond Effendi, that neither you nor I shall remain here tonight."

"What?"

Desmond glared angrily, but Ali remained unmoved.

"I am a man of few words," he said, in his simple, direct fashion; "but that which I saw last night was no fit thing for a man to see. Tonight I go. You, too, effendi, will leave the temple."

Brian Desmond was on fire, but he knew his man too well to show it. Moreover, he respected him.

"Be it so," he said, turned, and went back to his tent.

They laboured, those two, with pick and shovel and basket, from early morning until dusk. They worked as of old the slaves of Pharaoh worked. Not even under the merciless midday sun did they stay or slacken their herculean toils; and when, at coming of welcome evening, they threw down their tools in utter exhaustion, the narrow portals of the secret chamber were uncovered. Standing at the bottom of the shaft, sweat-begrimed, aching in every limb, the brown man and the white solemnly shook hands.

"Ali Mahmoud," said Desmond, "you are real British!"

"Desmond Effendi," the Egyptian answered, "you are a true Moslem!"

The desert toilet completed and the evening meal dispatched, Brian Desmond lit his pipe and stood staring out across the violet landscape toward the Valley of the Queens.

That day he had actually cleared the debris from before a door wrought of the red sandstone of Silsilis, which almost certainly was the portal of the secret Treasure Room. Despite the superstitious character of the natives, the spot was altogether too near to Luxor for the excavation to be left unguarded. Some predatory agent of a thieving dealer, or of an ambitious rival—for it had been well said that there is no honour among excavators—armed with suitable implements, might filch the treasure-trove destined to establish definitely the reputation of Brian Desmond.

Ali Mahmoud refused to remain—and Mme. de Medicis was waiting in the perfumed cabin of the dahabeah, where an incense burner sent up its smoke pencils of ambergris; and her golden eyes would be soft as the eyes of the gazelles.

But whosoever would retain the mastery of Moslems must first learn to retain the mastery of himself. Once let the idea that a place is haunted take root in the Arab mind, and, short of employing shackles, nothing could persuade a native to remain in that spot after sunset. Thus, at Karnak, the Bab el Abid, or Gate of the Slaves, a supposed secret apartment in the Temple of Mentu, is said to be watched over by a gigantic black afreet. No Egyptian would willingly remain alone in the vicinity of that gate by night.

Desmond entered his tent, trimmed and lighted the lamp, and wrote a note excusing himself and explaining his reasons. Sadi, the Persian poet, sings that love can conquer all; but Sadi lacked the opportunity of meeting a British archaeologist. Though every houri of Mohammed's paradise had beckoned him, Brian Desmond would not have been guilty of leaving the treasure of Taia unguarded.

Clapping his hands—a signal which Ali Mahmoud promptly answered—he handed the letter to the tall Egyptian.

"Give this personally to Mme. de Medicis," he said, "on the dahabeah *Nitocris*. Then do as you please."

"And you, effendi?"

"I agreed with you to leave the temple," Desmond answered. "I shall do so; but I did not agree not to return."

The fine face of Ali Mahmoud afforded a psychological study. Verbal subtlety is dear to the Arab mind. Desmond Effendi had tricked him, but tricked him legitimately.

"It is true," he answered; "but my heart misgives me."

He saluted Desmond gravely, and departed, his slippered feet making no noise upon the sandy ground. Like a shadow he glided from the tent door and was gone.

Desmond stood looking after the headman, and thinking of many things. The fires of his anger were by no means extinct; but Ali Mahmoud was staunch, and had laboured well. The night would pass, and the morrow held golden promise.

A faint, cool breeze fanned his brow, and about him lay that great peace which comes to Egypt with the touch of night. Vague sounds proceeded, for a time, from the direction of the Arab village, and once a pariah dog set up his dismal howling upon a mound not twenty yards away. Desmond could see the beast, painted in violet shadows against the sand; and, picking up a stone, he hurled it well and truly. With it went the last vapours of his rekindled wrath. The beautiful silence had become complete.

For long he stood there, smoking his pipe, and watching the eager velvet darkness claiming the land, until the perfect night of Egypt ruled the Thebaid, and the heavens opened their million windows that the angels might look upon the picture below.

Half regretfully, he turned and entered the tent. In the sandy floor his bottle of whisky was buried; in a bucket of water were the "baby

Polly" bottles. These latter he might reveal; but for Ali Mahmoud to detect him using strong liquor would be the signal for the headman's departure. That he so indulged was understood, but that he should keep his vice decently secret from every good Moslem was a *sine qua non*.

He helped himself to a peg, concealed the "vice" again, and set out to walk to the river, there to taunt himself with a sight of the twinkling lights of *madame's* dahabeah—and to carry out his pledge to Ali Mahmoud.

No more than ten paces had he gone when he became aware of a curious, cold tingling of his skin. The sensation was novel, but highly unpleasant. It gradually rose to his scalp—a sort of horrific chill quite unaccountable.

Remotely, sweetly, he heard, or thought he heard, a woman's voice calling his name:

"Brian! Brian!"

He stopped short. He felt his heart leap in his bosom. The voice had seemed to come from westward—from beyond the temple.

"Who's there?" he cried.

No one answered. A bat circled erratically overhead, as if blindly seeking some lost haven; then it swooped and was gone into some cranny of the great pylon.

"Brian! Brian!"

Again it came, more intimately, that sweet, uncanny crying of his name.

"Brian! Brian!"

Making for the moon-white angle of the great ruin, Desmond set out at a rapid pace. The woman, whoever she was, must be approaching by the path which skirted the temple—approaching from the valley below El Kurn, the Valley of the Queens.

He had almost gained the corner, wherefrom he could command a clear view of the path, when suddenly he pulled up. The icy finger of superstition touched him.

Who, or what, could be coming from the Tombs of the Queens at that hour of night? Breathing checked, muscles tensed, he stood listening.

Not a footfall could be heard, the very insects were still.

Deliberately, putting forth a conscious effort, he took the six remaining paces to the corner of the temple enclosure. No living thing was visible. Again a horrific tingling crept all over his skin and into his scalp. The opinions of the unknown stretched over him, and he stood in the shadow of fear.

"Is any one there?" he cried.

He shrank from the sound of his own voice, for it had a sinister and unfamiliar ring. The voice of the Thebaid answered him—the voice of the silence where altars were, of the valley where queens lie buried.

Panic threatened him, but he grimly attacked the ghostly menace, and conquered. His natural courage returning, he paced slowly forward along the silvery road that stretched to the gorge in the mountain. He stopped.

"My God!" he cried aloud. "What is the matter with me? What does it all mean?"

The moon-bathed landscape was swimming around him. A deadly nausea asserted itself. He had never swooned in his life, but he knew that he was about to do so now.

He turned, and began to stagger back to the tent.

Music aroused him—a dim chanting. Wearily he opened his eyes. Reflection was difficult, memory defied him; but he seemed to recall that at some time he had returned to the tent.

Yet he found himself in the temple!

That it *was* the Temple of Medinet Habu in which he stood, he was assured, although, magically, its character had changed. Yes—this was the Treasure Room, the scene of his excavation; but it was *intact!* The roof had been replaced. The apartment was filled with ancient Egyptian furniture. The air was heavy with a strange scent.

He was crouching like a spy, concealed behind a sort of screen. It was of carven wood, not unlike the *mushrebiyeh* screens of later Arab days; and through its many interstices he had a perfect view of the apartment.

Two women and a Nubian eunuch were in the room. The women were dressed, as Desmond had never seen living women attired in his life; yet he knew and recognised every ornament, every garment. The exquisite enamel jewellery, the scanty robes upon their slender ivory bodies, belonged to the Eighteenth Dynasty!

One, the small and more slender of the two, was of royal blood. This he knew by her dress. She spoke urgently to the other, whose face Desmond had not seen.

"Be quick, Uarda! I distrust him! Even how he may be spying upon us!"

The woman addressed turned—and he beheld Mme. de Medicis!

"Give me tile casket!" she said.

The first speaker took up a beautifully carven box of ebony and ivory, and placed it in the hands of the woman whom she had addressed as Uarda. Perhaps the judgment of Paris, the immortal shepherd, might have awarded the golden apple to the royal lady; but in the eyes of Desmond, watching, half stupefied, the movements of these two lovely Egyptians, incontestably the fairer was she whom he knew, in life, as Mme. de Medicis. He watched her greedily.

Somewhere in the great temple palace voices were chanting, sweetly.

The Nubian took the casket from the hands of Uarda and descended into a pit revealed by the displacement of a massive couch. Desmond, watching the women as they bent anxiously over the cavity, fell forward.

"Desmond Effendi!"

Desmond raised himself. Ali Mahmoud was supporting him.

He looked out from the tent to where rosy morn tinted the rugged lines of Medinet Habu.

"Effendi! I warned you! I warned you! And now you are stricken with fever!"

Desmond got to his feet. Clutching the tall Egyptian, he stood swaying for a moment, striving—wildly, at first, but with ever increasing self-control—to assemble the facts—the real facts—of the night.

Fever? No! In a flash of intuition the truth came to him. While he and Ali Mahmoud laboured through the previous day, some one— *some one*—had found and doctored his whisky. Even now he could recall the queer tang of it, which, in the tumult of mind that had been his at the time, he had ignored.

He had been drugged! But his dream—his dream of the Princess Taia and of her confidante?

His strength was returning with his clarity of mind. He shook off the supporting arm of Ali Mahmoud. He uttered a loud cry, and went staggering madly through the mighty courts of the temple.

His excavation below the floor of the sanctuary had been completed during the night. It opened, as he had conjectured, into a small square chamber—which was empty!

* * *

Paul van Kuyper stepped from the small boat to the deck of the dahabeah, bowing low to his beautiful hostess. Even in the desert, Mynheer van Kuyper contrived to preserve the manners, and, in a modified degree, the costume, of a fashionable boulevard lounger. As he stood there in the blaze of noonday sun, he was as truly representative of one school of archaeology as Brian Desmond, Working barefoot with his Arabs at Medinet Habu, was representative of another.

Van Kuyper's brown eyes flamed with admiration as he bent over the little white hand of Mme. de Medicis. She was seemingly unaffected by the great heat; she looked as cool as a morning rose. Hers were the toilet secrets of Diane de Poitiers, and the love lore of Thais.

Attended by four waiters from the Winter Palace, they lunched, and talked of many things; but always Van Kuyper's brown eyes spoke of passion. Yet when at last they were alone, with coffee such as may only be tasted in the East, and cigarettes of a sort that never leave Egypt except to go to Moscow:

"Quick—tell me!" he whispered, and glanced furtively around him. "What occurred last night at Medinet Habu?"

"How should I know what occurred, *monsieur?*"

Languidly Mme. de Medicis swept her black lashes upward, and languidly lowered them again, veiling the amber eyes.

"Ah!" Van Kuyper laughed. "But we understand each other! We are old allies, it is not so? When I learned from Abdul, who had been watching Desmond's camp since the work began, that the shaft was an old one, I followed the arranged plan. On Tuesday night he was nearly shot by Ali Mahmoud—Desmond's headman; but he brought great news! You received my letter?"

Madame inclined her head languidly.

"I have it in my bureau."

"Good! You had worked wonders thus far. Nearly a week ago the camp at Medinet Habu became deserted at night. Even the *ghafir* fled. How you worked upon the fear of the natives I do not know, but you succeeded. Only Ali Mahmoud and Desmond remained. As I told you, I took a double precaution. Desmond's buried bottle is a byword among the excavators. While he completed the clearing of the shift, Abdul dealt with this matter!"

"Excellent!" *madame* murmured.

"Your reports of Desmond's progress reached me daily, and last night, I acted. Abdul and Hassan es Suk were watching. Ali Mahmoud came to you here with a note. It was genius!"

"It was merely coincidence."

"What? You did not contrive it? No matter—it was good. Shortly afterward, Desmond succumbed to the drug, and Hassan came to fetch me."

"So?" *madame* murmured, dropped her half-smoked cigarette into the little brass tray.

Van Kuyper glanced at her uneasily, but proceeded:

"We opened the door. It was stiff work; but what we found, you know. I merely peeped at the contents of the casket, but *madame*— he seized and kissed her hand—"the cheque for a thousand pounds which reached you recently was not too much! Sail for Cairo in the morning. There will certainly be the usual official inquiry. I saw the casket safely on board your boat, and returned to my camp. Transport has been arranged to Alexandria, where my patron has a yacht lying."

"So?" *madame* murmured again, and delicately lighted a fresh cigarette. "Those Arabs are such liars!"

Paul van Kuyper bent forward, resting his manicured hands upon his knees. He had detected a coldness in the attitude of the beautiful woman. Always she was difficult, but today she was incomprehensible.

"Your meaning, *madame*?" he asked, and sued the glance of the amber eyes, but was foiled by lashes imperiously drooped.

"My meaning?" she returned. "It is so simple! What is this casket which you say you placed in my boat? And why do you refer so strangely to a cheque paid to me for a card debt?"

Van Kuyper came to his feet as if shot out of a trap. Every vestige of colour had fled from his flabby cheeks. A small table, with the coffee cups upon it, crashed over upon the carpet. He sought to speak, but she forestalled him.

"Your incorruptible Abdul is probably on his way to Persia," she said scornfully. "Why do you try to weave romances for *me*? You seem to suggest that I am here as your ally in some scheme to smuggle relics out of Egypt. I have a most damaging letter from you touching this plot!"

"By God!" Van Kuyper burst out hoarsely. "The police shall search this boat from stem to stem!"

"They will find your correspondence, my friend!" said Mme. de Medicis, and rose, queenly, sweeping the speaker with a glance of high disdain.

In the long, low cabin of the dahabeah *Nitocris*, Mme. de Medicis reclined upon a divan, its mattress gay with many silken cushions. Her flawless figure was draped wondrously in a robe conceived in Deccan gauzes. A cloud of delicate green caressed the pure modelling of her form, which shimmered alluringly as through the phantom haze of a Fayum sunset quickened to greater tenderness by an ultimate veil like the blush in the heart of a tulip. Keats's *Lamia* was not more magically lovely. The long, amber eyes were soft as enchanted lagoons; the shadows of the curved lashes rested upon flower-fresh cheeks.

Silver incense burners filled the air with the sensuous perfume of ambergris.

Brian Desmond entered, peering eagerly into the shadows cast by dim mosque lanterns swung from the ceiling. A casket of ebony and ivory, wrought with ancient Egyptian astronomical subjects, stood in the centre of the apartment. Beside it, heaped upon the carpet, lay ornaments richly chased and inlaid with strange gems.

"The ritual jewels!" he whispered. "The treasure of Princess Taia!"

"'Such things belong neither to the Egyptian government nor to any purse-proud collector,'" she whispered. The words were his own. "They belong to you!"

From the deck above to that perfumed cabin below stole the sound of a softly beaten *darabukkeh* and the mournful sweetness of a reed pipe. The tender-voiced singer of ghazals began, so softly that the music seemed indeed a ravishing sigh, to render the love plaint of Hafiz.

"If a cup of wine is spilled, and I have spilled it, what of that?"

CRIME TAKES A CRUISE

There was no one in sight in the narrow street. Nothing stirred its shadows; black shadows in contrast with blazing sunlight which touched the gallery of a tumbledown minaret rising above the squalor.

"Blessing and peace… O, Apostle of God."

A *mueddin* had just come out onto the gallery, chanting the *selam* as his kind have done on every Friday of the week for generations. It was half an hour before noon.

Blessing and peace! Shaun Bantry smiled a wry smile. To call for blessing and peace in a world which ignored blessings and had forgotten what peace meant rang the wrong bell. He paused at the door of the mosque, a modern, shabby, neglected, little place, and looked in. A very old beggar, blind in one eye, was entering. Otherwise, inhabitants of this quarter of Port Said remained undisturbed by the call of the Prophet.

What had become of the man wearing that unusual white coat with the faint pink stripe? Definitely, his car, an antique French sedan, had come this way. He pushed on, trying to ignore the mingled smells from the gutters.

Perhaps the description of Theo Leidler's attire which he had received from the porter at the Eastern Exchange Hotel that morning had been wrong. In chasing the man in a pink-striped coat he might be chasing a myth. In that one glimpse of him in the car Shaun hadn't had a chance to see his features.

He was wasting precious time. Ten minutes had elapsed since he lost sight of his quarry. A turning just beyond the mosque showed him an even narrower and, if possible, dirtier street. A little way along he saw two or three tables outside a native café. And in front of the tables, so as to fill up the rest of the thoroughfare, a grey sedan waited!

Shaun became aware that he was excited.

He might not fall down on this fantastic assignment after all! Luck was with him.

He had come to within ten paces of the café when a man wearing a white pink-striped coat came out, jumped into the sedan, and was driven away in the opposite direction.

Pursuit was out of the question. Shaun couldn't hope to pick up a taxi in the native quarter of Port Said. But this time he had seen the man's face——and it was the face of Theo Leidler, memorised from many photographs and detailed descriptions. This obscure café might give him the very link he was looking for. He went in.

The place was so dark that at first he could see less than nothing. The air had been poisoned with fumes of coffee, tobacco smoke, garlic and hot oil. As Shaun's eyes became used to the darkness, he saw that dilapidated couches lined two walls, small tables set before them. There were only five or six customers—obviously shopkeepers. He dropped down near one of them who sat alone.

A Nubian boy materialised out of deeper shadows. Shaun ordered coffee, in his fluent Arabic, and as the boy went away, lighted a cigarette and took a look round.

What business had Theo Leidler here?

He glanced at the man beside him, a man subtly different from the others, although he, too, probably had a shop somewhere. Grey-bearded, wearing a green turban cloth wrapped around his fez, he had the features of a bird of prey. Beard clutched in his hands, elbows propped on the low table, he sat staring straight before him.

Shaun looked down at his own table. The boy hadn't troubled to move a tray on which were a brass coffee pot and a china cup in a brass holder. Some sticky native coffee remained in the cup, and on the tray he saw the stub of an out-sized cigarette with a rose-petal tip. The brand was new to him.

The boy brought Shaun a similar tray and removed the dirty one. Shaun filled the tiny cup and turned to his neighbour.

"Good morning, *hadj*." He gave the Arab greeting, raising his cup. There was no reply, no faintest stirring. The vulture face remained immobile as a face carved in stone.

A surly old brute, apparently. Shaun, with his cast of features, deep tan, and ability to speak first-class Arabic, was used, when it suited him to pass for a true believer. What had he done wrong? His greeting had been correct, and he had kept his hat on.

Perhaps the *hadj* was deaf.

Shaun looked down at a glass which stood before the descendant of the Prophet. It was half filled with a colourless liquid which he suspected to be *râki*, a drink hard enough to knock out a strong man in one round. No fanatical Moslem, this! The fact encouraged him. Taking a fresh cigarette, he pretended to have trouble with his lighter, then turned to his silent neighbour.

"May I ask you for a light, O *hadji?*" He still spoke in Arabic.

There was no reply, no movement.

Shaun replaced the cigarette in his case and glanced swiftly around. No one (or no one visible) was paying any attention to him. Bending forward and sideways, as if in earnest conversation, he peered into the set face. Lightly, he touched the fingers clutching the grey beard, and then Shaun caught his breath.

In moments of climax Shaun's brain became icily cold—probably the reason why he was still alive. What he had to do now was to get out fast. He drank the coffee and clapped his hands.

When the Nubian boy materialized again out of the shadows, Shaun paid and stood up. As he turned away he bowed to his hawk-faced neighbour and, as if responding to a parting word, "Good day, *hadj,*" he said. "Peace be with you." Then Shaun raised his hand to his forehead and went out.

He walked swiftly until he came to the street of the tumble-down mosque, and only then allowed his pace to slacken.

He was doing some hard thinking. Now that he had got clear of the café and clear of clumsy native police inquiries he could act. The *hadj* must be identified. The link with Theo Leidler must be looked for.

And Leidler himself? Had Shaun stumbled by chance on the climax of his intrigue?

Evidence to break up a gang that had defied the European police and the US Secret Service for three years now seemed to lie within his grasp It was definitely known that Nazi loot of incalculable value had been passed from Paris to Istanbul and on into Egypt. In Egypt Theo Leidler had been waiting to take it over.

Why had Leidler gone to this café? Whom had he gone to meet? Shaun knew instinctively that it must have been the *hadj*.

Because the bearded *hadj* who had sat beside Shaun, chin in hands, elbows propped on the table… was *dead*!

* * *

Maureen Lonergan waved her hand at the group on the deck and walked down the gang plank. It wasn't that she disliked Mrs Simmonds and Shelley Downing but that she was rather sick of always being expected to go where the other *Antonia* passengers went.

"We're having early lunch at some casino on the beach," Shelley called after her. "It was up on the board this morning. See you there. Don't forget we sail at two."

Maureen had saved up hard so that she could take this Mediterranean cruise and she meant to enjoy every minute of it in her own way. The set excursions to "sights" and to night spots bored her. The Old World fascinated Maureen. She wanted to enter for awhile the real ways of its people, to see at close quarters the things she had read about.

The purser, who knew all about Maureen's passion for solitary exploring (she had been lost for three hours in the Muski while the passengers were "doing" Cairo), had advised her to complete her shopping in Port Said at Simon Arzt's. There, he assured her, she could buy anything from a pair of elephant's tusks to a packet of hairpins.

"Port Said isn't what it was under British rule," he warned her. "It's had a relapse."

Maureen had heard from a friend about a wonderful shop called Suleyman's. He had described it and where it was situated. "But don't go there alone," he had warned. "It's right in the old Arab quarter."

All the same, Maureen had made up her mind to go. It was silly to be afraid in broad daylight. But either the directions had been foggy or she had forgotten them, and apparently Suleyman was a common name in Port Said. When having wandered about for the best part of half an hour, she found herself lost on a chessboard of narrow native streets with no white face in sight, she had a sudden attack of nerves. Perhaps she had been crazy, after all, to wander into the Arab quarter by herself. And she hadn't the faintest idea of the way back!

Taxis there were none, but starved-looking mongrel dogs ferreted in the gutters and there were millions of flies. Although the sky was a dazzling blue, these streets were filled with mysterious shadows.

Oily-faced traders seated in cavernous shops leered at her openly. One, a fat, sinister jeweller, tried to force her inside. His touch made Maureen shudder.

She almost ran toward the open door of a little mosque and was turning in when a good-looking Arab boy appeared mysteriously beside her.

"Lady not to be afraid. My name Ali Mahmoud. Lady want to buy scarab ring? Very old, very cheap."

Maureen hesitated, looking anxiously into the Arab boy's face, then back at the fat jeweller who stood in the street watching them. She was desperately tempted to ask the boy to lead her to the ship, but stubbornly determined not be frightened.

"I want to go to a shop called Suleyman's. It has a brass lamp in front of it. If you can take me there I'll give you a dollar."

"Hadji Suleyman? I go. *American* dollar?"

"Yes, an American dollar."

"My lady will please to come this way."

Maureen was still doubtful but almost mechanically, she followed Ali Mahmoud. Five minutes later, to her intense relief, she found herself in front of Suleyman's shop. She sighed gratefully, handed the boy his promised dollar, and "If you can find me a taxi," she said, "I'll give you another."

"Taxicab, my lady? I go. Give me dollar now—or taximan won't come. You wait in shop."

Maureen gave him another dollar.

"Don't be long," she said.

She went into the shop, composure quite restored. And Suleyman's proved to be even more fascinating than described. The place was a mere hole in the wall, but the interior concealed an Ali Baba's cave, except that its treasures were tinsel. Maureen saw statuettes of Nile gods, scarab rings and necklaces. Bedawi slippers cunningly embroidered, and boxes filled with most unusual dress jewellery.

A wrinkled old woman who wore what looked like a brass anchor chain around her neck sat in an armchair. Her heavy-lidded eyes scarcely moved as Maureen came in. There was a smell of sandalwood.

Maureen took out a piece of green dress material and a pair of earrings she had bought at Simon Arzt's. The match was not a good one but it was the best she had been able to manage.

"Have you some beads anything like this?"

The old woman waved a hand covered in rings.

"All beads in that box."

Maureen began to inspect a most astonishing collection of bead and glass necklaces which lay in a cardboard box. They ranged from Egyptian enamel to gaudy paste diamonds. The light was poor, but she found one at last which, although altogether too gaudy, seemed more nearly to match the earrings than anything so far discovered.

"How much is this one, please?"

"Can sell nothing. Must wait till my husband come back."

"Oh! But I haven't time! The ship sails at two!"

Drooping lids were half raised. Maureen was inspected from head to foot by a pair of lancet-keen eyes.

"You pay American money?"

"Yes, if you like." Maureen had found out that dollar bills were talismans in Port Said. "How much is it?" she added.

The old woman shrugged so that her brass chain rattled.

"My husband go out. I never serve in here. I don't know price. Ten dollar?"

"Ten dollars! Good heavens! I couldn't think of it!"

"Five."

Maureen judged that the thing was probably worth fifty cents; but it seemed unlikely that she would find another before the ship sailed. Silently, she handed a five-dollar bill to the woman, the necklace was packed into a parcel, and Maureen went out.

There was no sign of Ali Mahmoud. But a man hurrying into Suleyman's as Maureen came out almost knocked her over. "Please forgive me," he murmured in a slightly accented voice.

Maureen met the glance of dark, ardent eyes and forced a smile. The man was not bad looking in a way, but it was a vaguely unpleasant way. And Maureen definitely didn't like his white coat with a pink stripe.

His glance lingered on her for only a moment. He seemed to be intensely pre-occupied, and with a quick "Forgive me," he hurried into the shop Maureen had just left.

With a little shrug at his abruptness, Maureen started back along the street in the direction from which she had come with Ali Mahmoud...

Shaun also was striding along, his thoughts racing. The *hadj's* death might be a natural death: some swift lesion of heart. But in his own heart Shaun knew it was murder: some deadly poison added to the *râki*, and equally swift in its action. He must get to the US Consulate on the waterfront. He must get to a safe phone.

He swung sharply to the right, down a street that was monotonously like all the others—native stores, bric-a-brac dealers. Before one shop hung a brass mosque lamp and the sign "Hadji Suleyman". He hurried on to the next corner.

A girl stood there, petite, slender, looking right and left in a rather bewildered way. He saw her fumble in a satchel swung from her shoulder, and he saw a small parcel drop as she did so.

Shaun was only two paces behind her. He checked his stride, picked up the parcel and stepped forward.

"You're losing your property, I'm afraid!"

"Oh, thank you!" Maureen turned swiftly. She met the glance of smiling grey eyes, saw a dark, sun-tanned face with clean-cut features, a man who wore a smart drill suit, who looked civilised.

Her eyes searched the smiling face.

"Heaven be praised, you're an American," Maureen murmured. "You see, I'm lost! I was trying to find the address of some beach place I'm to go for lunch."

Shaun was looking at a fresh-faced girl with frank blue eyes of the kind which in Ireland they say are put in with smutty fingers. A piquant face. She wore a white frock which left her arms bare, and a big sun-hat with a green veil.

"Are you with the Cunard cruise?"

"That's right."

"Then I expect lunch will be at the Casino. If we can find a taxi, the Consulate is right on the way. You can drop me off."

"But where do we find a taxi?"

"That's the problem!" Shaun grinned. "Mine as well as yours. Come on."

He took her arm, and Maureen found herself being hurried headlong forward by this attractive stranger.

"My name's Shaun Bantry," he volunteered, as they raced along.

"Maureen Lonergan!" She was breathless.

"Good Irish names." They came out onto Sharie el-Gâmi. "And our luck's in. Here's a taxi!"

Shaun held the door for Maureen, jumped in beside her and gave rapid orders in Arabic to the driver.

She looked aside at him, wondering why all the wrong men came on cruises. Shaun, considering Maureen as the taxi got under way, was wondering why most of the girls with whom his wandering life brought him in touch were so unlike Maureen. She had astonishingly long lashes, and her wavy chestnut hair under the white hat gleamed delightfully. As they talked, and his glance followed those exciting waves, out of the tail of his right eye he saw a grey sedan following the taxi.

Theo Leidler, dark eyes intent, was seated beside an Egyptian driver who wore a fez!

Shaun swore silently. He had slipped up somewhere. Leidler's suspicions were aroused. Or else—someone had given him away. Otherwise, why should Leidler follow him?

"There's a change of plan." Shaun spoke so sharply that Maureen was startled. "I'm going to drop you first, and take the taxi on…"

When she said goodbye to Shaun, Maureen found a strong contingent from the *Antonia* already halfway through lunch under the palm trees of the Casino. Shelley Downing, the queen of the cruise, was surrounded by her usual court. Mrs Simmonds near by, was lunching with other members of the cruise, and she invited Maureen to join them. When Maureen had begun her lunch: "How did you get on with your shopping, Maureen?" she inquired.

"I think I got everything," Maureen said. "Nothing really matches, of course!" Maureen took out a list and checked the items. "Green dye for white stockings. Wrong shade. Beads, earrings. Awful! But they won't look bad at night. Shoes!" A frown appeared between her level brows. "I've forgotten the shoes!"

Maureen considered the problem with all the seriousness which it called for. Her glance strayed vaguely from the group, and presently paused. She had seen a white coat with a pink stripe—and the man who wore it sat alone at the very next table!

Their glances met. He smiled and bowed slightly, and then turned away, but Maureen had the uncomfortable feeling that his attention was still fixed on her. For some unaccountable reason, she was suddenly frightened. Perhaps there was nothing in it. But it seemed queer to meet the man again here. Then she squared her shoulders and looked at her watch. Her mind was made up.

"Just time to get to Simon Arzt's. I'll skip lunch." She pushed her chair back. "They are sure to have something there." She stood up impetuously and hurried out to find a taxi, an easier matter at the Casino.

It was only moments later when the dark man put some money on a plate where a bill lay and unobtrusively followed...

When Maureen hurried into the big store her watch told her that she had less than twenty-five minutes to spare before the *Antonia* was due to sail. It was all very well to live dangerously, Maureen thought, but she mustn't miss the ship.

She ran along to the shoe department and once more pulled out the fragment of green material. A young Indian gentleman, with excellent manners and a leisurely style of speech which nearly drove her crazy, examined the sample for a long time.

"It is an unusual shade, madame." He sighed.

"Just bring me a lot of green, shoes. Size five. I must do the best I can."

"Yes, madame."

He walked away. His carriage was graceful and slow. Maureen saw him pause to discuss something with another customer, and when this conversation ended, he disappeared completely. Maureen, constantly looking at her watch, checked the passing seconds. The polite Indian had not returned when a sound dimly reached her ears. It was the deep warning note of the *Antonia's* whistle. She had just fifteen minutes to make the ship!

She was halfway to the door when the graceful salesman overtook her.

"Madame!" He dropped a litter of boxes at her feet. "There is plenty of time. Always American ladies are in such a hurry. Now, you see—" he opened a box—"these shoes, madame—"

"Are they my size?"

"But, yes, madame."

"They'll do!" Maureen fumbled frantically in her satchel. "The price, please?"

Maureen thrust several dollar bills into his hand, grabbed the box and ran.

Out on the street she stood still for a moment, trying to get her bearings. No taxi was in sight.

Panic threatened, but Maureen conquered it.

She had come straight from the ship to Simon Arzt's and she *must* remember the way... Of course! It suddenly came back to her!

Looking all the time for a taxi, she set out, almost running. Would they delay sailing if she hadn't come on board?

Whatever would happen to her if she got left behind in Port Said?

* * *

When he dropped Maureen at the Casino, Shaun had found himself badly puzzled to learn that Theo Leidler's grey sedan was no longer following. It seemed as if his theory that Leidler had identified him must be wrong.

But if Leidler wasn't tailing *him*, who *was* he tailing?

Shaun drove straight to the US Consulate. There was much to do, and little time to do it.

First, he called the chief of police, to tell him that a dead man was sitting in a certain café in the Arab quarter—unless someone had jogged his elbow, in which case he would be lying on the floor.

The first ship scheduled to leave Port Said that day was the *Antonia* at two o'clock; so Shaun's next call was to Cook's who were managing the cruise.

What he learned there convinced him that his time was even more limited than he had supposed.

Theo Leidler had just booked a passage on the *Antonia*!

"Hold one for me!" He hung up.

Shaun glanced at his watch. He couldn't hope to get to the café and back.

But there were so many things he must know.

He drove to his hotel, bundled his kit into a bag, paid his bill, and made a dash for the police station.

He spent all of fifteen precious minutes with the chief of police, and then raced to Cook's to pick up his steamer ticket.

His taxi wasn't far from the docks when another car caught his eye. A grey sedan—surely, it was Leidler's—sped past, swerved in, was pulled up with screaming brakes. The Egyptian driver sprang out. This street was nearly deserted. Heavy shadows, cast by a dock building, lay blackly across it. Shaun had a hazy impression of a slight figure, running.

Then, that flying shape and Egyptian as well were hidden from him by the sedan.

"Stop!"

But Shaun was out on the running-board before his taximan had tune to obey the order. He jumped, took one swift look, and hurled himself forward.

The Egyptian was dragging the girl into the sedan!

The hoarse warning of the *Antonia*'s fog whistle blared deafeningly.

Shaun saw that the Egyptian driver had one arm around his struggling captive and a hand pressed over her mouth. He nearly had her into the sedan when Shaun's kick, calculated to thrust his backbone through his scalp, sent the man reeling to the ground. The girl slumped dizzily onto the car step. Shaun caught her. *"Maureen"* he said tensely.

She didn't reply. Her eyes were closed, the lashes looking preposterously long as they drooped on her cheeks.

The *Antonia's* whistle roared a final warning as Shaun stooped and lifted Maureen. She was light as a child as he carried her to the taxi. "Right onto the dock," he told the man. "Drive like blazes…"

On board the *Antonia* the third officer came up to Lorkin, the purser, who stood at the head of the gangway. "Captain's compliments." He winked an ironic wink. "He wants to know if you've got all your sheep in their pens."

"Damn it, no! No! What d'you suppose I am standing here for?" Lorkin was in a very bad humour. "Two new passengers wished onto me by Cook's at the last minute—not arrived. And my pet headache—Miss Maureen Lonergan."

"Very attractive," the third murmured. "But the pilot's getting fussy."

"Tell him to jump in the ditch! My compliments to the captain—and I'm three passengers short."

On the deck above, rails were crowded. A rumour had spread that somebody was missing. This rumour gained strength when yet another deafening bellow came from the great ship's whistle. Shelley Downing, always in the know, ran up to Mrs Simmonds. "It's Maureen who's missing," she said, "and Maureen was lunching with *you*!"

Mrs Simmonds turned an anxious face.

"I know she was. But she rushed off at the last minute to Simon Arzt's. Are you sure it's Maureen?"

"I just had the news—official!" Shelley nodded, and ran off, birdlike, to exploit her information. Mrs Simmonds turned again to the rail. A sudden commotion arose. A girl was being supported to the gangway by a man in a drill suit! She seemed to be ill. A boy followed on, carrying a leather grip. As they climbed up slowly to the deck Shelley cried shrilly, "It's Maureen!" and rushed to greet her.

A husky roar through a megaphone came from the bridge: "Strike that gangway!"

"Strike that gangway!" a voice echoed from the dockside.

The heavy gangway had begun to swing clear, when a man came running. Two Arabs ran sweating behind him shouldering baggage.

"Hold it!" the dockside voice commanded.

Down came the gangway—and up climbed the belated passenger who wore a white coat, with a faint pink stripe. The Arab boys dropped their loads on the deck and raced down again to shore. "Strike that blasted gangway!" This final order from the bridge threatened to split the megaphone.

The gangway was swung clear of the ship.

Captain William McAndrew, RNUR, DSO, loved discipline and hated cruises…

* * *

"You're quite sure you feel all right?"

Maureen, lying on a bed in the surgery, looked up into Shaun Bantry's worried face with a sort of wonder. She had never expected to see him again.

"Quite sure."

"But a lucky escape," the ship's doctor declared. "And a most mysterious outrage."

"I couldn't agree with you more." Shaun stared at the doctor. "An attempt at abduction in broad daylight! What was the stuff on the sponge?"

"Ethyl chloride. No bad after effects."

"They gave it to me when I had my operation for tonsils." Maureen spoke in a low voice. "That was years back but I remember the smell." She sat up on the bed, smoothing her disordered hair. "You've been very kind, Mr Bantry. First you picked up my silly beads, and then you saved me from that awful man, and—" she forced a smile—"this time I have really taken you out of your way!"

"Not a bit of it! I booked a passage at Cook's half an hour ago!"

He grinned cheerfully, waved his hand and walked out of the surgery, leaving Maureen to think about the look in his eyes and to wonder if it could be possible that he had joined the *Antonia* just because... But, no! That idea was plain silly—stupid vanity.

Shaun, unpacking the one grip with which he had travelled from Paris to Istanbul, Istanbul to Cairo and Cairo to Port Said, was thinking he was lucky to have got a comfortable outside room at such short notice, and asking himself how long he was likely to occupy it. His job demanded swift decisions. The fact that Maureen was a passenger on the *Antonia* had helped him to make this one.

It seemed oddly like fate. He wondered if at last he had met the right woman. Certainly, that flushed piquant face all too often got between him and his job. But the job was what mattered first, and Shaun confessed himself to be the most hopelessly mystified man at that hour afloat on the Mediterranean. Why had Theo Leidler booked passage on the *Antonia*?

And was he really aboard? It was Leidler's driver who had attacked Maureen. Perhaps Leidler had made a last-minute change of plan or waited so long that he missed the ship. If that had happened, Shaun would feel like a hundred per cent, pure idiot. In the excitement of getting Maureen safely aboard, he would have let his quarry slip. He hadn't even the vaguest idea of the ship's next port of call.

Striding swiftly, he went up on deck.

Cruise passengers were crowding aft for a last glimpse of Port Said. Shaun attracted a lot of attention. He had been pointed out by Shelley Downing as the man who helped Maureen up the gangway. But he remained completely indifferent to the stares. He was looking for Leidler.

Suddenly he found Maureen, forward on the promenade deck, lying on a long chair. Then, the shock came. Theo Leidler sat very close to her, deep in earnest conversation.

Maureen looked up, beckoned eagerly, and Shaun, trying to show no sign of the utter bewilderment he felt, joined them.

She raised her glance to Leidler. "This is Mr Shaun Bantry."

Leidler showed two rows of perfect teeth. The effort could not be called a smile. He had changed into a smart white linen suit. Shaun noted that his perfectly waved hair was almost blue-black.

"I'm delighted to meet you, Mr Leidler."

"Won't you sit down? The next chair belongs to Mrs Simmonds. She won't mind." Shaun sat down. "I was just telling Mr Leidler about what happened to me this morning."

Shaun glanced across at Leidler. The situation demanded tact. "Queer affair, wasn't it?" He met the gaze of illegible dark eyes. "Even in Port Said today such an outrage is unusual, wouldn't you say?"

"More than unusual!" Theo Leidler had a slight accent: he was believed to be Romanian. "I can only suppose that Miss Lonergan had attracted the attention of some wealthy Egyptian connoisseur. It was *most* fortunate that someone was near."

"I thought so, too. And your theory is good. Except that old French sedan hardly looked like the property of a pasha."

Leidler shrugged his shoulders.

"You wouldn't expect him to send his own automobile on such a business?"

"No." Shaun looked thoughtful. "I expect it was hired for the purpose. I'm sorry that I hadn't time to call the police."

"Then the man got clear away?" A faint note of eagerness crept into Leidler's voice.

"I'm afraid he did. But I hope I broke his jaw." Shaun took out his cigarette case. "Of course, I could send the police a radio."

"By now it would be useless," Leidler decided. "Nothing could be done about it."

But Shaun was thinking that a lot of things could be done about it, for some of which he had already arranged. One point became clear. Unless Leidler's acting was superlative, he had no suspicions. Quite definitely, he hadn't been tailing Shaun that morning. *Then he must have been following Maureen!*

In the name of sanity, what for? Shaun had no idea how long Leidler had known her, but the "wealthy connoisseur" he had mentioned might be Leidler himself. If the abduction had succeeded, he wouldn't have come on board. Some watcher must have passed the news of its failure to him, wherever he was waiting; and Leidler had rushed to join the ship.

The *Antonia* had followed a lazy course around the Mediterranean and now was heading back to the States. The return run would be along the African coast: next port of call Tunis. Shaun wondered if Leidler might intend to leave the ship there and then decided angrily to abandon conjecture.

All his deductions were being proved wrong. He must get more data, and do some hard thinking. When a radio message was brought to him, he made it an excuse to go. Maureen, left alone with Theo Leidler, gave Shaun an almost pathetic look as he walked away.

Shaun went below and made the acquaintance of Lorkin, the purser. He asked for certain information. Lorkin, who had had a trying morning, was far from amiable. "This is a British ship, you know. I should have to get the Old Man's okay."

Shaun gave Lorkin a cheerful grin. "Old Man in as bad a humour as you are?"

"Worse." Lorkin opened a locker and exposed a row of bottles. "Capitan McAndrew is a martinet. The hitch in Port Said has ruined his day. Scotch or bourbon?"

It was easy after that.

Two more radiograms were brought to Shaun in the purser's room. After he had read them he felt pleased with the work of the Port Said police but more completely fogged than ever about the relationship between Theo Leidler and Maureen. He was inclined to feel unhappy, but didn't blame the purser's whisky.

Lorkin had produced all the information he had on Leidler. The man had crossed twice before in the *Antonia* on her usual run from Southampton to New York. His United States passport described him as a business manager.

He had always come aboard at Cherbourg. "Hell of a lad for the ladies," was Lorkin's only comment.

"He's the hell of a lad altogether," Shaun assured him. "Theo Leidler is the big shot of the most successful gang of loot traffickers operating between Europe and the United States. Before this ship docks in New York I intend to prove it."

Shaun had many things to keep him busy. He positively haunted the radio office, sending and receiving messages. At five o'clock he took a walk around. He discovered Maureen and Mrs Simmonds having tea on deck. Leidler was in attendance.

Shaun joined the party but declined tea.

"Isn't the Mediterranean a simply wonderful blue?" Mrs Simmonds said.

"Yes." Shaun glanced at Maureen, "It's the colour of some Irish eyes."

Maureen began speaking, quickly. "I'm going back to my room after tea, to work until cocktail time. I shan't have my dress ready for St Patrick's night if I don't."

"St Patrick's night? That's tomorrow, isn't it? Some special jamboree?"

"A fancy dress ball." Maureen met Shaun's lingering gaze. "With prizes."

Shaun moved quickly, as Maureen stood up, to help her out of her long chair. Their glances met. "I shall be through by six o'clock." Maureen spoke softly.

"May I call for you?"

She nodded, smiled at Theo Leidler, who was frowning, and hurried away.

Shaun sat down again, but Leidler didn't seem disposed to stay.

He hesitated for a moment, his glance following the slim figure, then bowed in his Continental way to Mrs Simmonds, ignored Shaun, and walked off in the opposite direction.

"You know—" Shaun turned to Mrs Simmonds, "I don't understand that man."

"I don't think I want to!"

"Oh, you feel like that about him? Is he an old friend of Miss Lonergan's?"

"She never saw him until this morning!"

This was what Shaun wanted to know, and he soon knew all that Mrs Simmonds had to tell him: Maureen's first meeting with Theo Leidler outside some shop (she didn't know the name) in the Arab quarter; her second during lunch at the Casino; how, from the moment he came on board Leidler had tried to monopolise her. Shaun felt better about everything as he hurried back to his room.

When Shaun knocked on Maureen's door at six o'clock, she came out at once. She had changed her frock, and, Shaun thought, was a radiant vision. "Your dress looks as though it came from Paris."

Maureen laughed. She was very happy. "It didn't. It came from New York. Oh! We're going the wrong way! The bar's upstairs."

"We're not going to the bar. You don't mind? We've having drinks in the purser's quarters—just you and me, and Mrs Simmonds and Lorkin. Too dull?"

"Oh, no!" When Maureen's eyes were turned to Shaun they seemed to be dancing. "If it isn't too dull for *you*."

"Just thought I'd like you all to myself—if only for a few minutes."

They were outside the purser's door before Maureen spoke again.

"How do you manage these things? You're not a director of the line, are you?"

Shaun smiled holding the curtain aside for Maureen. "Not my kind of luck. But my own kind is pretty good."

Shaun now had all the information he was likely to get from Port Said. All that remained was to pin some evidence of his crimes on Leidler. But how could he be sure Leidler really had such evidence among his belongings?

And where did Maureen come in?

At one time, watching Maureen on deck with Leidler, Shaun asked himself whether it could be possible that this naïve little girl knew more about the matter than she pretended. Mrs Simmonds had seemed to clear her of any past acquaintance with Leidler. Shaun was far too experienced in the Secret Service game to discount other possibilities. He had been fooled before. But somehow this particular two and two didn't seem to make four. Maureen, almost eagerly, had told him all about herself, how hard she had worked and saved up for this cruise. She was a fashion artist and dress designer, and apparently a successful one. The dress she planned to wear on St Patrick's night was of her own designing.

Shaun sauntered up to Maureen and took out his cigarette case. She opened a box which lay beside her. "Won't you try one of these?"

Shaun drew a deep breath. The box was half full of uncommonly long cigarettes, *rose-tipped*. It was the stub of one of these which he had seen on a brassy tray in the Arab café—near the dead man!

"Highly exotic! Where did you get them?"

"They come from Istanbul. Mr Leidler insisted on presenting me with a dozen boxes…"

* * *

For St Patrick's night a space had been cleared for dancing in the *Antonia's* dining room. Green candles decorated the tables and on each were bunches of shamrock especially shipped from Ireland. Weather was ideal, the Mediterranean like a lake.

Shaun, looking clean-cut and bronzed in his white tuxedo, sat watching the fancy dresses as singly and in pairs the passengers came in to dinner. Some won applause; others laughs. Most of the dresses were of the stock variety and only a few of the women had made any attempt to rise to the special occasion.

Nothing like enthusiasm was shown until Maureen made a rather timid entrance. She wore a lace frock covered with hand-painted shamrocks, leaving her arms and shoulders bare; green shoes, green silk gloves. Emerald earrings, too large for her small ears, and a blazing green and white necklace, completed the ensemble.

Amid the cries and clapping of hands, Shaun stood silent, staring like a man struck dumb. Maureen, who seemed to be really frightened, cast an anxious glance around. She saw Shaun, smiled more happily, and waved her hand. He waved back and as Maureen went to her table at the other end of the room, sat down with a sudden sickening feeling that he wanted to clutch his head.

Maureen looked unreally lovely—but tonight it wasn't this that had overpowered him. Now he was racked by doubt, mentally lost in a fog of hopeless misunderstanding…

When dancing began, it was a long time before he managed to get Maureen for a partner. Even then, while Leidler danced with Shelley Downing, the dark man's glance followed Maureen ravenously about the room. Shelley had come as a leprechaun. It was plain that she knew nothing of the Irish climate, for she evidently thought leprechauns wore next to no clothes.

"Your friend, Theo," said Shaun, when he and Maureen were alone in the crowd of dancers, "seems to regard you as his private property!"

"Yes. He's getting to be a real nuisance." Maureen changed this subject quickly. "Do you think I deserve the first prize? Mr Lorkin says I shall win it."

"You have *my* vote, Maureen. Your dress is a dream. Did you have the earrings and necklace already, or are they those you bought in Port Said?"

"In Port Said I got the earrings at Simon Arzt's, and the shoes. I dyed my own stockings! The necklace I picked up at Suleyman's."

The band stopped, showed signs of resting; but Shaun, into whose mind the name, *Suleyman,* had crashed as a revelation, applauded persistently. Leidler, who had led Shelley back to her table, watched Maureen like a hungry wolf preparing to spring on a gazelle. The band started again. As Shaun and Maureen resumed dancing: "You *did* say Suleyman's, didn't you?" Shaun asked.

"Yes. Hadji Suleyman's. Do you know it? I'd just come from there when—I met you. It was the necklace you picked up!"

And then, while relief flooded through Shaun, Maureen laughingly told him all about the queer old woman who didn't know the price of anything, but all the same had charged her five dollars for a trinket worth fifty cents. "It's so heavy! It's fraying my neck. I'm going to my room in a minute to take it off."

Shaun started to remonstrate but the band stopped just then and they were hemmed in the crowd. "I'll only be a minute," Maureen said, and before Shaun could stop her she was gone.

Back in her cabin, Maureen dropped the heavy necklace on her dresser and paused to adjust her hair and make-up with hasty care. Then she ran out to return to the dance. For a moment she hesitated by a dark alleyway next to her room. She had a sense that someone was standing there in the shadows. Then she hurried on.

Maureen had hardly turned the corner by the purser's office when Shaun stepped out of the shadowy alleyway, glanced swiftly left and right, then opened the door of Maureen's room and glided inside. He reclosed the door. He had had no more time than to take cover when another man came in!

The second visitor wasted not a moment. He scooped up the green necklace, inhaling sharply, moved away, was about to turn, when: "What's the hurry, Leidler?" a casual voice inquired.

In a wing of Maureen's mirror, his own face suddenly blanched under the bronze, Theo Leidler saw Shaun Bantry standing at his elbow, holding an automatic.

"I'm here—" Leidler swallowed audibly—"at Miss Lonergan's request—"

"Sure you are! But at my request you're coming along to see the captain. No! Leave the necklace in your pocket!"

In Captain McAndrew's quarters the story was told, that grim seaman presiding over the meeting. Shaun Bantry had done most of the talking.

"The Egyptian police have recovered an unusual cigarette stub left behind in the café. And they have a glass of *râki* which Hadji Suleyman was drinking. It had enough dope in it to kill ten men!"

Leidler moistened dry lips. "What has this to do with me?"

"Six witnesses have described you—and *I* saw you come out of the café. You may have meant just to send Suleyman to sleep. Instead, you sent him to Paradise! Don't waste your breath to interrupt me. We have the facts in line. I've figured out the set-up at Suleyman's."

Shaun paused to light a cigarette. An armed quarter-master who stood behind Leidler's chair looked hypnotised. Lorkin was studying the captain's angry face.

"When an agent of the gang dumped a valuable piece there,

Suleyman put it in amongst a lot of junk. If there was any trouble he could say he'd bought it for a few *piastres* and didn't know its value. But he was taking big risks. And he wanted a big cut on profits."

"You're talking nonsense!" Leidler broke in hotly.

"Silence!" Captain McAndrew spoke in his bridge voice.

"You met at the café to settle terms. You had found out that Suleyman's wife knew nothing about her husband's underground connections, had no knowledge of precious stones. But *he* had! Having put Suleyman to sleep, you counted on getting this—" he pointed to the necklace lying on the captain's desk—"for the price of a packet of cigarettes. Maybe you were desperate. It might have been your last deal. I'm just guessing. In any case, it is your last deal, Leidler."

Leidler's eyes darted furtively around the room, seeking a means of escape. Then, seeing the hopelessness of his situation, he shrugged his shoulders in an elegant gesture.

"Well...well," boomed Captain McAndrew. "Have you anything to say for yourself, man?"

Leidler smiled thinly. "In moments of this sort," he said, "I find it better to keep my own counsel."

The Captain stirred impatiently. "As you wish." He nodded to the quartermaster. 'Take the prisoner below. Mr Bantry, congratulations on a fine piece of work."

Now it was Shaun's turn to smile. "I've been waiting a long time to play out this little scene, sir," he said, softly. "Now I feel at sort of a loose end."

It was very late when Shaun leaned on the rail beside Maureen looking out across a dark Mediterranean. The band had packed up.

St Patrick's night was over, dawn not far away. "What's that light, Shaun, over there? Not on the African side."

"Malta."

They were silent for a while. Shaun's hand lay over Maureen's on the rail.

"Shaun, will you tell me something—now?" Her voice was barely audible above the lullaby of the sea as it swept the bows of the big ship.

"Anything."

"What really happened tonight?" She turned to him and her eyes were bright in the dim lights along the deck. "And why was my necklace stolen from my room? It only cost me five dollars!"

Shaun put his arm around her shoulders. "Five dollars was what it cost *you*, Maureen. But that necklace has been valued at two hundred and fifty thousand!"

"Shaun!"

He smiled down at her. "The emeralds alone are worth a fortune, without the diamonds. It's the famous necklace which Catherine II of Russia presented to Marie Antoinette."

She was silent a moment, shivering a little till his arm tightened around her and she was drawn against him. Her eyes were lifted, and now there was laughter behind their serious depths. "And that's what you were after all the time?" she asked.

"All the time," he agreed, solemnly.

"And nothing else?"

"Darling!" was what Shaun said.

A HOUSE POSSESSED

I strode briskly up the long beech avenue. The snow that later was to carpet the drive, and to clothe the limbs of the great trees, now hung suspended in dull grey cloud banks over Devrers Hall. Thus I first set eyes upon the place.

W. Earl Ryland had seen it from the car when motoring to Stratford, had delayed one hour and twenty-five minutes to secure the keys and look over the house, and had leased it for three years. That had been two days ago. Now, as I passed the rusty, iron gates and walked up the broad stairs of the terrace to the front door, the clatter of buckets and a swish of brushes told me that the workmen were busy within. It is, after all, a privilege to be the son of a Wall Street hustler.

Faithful to my promise, I inspected the progress made by the decorating contractor, and proceeded to look over the magnificent old mansion. Principally, I believe, it was from designs by Vanbrugh. The banqueting hall impressed me particularly with its fretwork ceiling, elaborate mouldings, and its large, stone-mullioned windows with many-hued, quarrel-pane lattices.

I had this wing of the building quite to myself, and passing through into what may have been a library, I saw at the farther end a low, arched door in the wall. It was open, and a dim light showed beyond. I approached it, passed down six stone steps and found myself in a small room, evidently of much earlier date than the rest of the house.

It had an elaborately carved chimney piece reaching to the ceiling, and the panelling was covered with extraordinary designs. One small window lighted the room. Before the window, his back towards me, stood a cowled monk!

At my gasp of mingled fear and surprise, he turned a red, bearded face to me. To my great amazement, I saw that the mysterious intruder was smoking a well-coloured briar!

"Did I frighten you?" he inquired, with a strong Irish brogue. "I'm sorry! But it's years since I saw over Devrers, and so I ventured to trespass. I'm Father Bernard from the monastery yonder. Are you Mr Ryland?"

I gasped again, but with relief. Father Bernard, broad-shouldered and substantial, puffing away at his briar, was no phantom after all, but a very genial mortal.

"No," I replied. "He will be down later. I am known as Cumberly."

He shook my hand very heartily; he seemed on the point of speaking again, yet hesitated.

"What a grand old place it is," I continued. "This room surely, is older than the rest?"

"It is part of the older mansion," he replied, "Devereaux Hall. Devrers is a corruption."

"Devereaux Hall," I said. "Did it belong to that family?"

Father Bernard nodded.

"Robert Devereaux, Earl of Essex, owned it. There's his crest over the door. He never lived here himself, but if you can make out medieval Latin, this inscription here will tell you who did."

He watched me curiously while I struggled with the crabbed characters:

"Here by grace of his noble patron, Robert Devereaux, my lord of Essex," I read, "laboured Maccabees Nosta of Padua, a pupil of Michel de Notredame, seeking the light."

"Nosta was a Jewish astrologer and magician," explained the monk, "and according to his own account, as you see, a pupil of the notorious Michel de Notredame, or Nostradamus. He lived here under the patronage of the Earl until 1601, when Essex was executed. Legend says that he was not the pupil of Nostradamus, but his master the devil, and that he brought about the fall of his patron. What became of Nosta of Padua nobody knows."

He paused, watching me with something furtive in his blue eyes.

"I'm a regular guidebook, you're thinking?" he went on. "Well, so I am. We have it all in the old records at the monastery. A Spanish family acquired the place after the death of Robert Devereaux—the Miguels, they called themselves. They were shunned by the whole country; and it's recorded that they held Black Masses and Devil's Sabbaths here in this very room!"

"Good heavens!" I cried. "The house has an unpleasant history!"

"The last of them was burned for witchcraft in the marketplace at Ashby, as late as 1640!"

I suppose I looked as uncomfortable as I felt, glancing apprehensively about the gloomy apartment.

"When Devereaux, or Devrers, Hall was pulled down and rebuilt, this part was spared for some mysterious reason. But let me tell you that from 1640 till 1863—when a Mr Nicholson leased it—nobody has been able to live here!"

"What do you mean? Ghosts?"

"No, fires!"

"Fires!"

"That same! If you'll examine the rooms closely, you'll find that some of them have been rebuilt and some partially rebuilt, at dates long after Vanbrugh's day. It's where the fires have been! Seven poor souls have burned to death in Devrers since the Miguels' time, but the fires never spread beyond the rooms they broke out in!"

"Father Bernard," I said, "tell me no more at present! This is horrible! Some of the best friends I have are coming to spend Christmas here!"

"I'd have warned Mr Ryland if he'd given me time," continued the monk. "But it's likely he'd have laughed at me for my pains! All you can do now, Mr Cumberly, is to say nothing about it until after Christmas. Then induce him to leave. I'm not a narrow-minded man, and I'm not a superstitious one, I think, but if facts are facts, Devrers Hall is *possessed*!"

The party that came together that Christmas at Devrers Hall was quite the most ideal that one could have wished for or imagined. There was no smartset boredom, for Earl's friends were not smart set bores. Old and young there were, and children too. What Christmas gathering is complete without children?

Mr Ryland, Sr, and Mrs Ryland were over from New York, and the hard-headed man of affairs proved the most charming old gentleman one could have desired at a Christmas party. A Harvard friend of Earl's, the Rev. Lister Hanson, Mrs Hanson, Earl's sister, and two young Hansons were there. They, with Mrs Van Eyck, a pretty woman of thirty whose husband was never seen in her company, completed the American contingent.

But Earl had no lack of English friends, and these, to the round number of twenty, assisted at the Christmas housewarming.

On the evening of the twenty-third of December, as I entered the old banqueting hall bright with a thousand candles, the warm light from the flaming logs danced upon the oak leaves, emblems of hospitality which ornamented the frieze. Searching out strange heraldic devices upon the time-blackened panelling, I stood in the open door in real admiration.

A huge Christmas tree occupied one corner by the musicians' gallery, and around this a group of youngsters had congregated, looking up in keen anticipation at the novel gifts which swung from the frosted branches. Mr Ryland, Sr, his wife and another grey-haired lady, with Father Bernard from the monastery, sat upon the black oak settles by the fire; they were an oddly assorted, but merry group. In short, the interior of the old hall made up a picture that would have delighted the soul of Charles Dickens.

"It's just perfect, Earl!" came Hanson's voice.

I turned, and saw that he and Earl Ryland stood at my elbow.

"It will be, when Mona comes!" was the reply.

"What has delayed Miss Verek?" I asked. Earl's fiancée, Mona Verek, and her mother were to have joined us that afternoon.

"I can't quite make out from her wire," he answered quietly, a puzzled frown ruffling his forehead. "But she will be here by tomorrow, Christmas Eve."

Hanson clapped him on the back and smiled. "Bear up, Earl," he said. "Hello! Here comes Father Bernard, and he's been yarning again. Just look how your governor is laughing."

Earl turned, as with a bold gait the priest came towards them, his face radiating with smiles, his eyes alight with amusement. It was certainly a hilarious group the monk had left behind him. As he joined us, he linked his arm in that of the American clergyman and drew him aside for a private chat, I thought what a broad-minded company we were. When the two, in intimate conversation, walked off together, they formed one of the most pleasant pictures imaginable. The true spirit of Christmas reigned.

I passed to an oak settee where Justin Grinley, his wife and small daughter were pulling crackers with Mrs Hanson, just as young Lawrence Bowman appeared from a side door.

"Have you seen Mrs Van Eyck?" he inquired quickly.

No one had seen her for some time, and young Bowman hurried off upon his quest.

Grinley raised quizzical eyebrows, but said nothing. In point of fact, Bowman's attentions to the lady had already excited some comment; but Mrs Van Eyck was an old friend of the Rylands, and we relied upon her discretion to find a nice girl among the company—there were many—to take the romantic youth off her hands.

Father Bernard presently beckoned to me from the door beneath the musicians' gallery.

"You have, of course, said nothing of the matters we know of?" he asked as I joined him.

I shook my head, and the monk smiled around on the gathering.

"The old sorcerer's study is fitted up as a cozy corner, I see," he continued, "but between ourselves, I shouldn't let any of the young people stay long in there!" He met my eyes seriously.

"If, indeed, the enemy holds power within Devrers, I think there is no likely victim among you tonight. The legend of Devrers Hall, you must know, Mr Cumberly, is that Maccabees Nosta, or the arch enemy in person, appears here in response to the slightest evil thought, word or deed within the walls! If any company could hope to exclude him, it is the present!" This he said half humorously and with his eyes roaming again over the merry groups about the great lighted room. "But, please God, the evil has passed."

He was about to take his leave, for he came and went at will, a privileged visitor, as others of the Brotherhood. I walked with him along the gallery, lined now with pictures from Earl Ryland's collection. One of the mullioned windows was open.

Out of the darkness we looked for a moment over the dazzling white carpet which lay upon the lawn, to where a fairy shrubbery, backed by magical, white trees, glittered as though diamond-dusted under the frosty moon. A murmur of voices came, and two figures passed across the snow: a woman in a dull red cloak with a furred collar and a man with a heavy travelling coat worn over his dress clothes. His arm was about the woman's waist.

The monk made no sign, leaving me at the gallery door with a deep "Good night."

But I saw his cowled figure silhouetted against a distant window, and his hand was raised in the ancient form of benediction.

Alone in the long gallery, something of the gaiety left me. By the open window, I stood for a moment looking out, but no one was visible now. The indiscreet dalliance of Mrs Van Eyck with a lad newly down from Cambridge seemed so utterly out of the picture. The lawn on that side of the house was secluded, but I knew that Father Bernard had seen and recognised them. I knew, too, the thought that was in his mind. As I passed slowly back towards the banqueting hall, my footsteps striking hollowly upon the oaken floor, that thought grew in significance. Free as I was, or as I thought I was, from the medieval superstitions which possibly were part of the monk's creed, I shuddered at remembrance of the unnameable tragedies which this gallery might have staged.

It was very quiet. As I came abreast of the last window, the moonlight through a stained quarrel pane spread a red patch across the oaken floor, and I passed it quickly. It had almost the look of a fire burning beneath the woodwork!

Then, through the frosty, night air, I distinctly heard the great bell tolling out, from up the beech avenue at the lodge gate.

I was anxious to know what it meant myself. But Earl, whose every hope and every fear centred in Mona Verek, out ran me easily. I came up to the lodge gates just as he threw them open in his madly impulsive way. The lodge was unoccupied, for the staff was incomplete, and a servant had fastened the gates for the night after Father Bernard had left.

The monk could not have been gone two minutes, but now in the gateway stood a tall man enveloped in furs, who rested one hand upon the shoulder of a chauffeur. It had begun to snow again.

"What's the matter?" cried Ryland anxiously, as the man who attended to the gates tardily appeared. "Accident?"

The stranger waved his disengaged hand with a curiously foreign gesture, and showed his teeth in a smile. He had a black, pointed beard and small moustache, with fine, clear-cut features and commanding eyes.

"Nothing serious," he replied. Something in his voice reminded me of a note in a great organ, it was so grandly deep and musical. "My man was blinded by a drive of snow and ran us off the road. I fear my ankle is twisted, and the car being temporarily disabled…"

With the next house nearly two miles away, that was explanation enough for Earl Ryland. Very shortly we were assisting the distinguished-looking stranger along the avenue, Earl pooh-poohing his protests and sending a man ahead to see that a room would be ready. The snow was falling now in clouds, and Ryland and I were covered. At the foot of the terrace stairs, with cheery light streaming out through the snow-laden air, I noted something that struck me as odd, but at the time as no more than that.

Not a flake of snow rested upon the stranger, from the crown of his black fur cap to the edge of his black fur coat!

Before I had leisure to consider this circumstance, which a moment's thought must have shown to be a curious phenomenon, our unexpected visitor spoke.

"I have a slight face wound, occasioned by broken glass," he said. For the first time, I saw that it was so. "I would not alarm your guests unnecessarily. Could we enter by a more private door?"

"Certainly!" cried Ryland heartily. "This way, sir."

So, unseen by the rest of the party, we entered by the door in the tower of the south wing and lodged the stranger in one of the many bedrooms there. He was profuse in his thanks, but declined any medical aid other than that of his saturnine man. When the blizzard had somewhat abated, he said, the man could proceed to the wrecked car and possibly repair it well enough to enable them to continue their journey. He would trespass upon our good nature no longer; an hour's rest was all that he required.

"You must not think of leaving tonight," said Ryland cordially. "I will see that your wants are attended to."

His man entered, carrying a bag; we left him descending again to the hall.

"Why!" cried Earl. "I never asked him his name and never told him mine!"

He laughed at his own absentmindedness, and we rejoined his guests. But an indefinable change had come over the party. The blizzard was increasing in violence, so that now it shrieked around Devrers Hall like a regiment of ghouls. The youthful members, numbering five, had been sent off to bed, and into the hearts of the elders of the company had crept a general predilection for the fireside. Our entrance created quite a sensation.

"Why," cried Ryland, "I believe you took us for bogeys. Who's been telling ghost stories?"

Mrs Van Eyck stretched a dainty foot to the blaze and writhed her white shoulders expressively.

"Mr Hanson has been talking about the Salem witch trials," she said, turning her eyes to Earl. "I don't know why he likes to frighten us!"

"There was an alleged witch burned at Ashby, near here, as recently as 1640," continued Hanson. "I remember reading about it in a work on the subject; a young Spanish woman, of great beauty, too, called Isabella de Miguel, I believe."

I started. The conversation was turning in a dangerous direction. Old Mr Ryland laughed, but not mirthfully.

"Quit demons and witches," he said. "Let's find a more humorous topic, not that I stand for such nonsense."

Three crashing blows, sounding like those of a titanic hammer on an anvil, rang through the house. An instant's silence followed, then a frightened chorus: "What was that?"

No one could imagine, and Earl had been as startled as the rest of us. He ran from the room, and I followed him. The wind howled and whistled with ever increasing violence. At the low arched door leading to the domestic offices, we found a group of panic-stricken servants huddled together.

"What was that noise?" asked Earl sharply.

His American butler, Knowlson, who formed one of the group,

came forward. "It seemed to come from upstairs, sir," he said. "But I don't know what can have caused it."

"Come and look, then."

Up the massive staircase we went, Knowlson considerably in the rear. But though we searched everywhere assiduously, there was nothing to show what had occasioned the noise. Leaving Ryland peeping in at his two small nephews, who proved to be slumbering peacefully, I went up three steps and through a low archway, and found myself in the south wing. The only occupant, as far as I knew, was the injured stranger. A bright light shone under his door, and I wondered how many candles he had burning.

I knocked.

A gust of wind shrieked furiously around the building, then subsided to a sound like the flapping of wings.

The door was opened a few inches. The light almost dazzled me. I had a glimpse of the unbidden guest, and saw that he wore a loose dressing gown of an unusual shade of red.

"Has anything disturbed you?" I asked.

"No," he replied, with much concern in his deep, organ voice, yet his black eyes were laughing. "Why do you ask?"

"We heard a strange noise," I answered shortly. "Is your ankle better?"

"I thank you—very much," he said. "I am awaiting my man's report respecting the state of the car."

There was nothing in his handsome dark face, in his deep voice, or even in his laughing eyes to justify it, but at that moment I felt certain, beyond any possibility of doubt, that the noise had come from his room. I wanted to run! In fact, I do not know how I might have acted, if Ryland hadn't joined me.

"Sorry to have disturbed you," came his jovial tones, "but the house is full of funny noises! By the way, I forgot to mention that my name is Wilbur Earl Ryland, and I hope you'll stay just as long as it suits you!"

"I thank you," was the unemotional reply. "You are more than kind. I am Count de Stano of Padua. Good night."

He closed the door.

Again came the wind, shrieking around the end of the wing like a troop of furies; and again came an uncanny flapping. Earl caught at my arm.

"What is it?"

"Did you hear—someone laughing?"

"No," I said unsteadily. "It was the howling of the blizzard."

At the landing, he turned to me again.

"What had the Count burning in his room?" he muttered. "That wasn't candlelight!"

We found a crowd awaiting us at the foot of the staircase. No one was anxious to go to bed, and arrangements were made by several of the more nervous to share rooms.

"Has the Count's chauffeur returned?" Earl asked Knowlson.

"He's just come into the servants' hall now, sir. He—"

"Lock up, then."

"He'd been out in all that snow sir!"

"Well?"

"There wasn't a sign of any on his coat."

The man's voice shook and he glanced back at the group of servants, none of whom seemed disposed to return to their quarters.

"He wore another over it, ass!" snapped Ryland. "Set about your business, all of you! You are like a pack of children."

We experienced no further alarms, save from the uncanny howling of the wind, but there were no more ghost stories. Those who went to bed ascended the great oak staircase in parties. Mr Ryland, Earl and I were the last to go, and we parted at last without reference to the matter, of which, I doubt not, all of us were thinking.

Sleep was almost impossible. My quaint little oak-panelled room seemed to rock in a tempest which now had assumed extraordinary violence. For hours I lay listening for that other sound which was not the voice of the blizzard and which, although I had belittled, I had heard as clearly as Earl had heard it.

I detected it at last, just once—a wild, demoniacal laugh.

I leaped to the floor. The sound had not been within the house, I thought, but outside. Clenching my teeth in anticipation of the icy gust which would sweep into the room, I slightly opened the heavily leaded window. The south wing was clearly visible.

Out from the small, square window of the study of Maccabees Nosta poured a beam of fiery light, staining the snowflakes as they swirled madly through its redness.

A moment it shone, and was gone.

I pulled the window fast.

Strange needs teach us strange truths. I was sure in that hour that the simple faith of Father Bernard Was greater than all our wisdom, and I would have given much for his company.

For me the pleasures and entertainments of the ensuing day were but gnawing anxieties and fruitless vigils. Who was the man calling himself de Stano? *Stano* was merely a play on *Nosta*. To what place had his chauffeur taken his car to be repaired? Why did He avoid Father Bernard, as that morning I had seen him do? De Stano claimed acquaintance with mutual friends, all of them absent. Earl was too hospitable. A man who could walk, even with the aid of a big ebony stick, could reach the station in a borrowed car and proceed on his journey.

Devrers Hall was nearly empty, but by one pretext or another I had avoided joining any of the parties. As I stood smoking on the terrace, Mrs Van Eyck came out, dressed in a walking habit which displayed her lithe figure almost orientally.

"Mr Bowman and I are walking over to the monastery. Won't you join us, Mr Cumberly?" she said.

"Thank you, but some unexpected work has come to hand and I fear I must decline! Have you seen our new guest recently?"

"The Count? Yes, just a while ago. What a strange man! Do you know, Mr Cumberly, he almost frightens me."

"Indeed!"

"He is a most accomplished hypnotist! Oh, I must show you! He was angry with me for being sceptical, you know, and suddenly challenged me to touch him, even with my little finger. I did, look!"

She had pulled off her glove and held out her hand. The top of one finger was blistered, as by contact with fire!

"Hypnotic suggestion, of course," she said laughingly. "He is not always red hot."

She laughed gaily as young Bowman came out; the two walking off together.

I re-entered the house.

None of the servants had seen the Count, and when I knocked at his door there was no reply. Passing back along the corridor I met Lister Hanson.

"Hello!" I said. "I thought you were out with the others."

"No. I had some trivial matters to attend to; Majorie and the youngsters have gone skating."

I hesitated.

"Is Earl with them?"

Hanson laughed.

"He has motored over to the station. Mona Verek is due some time within the next three hours."

Should I confide in him? Yes, I decided, for I could contain my uncanny suspicions no longer.

"What is your opinion of this de Stano?" I asked abruptly.

Hanson's face clouded.

"Curiously enough, I have not met him," he replied. "He patently avoids me. In fact, Cumberly, very few of the folks *have* met him. You must have noticed that on one pretence or another he has avoided being present at meals? Though he is living under the same roof, I assure you the bulk of us *have never seen him.*"

It was sufficient. I at any rate felt assured of a hearing; and, drawing Hanson into my own room, I unfolded to him the incredible suspicions which I dared to harbour and which were shared by Father Bernard.

At the end of my story, the young clergyman sat looking out the window. When he turned his face to me, it was unusually serious.

"It is going back to the Middle Ages," he said, "but there is nothing in your story that a Churchman may not believe. I have studied the dark pages of history which deal with witchcraft, demonology and possession, I have seen in Germany the testimonies of men as wise as any we have today. Although I can see your expected incredulity and scepticism, I assure you I am at one with Father Bernard upon this matter. The Count de Stano, whoever or whatever he is, must quit this house."

"But what weapons have we against—"

"Cumberly, if some awful thing in the shape of man is among us, that thing has come in obedience to a summons. Do you know the legend of Devrers Hall; the dreadful history of the place?"

I nodded, greatly surprised.

"You wonder where I learned it? You forget that I have dipped deeply into these matters. Directly after the party broke up, I had intended to induce Earl to leave. Cumberly, the place is unclean."

"Is there no way of ridding it of—"

"Only by defeating the thing which legend says first appeared here as Maccabees Nosta. And which of us, being human, can hope to brave that ordeal?"

I was silent for some time.

"We must remember, Hanson," I said, "that, regarding certain undoubtedly weird happenings in the light of what we know of Devrers, we may have deceived ourselves."

"We may," he agreed. "But we dare not rest until we know that we *have*."

So together we searched the house for Count de Stano, but failed to meet with him. The storm of the previous night had subsided, and dusk came creeping upon a winter landscape which spoke only of great peace. The guests began to return, in parties, and presently Earl Ryland arrived, looking very worried.

"Mona's missed her train," he said. "There seems to be a fatality about the thing."

Hanson said nothing at the time, but when Earl had gone upstairs to dress, he turned to me.

"You know Mona Verek, of course?"

"Quite well."

"She justifies all his adoration, Cumberly. She is the nearest thing to an angel that a human can be. I agree with Earl that there is a fatality in her delay! He is going off again after dinner. You know how dreadfully impulsive he is, and I have always at the back of my brain the idea that we may be deluding ourselves."

It was close to the dinner hour now, and I hurried to my room to dress. The quaint little window, as I already have mentioned, commanded a view of the south wing, and as I stooped to the oaken window seat, groping for the candles, my gaze strayed across the snow-carpeted lawns to where the shrubbery loomed greyly in the growing December dusk.

Two figures passed hurriedly in by the south entrance, Lawrence Bowman and Marie Van Eyck. They would have quick work to dress. I found the candles, then dropped them and stood peering from the window with a horror upon me greater than any I yet had known in that house.

A few paces behind the pair, footsteps were forming in the snow—the footsteps of one invisible, who followed, who came to the southern door and who entered after them. Faint wreaths as of steam floated over the ghostly trail.

"My God!" I whispered. "My God!"

How I dressed, Heaven only knows. I have no recollection of anything until, finding myself at the foot of the great staircase, I said to Knowlson, struggling to make my voice sound normal, "Is the Count de Stano in?"

"I think not, sir. I believe he is leaving this evening. But I have never seen the Count personally, sir."

Looking in at the door of the long apartment which Earl had had converted into a billiard room, I found Bowman adjusting his tie before a small mirror.

"Have you seen the Count?" I asked shortly.

"Yes. He is talking to Marie—to Mrs Van Eyck—in the lounge."

I set off briskly. There was but one door to the old study, now the lounge. I hoped (and feared, I confess) to meet the Count there face to face.

The place was only lighted by the crackling wood fire on the great hearth and Mrs Van Eyck alone stood leaning against the mantelpiece, the red gleam of the fire upon her bare shoulders.

"I had hoped to find the Count here," I said, as she turned to me.

"Surely you passed him? He couldn't have reached farther than the library as you came in."

I shook my head, and for a moment Mrs Van Eyck looked almost afraid.

"Are you sure?" she asked. "I can't understand it. He is leaving almost immediately, too."

Her hands were toying with a curious little ornament suspended by a chain about her neck. She saw me looking at it and held it up for my inspection.

"Isn't it odd?" she laughed rather uneasily. "The Count tells me that it is an ancient Assyrian love charm."

It was a tiny golden calf, and, unaccountably, I knew that I paled as I looked at it.

The gong sounded.

I met Lister Hanson at the door of the banqueting hall. His quest had proved as futile as mine.

We were a very merry dinner party. Again it seemed impossible to credit the idea that malign powers were at work in our midst. Earl Ryland made himself the object of much good-humoured jest by constantly glancing at his watch.

"I know it's rude," he said, "but you don't know how anxious I am about Mona."

When at last dinner was over, he left the old people to do the honours and rushed away in his impetuous, schoolboy fashion to the waiting car, and so off to the station.

Hanson touched me on the shoulder.

"To the Count's room first," he whispered.

We slipped away unnoticed and mounted the staircase. On the landing we met Mrs Van Eyck's maid carrying an armful of dresses.

"Are you packing?" rapped Hanson, with, a sudden suspicion in his voice.

"Yes, sir," replied the girl. "My lady has had a message and must leave tonight."

"Have you seen the Count de Stano?"

"A tall, dark gentleman, carrying a black stick? He has just gone along the passage, sir."

Hanson stood looking after the maid for a moment.

"I have heard of no messenger," he said, "and Van Eyck is due on Christmas morning."

Along the oak-lined passage and up into the south wing we went. The Count's room was empty. There was no fire in the hearth, but the heat of the place was insupportable, although the window was open.

Something prompted me to glance out. From the edge of the lawn below, across to the frosted shrubbery, extended a track of footprints.

"Look Hanson!" I said and grasped his arm. "Look! And tell me if I dream!"

A faint vapour was rising from the prints.

"Let's get our coats and see where they lead," he said quietly.

It was with an indescribable sense of relief that I quitted the room which the Count de Stano had occupied. We got our coats and prepared to go out. With a suddenness which was appalling, the wind rose and, breaking in upon the frozen calm of the evening, shrieked about Devrers Hall with all the fury of a high gale. With it came snow.

Through that raging blizzard, we fought our way around the angle of the house, leaving the company preparing for the dance in the banqueting hall.

Not a track was to be seen, and the snow was falling in swirling clouds.

We performed a complete circuit of the hall, and in the huge yard we found lamps and lanterns burning. Lawrence Bowman's man was preparing his car for the road; he was driving Mrs Van Eyck to the station, the man said. But both Hanson and I quickly noted that young Bowman's luggage was strapped in place.

Retracing our steps, we saw two snow-covered figures ahead of us, a woman in a dull-red cloak and a man in a big motor coat. They passed on to the terrace, and into the light streaming from the open doors. Eary Ryland had returned. His big Panhard stood at the steps.

"My God! Look!" gasped Hanson, and dragged me back.

I knew what to expect, yet at sight of it my heart stood still. Steaming footprints appeared, hard upon those of Mrs Van Eyck and Bowman. They pursued a super-natural course on the terrace steps, stopped, and passed away around the north angle of the hall.

"May Heaven protect all here tonight!" prayed the clergyman fervently. "Follow, follow, Cumberly! At all costs we must follow!" he continued hoarsely.

Which of us trembled the more violently, I do not know. Passing the cheery light of the open doors, we traced the devilish tracks before us. The wind had dropped as suddenly as it had arisen, but snow still fell lightly. Then, from the angle of the great house, we saw a sight which robbed us of what little courage we retained.

Glaring in at the window of the room known as the lantern room, with the light of a great log fire and many candles playing fully upon its malignant face, crouched a red-robed figure. A demon of the Dark Ages it seemed, that clutched and mewed and muttered as it glared. It crouched lower, and lower, then drew back and held its arms before its awful face, thrusting away from it that which approached the window from within. It turned and fled with a shriek unlike anything human or animal, and was gone, leaving behind it steaming footprints in the snow.

A slim shape showed darkly behind the lattice, and the cold light reflected from the snow touched the pure, oval face of Mona Verek.

We fought our way back to the terrace.

"The curse of Devrers Hall in its true form," muttered Hanson, "in the red robe of Maccabees Nosta, the Uniform of Satan!"

We could not and dared not, speak of what we had seen, but the gaieties of the night left us cold. As the hours passed and still nothing occurred to break the serenity of the happy gathering, my forebodings grew keener.

Yet, whenever I looked at Mona Verek, fair and fragile, with wonderful blue eyes—which often made me fear that already she was more than half a creature of another sphere—I found new courage.

It was Hanson who first noticed that Mrs Van Eyck and Bowman were missing.

He drew my attention to it at the instant when the tempest, for a while quiescent, awoke to renewed fury.

"Did you hear that?" he whispered.

I saw Earl glance up quickly from an intimate chat with Mona.

Mingled with the song of the storm had arisen fiendish laughter again and the sound of dull flapping. It seemed like the signal for what was to befall.

Knowlson, ghastly white, rushed into the hall.

"Mr Ryland! Mr Ryland!" he cried unceremoniously.

In an instant we were all flocking about the door. Bowman's man, trembling, stood outside.

"I don't know what's become of him, sir," he said tremulously. "He and Mrs Van Eyck were to have started at eleven-thirty, and, going in to look for him in the lounge—Oh, my God, sir!—I saw something like a great owl go in at the window."

We delayed no longer. Out into the blizzard we poured and over the snow to the south wing.

Blue, spirituous flames were belching from the window of the astrologer's study! One shrill scream reached our ears, to be drowned by the mighty voice of the wind.

"Impossible to get in the window," cried Ryland. "Around through the library. Form up a line to pass buckets, Knowlson!"

As we rushed up the snow-carpeted terrace steps, Hanson fell. Someone stayed to attend to him. Ryland and I ran on through the house and entered the library together. It was in darkness, but the ancient, iron-studded door leading down into the study was outlined in blue light.

I leapt forward in the gloom, my hand outstretched, and something interposed between me and the door—something fiery. With a muffled yell, I drew back...

Ryland passed me. His form vaguely silhouetted against that weird glow, I saw him raise his arms as if to shield his face. An evidently irresistible force hurled him back, and he fell with a crash at the feet of those who crowded the entrance to the library.

"Oh! My God!" he groaned, struggling to his feet. "*What* is before that door?"

A sound like the roaring of a furnace came from within, with a dull beating on the oak. We stood there in the dark, watching the door. Someone pushed to the front of the group.

"Keep back, Masters," said Ryland huskily. "My arms are burned to the elbows. Some hellish thing stands before the door. Keep back, man, till we get lights: Bring lights! Bring lights!"

At that we withdrew from the dark library, until we all stood outside in the hall. Some of us muttered what prayers we. knew, while the furnace roared inside and the storm shrieked outside.

There have been some with whom I have discussed these events, who were convinced that these were the result of hallucination combined with the unsuspected presence of an accomplished illusionist and remorseless jester, but I am convinced otherwise.

Mona Verek approached from the direction of the banqueting hall, two trembling servants following with lights. She was very pale, but quite composed.

"Mona!" began Earl, huskily. "There's devil's work! This is no place—"

She stopped him with a quiet little gesture, and took a lamp from one of the men.

"Mr Hanson has explained to me, Earl," she said. "He is disabled, or he would be here. I quite understand that there is nothing in the library that can harm me. It. can only harm those who fear it. I will unlock the door, Earl, I have promised."

"Mona! Hanson has asked *you*—"

"You don't understand. He has asked me, because for me there is no danger."

He would have stopped her, but he forgot his injured arms, and was too late. She went in, believing she would be protected.

Protected she was.

No invisible flame seared her, nothing contested her coming. Entering behind her, we saw her stoop and unlock the door. A cloud of oily, blue-black smoke belched out.

We had thought to find those within past aid, but up the steps Lawrence Bowman staggered, dragging the insensible form of Marie Van Eyck.

"Thank God!" said old Mr Ryland devoutly.

There was a piercing, frenzied shriek. All heard it with horror. One of the Library windows banged open, and a cloud of snow poured into the room.

"There's someone getting out," cried a man's voice.

"De Stano!" yelled Earl.

Several of us leaped to the window. In the stormy darkness, a red something was racing over the snow towards the beech avenue. The wind dropped, and from the monastery a bell rang.

"The midnight service," I said.

At the first stroke the red figure stopped dead, turned, and seemed to throw up its arms. It was at that moment, I was told by those near the door, that the strange flames died away in the ancient study, leaving only some charred woodwork to show where the fire had been. The blizzard howled again madly. I was not the only one there who heard amid its howling the sound as of flapping wings.

Mona Verek and Bowman were bending over the insensible woman. Upon her flesh was burned a clear impression of a calf, but the little image itself was missing.

The wind died away, no more snow fell and suddenly, as if a curtain had been raised from before it, the moon sailed into the skies. Marie Van Eyck opened her eyes and looked about her with an expression I shall never forget.

"The fire!" she whispered. "The fire! What is it?"

The bell ceased tolling.

"It is Christmas morning!" said Mona Verek.

ABOUT THE AUTHOR

Sax Rohmer was born Arthur Henry Ward in 1883, in Birmingham, England, adding "Sarsfield" to his name in 1901. He was four years old when Sherlock Holmes appeared in print, five when the Jack the Ripper murders began, and sixteen when H.G. Wells' Martians invaded.

Initially pursuing a career as a civil servant, he turned to writing as a journalist, poet, comedy sketch writer, and songwriter in British music halls. At age 20 he submitted the short story "The Mysterious Mummy" to *Pearson's* magazine and "The Leopard-Couch" to *Chamber's Journal*. Both were published under the byline "A. Sarsfield Ward."

Ward's Bohemian associates Cumper, Bailey, and Dodgson gave him the nickname "Digger," which he used as his byline on several serialized stories. Then, in 1908, the song "Bang Went the Chance of a Lifetime" appeared under the byline "Sax Rohmer." Becoming immersed in theosophy, alchemy, and mysticism, Ward decided the name was appropriate to his writing, so when "The Zayat Kiss" first appeared in *The Story-Teller* magazine in October,

1912, it was credited to Sax Rohmer.

That was the first story featuring Fu-Manchu, and the first portion of the novel *The Mystery of Dr. Fu-Manchu*. Novels such as *The Yellow Claw, Tales of Secret Egypt, Dope, The Dream Detective, The Green Eyes of Bast*, and *Tales of Chinatown* made Rohmer one of the most successful novelists of the 1920s and 1930s.

There are fourteen Fu-Manchu novels, and the character has been featured in radio, television, comic strips, and comic books. He first appeared in film in 1923, and has been portrayed by such actors as Boris Karloff, Christopher Lee, John Carradine, Peter Sellers, and Nicolas Cage.

Rohmer died in 1959, a victim of an outbreak of the type A influenza known as the Asian flu.

APPRECIATING DR. FU-MANCHU

BY LESLIE S. KLINGER

The "yellow peril"—that stereotypical threat of Asian conquest—seized the public imagination in the late nineteenth century, in political diatribes and in fiction. While several authors exploited this fear, the work of Arthur Henry Sarsfield Ward, better known as Sax Rohmer, stood out.

Dr. Fu-Manchu was born in Rohmer's short story "The Zayat Kiss," which first appeared in a British magazine in 1912. Nine more stories quickly appeared and, in 1913, the tales were collected as *The Mystery of Dr. Fu-Manchu* (*The Insidious Dr. Fu-Manchu* in America). The Doctor appeared in two more series before the end of the Great War, collected as *The Devil Doctor* (*The Return of Dr. Fu-Manchu*) and *The Si-Fan Mysteries* (*The Hand of Fu-Manchu*).

After a fourteen-year absence, the Doctor reappeared in 1931, in *The Daughter of Fu-Manchu*. There were nine more novels, continuing until Rohmer's death in 1959, when *Emperor Fu-Manchu* was published. Four stories, which had previously appeared only in magazines, were published in 1973 as *The Wrath of Fu-Manchu*.

The Fu-Manchu stories also have been the basis of numerous

motion pictures, most famously the 1932 MGM film *The Mask of Fu-Manchu*, featuring Boris Karloff as the Doctor.

In the early stories, Fu-Manchu and his cohorts are the "yellow menace," whose aim is to establish domination of the Asian races. In the 1930s Fu-Manchu foments political dissension among the working classes. By the 1940s, as the wars in Europe and Asia threaten terrible destruction, Fu-Manchu works to depose other world leaders and defeat the Communists in Russia and China.

Rohmer undoubtedly read the works of Conan Doyle, and there is a strong resemblance between Nayland Smith and Holmes. There are also marked parallels between the four doctors, Petrie and Watson as the narrator-comrades, and Dr. Fu-Manchu and Professor Moriarty as the arch-villains.

The emphasis is on fast-paced action set in exotic locations, evocatively described in luxuriant detail, with countless thrills occurring to the unrelenting ticking of a tightly-wound clock. Strong romantic elements and sensually described, sexually attractive women appear throughout the tales, but ultimately it is the *fantastic* nature of the adventures that appeal.

This is the continuing appeal of Dr. Fu-Manchu, for despite his occasional tactic of alliance with the West, he unrelentingly pursued his own agenda of world domination. In the long run, Rohmer's depiction of Fu-Manchu rose above the fears and prejudices that may have created him to become a picture of a timeless and implacable creature of menace.

A complete version of this essay can be found in *The Mystery of Dr. Fu-Manchu*, also available from Titan Books.

ALSO AVAILABLE FROM TITAN BOOKS:

THE COMPLETE FU-MANCHU SERIES

Sax Rohmer

Available now:

THE MYSTERY OF DR. FU-MANCHU

THE RETURN OF DR. FU-MANCHU

THE HAND OF DR. FU-MANCHU

DAUGHTER OF FU-MANCHU

THE MASK OF FU-MANCHU

THE BRIDE OF FU-MANCHU

THE TRAIL OF FU-MANCHU

PRESIDENT FU-MANCHU

THE DRUMS OF FU-MANCHU

THE SHADOW OF FU-MANCHU

RE-ENTER FU-MANCHU

EMPEROR FU-MANCHU

WWW.TITANBOOKS.COM

THE SEVENTH BULLET
by Daniel D. Victor

THE WHITECHAPEL HORRORS
by Edward B. Hanna

DR. JEKYLL AND MR. HOLMES
by Loren D. Estleman

THE ANGEL OF THE OPERA
by Sam Siciliano

THE GIANT RAT OF SUMATRA
by Richard L. Boyer

THE PEERLESS PEER
by Philip José Farmer

THE STAR OF INDIA
by Carole Buggé

THE WEB WEAVER
by Sam Siciliano

THE TITANIC TRAGEDY
by William Seil

SHERLOCK HOLMES VS. DRACULA
by Loren D. Estleman

THE GRIMSWELL CURSE

by Sam Siciliano

THE DEVIL'S PROMISE

by David Stuart Davies

THE ALBINO'S TREASURE

by Stuart Douglas

THE WHITE WORM

by Sam Siciliano

Coming soon:

MURDER AT SORROW'S CROWN

by Steven Savile & Robert Greenberger

THE RIPPER LEGACY

by David Stuart Davies

THE COUNTERFEIT DETECTIVE

by Stuart Douglas

THE MOONSTONE'S CURSE

by Sam Siciliano

WWW.TITANBOOKS.COM

For more fantastic fiction, author events, exclusive
excerpts, competitions, limited editions and more

VISIT OUR WEBSITE
titanbooks.com

LIKE US ON FACEBOOK
facebook.com/titanbooks

FOLLOW US ON TWITTER
@TitanBooks

EMAIL US
readerfeedback@titanemail.com